The Dreamer And Other Stories of Saki

Hector Hugh Munro

Om Books International

This edition first published in 2020 by

Om Books International

Corporate & Editorial Office
A-12, Sector 64, Noida 201 301
Uttar Pradesh, India
Phone: +91 120 477 4100
Email: editorial@ombooks.com
Website: www.ombooksinternational.com

Sales Office
107, Ansari Road, Darya Ganj,
New Delhi 110 002, India
Phone: +91 11 4000 9000
Fax: +91 11 2327 8091
Email: sales@ombooks.com
Website: www.ombooks.com

Compiled by: Vineetha Mokkil

ISBN: 978-93-53763-60-2

Printed in India

10 9 8 7 6 5 4 3 2 1

British author Hector Hugh Munro (December 18, 1870–November 14, 1916) wrote under the pen name, Saki. Munro was born in Akyab, Myanmar (formerly known as Burma) in 1870. His mother, Mary, died when he was only two years old. After her death, the three Munro children were sent back to Britain to live with their strict, puritanical grandmother and aunts. At 23, Munro joined the military police in Myanmar. After suffering from bouts of malaria, he resigned from his post and went back to Britain in 1895. In 1896, he joined the *Westminster Gazette* as a political sketch writer. His sketches were later published as *The Westminster Alice* and *The Not So Stories*.

Munro's historical work, *The Rise of the Russian Empire*, was published in 1900. He became the Balkan correspondent of *The Morning Post* in 1902. His story, 'Reginald', appeared in book form in 1904, *Reginald in Russia* in 1910, *The Chronicles of Clovis* in 1911, and *Beasts and Super-Beasts* in 1914. The rest of his stories were published posthumously. Munro also wrote two novels, *The Unbearable Bassington* (1912) and *When William Came* (1913) as well as three short plays.

When World War I broke out in 1914, Munro enlisted in the ranks. He was killed in France on November 13, 1916, by German sniper fire during the Battle of Ancre.

Contents

1. Reginald on Christmas Presents

I wish it to be distinctly understood (said Reginald) that I don't want a "George, Prince of Wales" Prayer-book as a Christmas present. The fact cannot be too widely known.

There ought (he continued) to be technical education classes on the science of present-giving. No one seems to have the faintest notion of what anyone else wants, and the prevalent ideas on the subject are not creditable to a civilised community.

There is, for instance, the female relative in the country who "knows a tie is always useful," and sends you some spotted horror that you could only wear in secret or in Tottenham Court Road. It might have been useful had she kept it to tie up currant bushes with, when it would have served the double purpose of supporting the branches and frightening away the birds – for it is an admitted fact that the ordinary tomtit of commerce has a sounder aesthetic taste than the average female relative in the country.

Then there are aunts. They are always a difficult class to deal with in the matter of presents. The trouble is that one never catches them really young enough. By the time one has educated them to an appreciation of the fact that one does not wear red woollen mittens in the West End, they die, or quarrel with the family, or do something equally inconsiderate. That is why the supply of trained aunts is always so precarious.

There is my Aunt Agatha, par example, who sent me a pair of gloves last Christmas, and even got so far as to choose a kind that was being worn and had the correct number of buttons. But – *They were nines*! I sent them to a boy whom I hated intimately: he didn't wear them, of course, but he could have – that was where the bitterness of death came in. It was nearly as consoling as sending white flowers to his funeral. Of course I wrote and told my aunt that they were the one thing that had been wanting to make existence blossom like a rose; I am afraid she thought me frivolous – she comes from the North, where they live in the fear of Heaven and the Earl of Durham. (Reginald affects an exhaustive knowledge of things political, which furnishes an excellent excuse for not discussing them.) Aunts with a dash of foreign extraction in them are the most satisfactory in the way of understanding these things; but if you can't choose your aunt, it is wisest in the long-run to choose the present and send her the bill.

Even friends of one's own set, who might be expected to know better, have curious delusions on the subject. I am NOT collecting copies of the cheaper editions of Omar Khayyam. I gave the last four that I received to the lift-boy, and I like to think of him reading them, with Fitzgerald's notes, to his aged mother. Lift-boys always have aged mothers; shows such nice feeling on their part, I think.

Personally, I can't see where the difficulty in choosing suitable presents lies. No boy who had brought himself up properly could fail to appreciate one of those decorative bottles of liqueurs that are so reverently staged in Morel's window – and it wouldn't in the least matter if one did get duplicates. And there would always be the supreme moment of dreadful uncertainty whether it was *crème de menthe* or Chartreuse – like the expectant thrill on seeing your partner's hand turned up at bridge. People may say what they like about the decay of Christianity; the religious system that produced green Chartreuse can never really die.

And then, of course, there are liqueur glasses, and crystallised fruits, and tapestry curtains, and heaps of other necessaries of life that make really sensible presents – not to speak of luxuries, such as having one's bills paid, or getting something quite sweet in the way of jewellery. Unlike the alleged Good Woman of the Bible, I'm not above rubies. When found, by the way, she must have been rather a problem at Christmas-time; nothing short of a blank cheque would have fitted the situation. Perhaps it's as well that she's died out.

The great charm about me (concluded Reginald) is that I am so easily pleased.

But I draw the line at a "Prince of Wales" prayer-book.

2. Reginald On The Academy

"One goes to the Academy in self-defence," said Reginald. "It is the one topic one has in common with the Country Cousins."

"It is almost a religious observance with them," said the Other. "A kind of artistic Mecca, and when the good ones die they go –"

"To the Chantrey Bequest. The mystery is what they find to talk about in the country."

"There are two subjects of conversation in the country: Servants, and Can fowls be made to pay? The first, I believe, is compulsory, the second optional."

"As a function," resumed Reginald, "the Academy is a failure."

"You think it would be tolerable without the pictures?"

"The pictures are all right, in their way; after all, one can always *look* at them if one is bored with one's surroundings, or wants to avoid an imminent acquaintance."

"Even that doesn't always save one. There is the inevitable female whom you met once in Devonshire, or the Matoppo Hills, or somewhere, who charges up to you with the remark that it's funny how one always meets people one knows at the Academy. Personally, I *don't* think it funny."

"I suffered in that way just now," said Reginald plaintively, "from a woman whose word I had to take that she had met me last summer in Brittany."

"I hope you were not too brutal?"

"I merely told her with engaging simplicity that the art of life was the avoidance of the unattainable."

"Did she try and work it out on the back of her catalogue?"

"Not there and then. She murmured something about being 'so clever.' Fancy coming to the Academy to be clever!"

"To be clever in the afternoon argues that one is dining nowhere in the evening."

"Which reminds me that I can't remember whether I accepted an invitation from you to dine at Kettner's to-night."

"On the other hand, I can remember with startling distinctness not having asked you to."

"So much certainty is unbecoming in the young; so we'll consider that settled. What were you talking about? Oh, pictures. Personally, I rather like them; they are so refreshingly real and probable, they take one away from the unrealities of life."

"One likes to escape from oneself occasionally."

"That is the disadvantage of a portrait; as a rule, one's bitterest friends can find nothing more to ask than the faithful unlikeness that goes down to posterity as oneself. I hate posterity – it's so fond of having the last word. Of course, as regards portraits, there are exceptions."

"For instance?"

"To die before being painted by Sargent is to go to heaven prematurely."

"With the necessary care and impatience, you may avoid that catastrophe."

"If you're going to be rude," said Reginald, "I shall dine with you to-morrow night as well. The chief vice of the Academy," he continued, "is its nomenclature. Why, for instance, should an obvious trout-stream with a palpable rabbit sitting in the foreground be called 'an evening dream of unbeclouded peace,' or something of that sort?"

"You think," said the Other, "that a name should economise description rather than stimulate imagination?"

"Properly chosen, it should do both. There is my lady kitten at home, for instance; I've called it Derry."

"Suggests nothing to my imagination but protracted sieges and religious animosities. Of course, I don't know your kitten" –

"Oh, you're silly. It's a sweet name, and it answers to it – when it wants to. Then, if there are any unseemly noises in the night, they can be explained succinctly: Derry and Toms."

"You might almost charge for the advertisement. But as applied to pictures, don't you think your system would be too subtle, say, for the Country Cousins?"

"Every reformation must have its victims. You can't expect the fatted calf to share the enthusiasm of the angels over the prodigal's return. Another darling weakness of the Academy is that none of its luminaries must 'arrive' in a hurry. You can see them coming for years, like a Balkan trouble or a street improvement, and by the time they have painted a thousand or so square yards of canvas, their work begins to be recognised."

"Someone who Must Not be Contradicted said that a man must be a success by the time he's thirty, or never."

"To have reached thirty," said Reginald, "is to have failed in life."

3. Reginald At The Theatre

"After all," said the Duchess vaguely, "there are certain things you can't get away from. Right and wrong, good conduct and moral rectitude, have certain well-defined limits."

"So, for the matter of that," replied Reginald, "has the Russian Empire. The trouble is that the limits are not always in the same place."

Reginald and the Duchess regarded each other with mutual distrust, tempered by a scientific interest. Reginald considered that the Duchess had much to learn; in particular, not to hurry out of the Carlton as though afraid of losing one's last 'bus. A woman, he said, who is careless of disappearances is capable of leaving town before Good-wood, and dying at the wrong moment of an unfashionable disease.

The Duchess thought that Reginald did not exceed the ethical standard which circumstances demanded.

"Of course," she resumed combatively, "it's the prevailing fashion to believe in perpetual change and mutability, and all that sort of thing, and to say we are all merely an improved form of primeval ape – of course you subscribe to that doctrine?"

"I think it decidedly premature; in most people I know the process is far from complete."

"And equally of course you are quite irreligious?"

"Oh, by no means. The fashion just now is a Roman Catholic frame of mind with an Agnostic conscience: you get the medieval picturesqueness of the one with the modern conveniences of the other."

The Duchess suppressed a sniff. She was one of those people who regard the Church of England with patronising affection, as if it were something that had grown up in their kitchen garden.

"But there are other things," she continued, "which I suppose are to a certain extent sacred even to you. Patriotism, for instance, and Empire, and Imperial responsibility, and blood-is-thicker-than-water, and all that sort of thing."

Reginald waited for a couple of minutes before replying, while the Lord of Rimini temporarily monopolised the acoustic possibilities of the theatre.

"That is the worst of a tragedy," he observed, "one can't always hear oneself talk. Of course I accept the Imperial idea and the responsibility. After all, I would just as soon think in Continents as anywhere else. And some day, when the season is over and we have the time, you shall explain to me the exact blood-brotherhood and all that sort of thing that exists between a French Canadian and a mild Hindoo and a Yorkshireman, for instance."

"Oh, well, 'dominion over palm and pine,' you know," quoted the Duchess hopefully; "of course we mustn't forget that we're all part of the great Anglo-Saxon Empire."

"Which for its part is rapidly becoming a suburb of Jerusalem. A very pleasant suburb, I admit, and quite a charming Jerusalem. But still a suburb."

"Really, to be told one's living in a suburb when one is conscious of spreading the benefits of civilisation all over the world! Philanthropy – I suppose you will say *that* is a comfortable delusion; and yet even you must admit that whenever want or misery or starvation is known to exist, however distant or difficult of access, we instantly organise relief on the most generous scale, and distribute it, if need be, to the uttermost ends of the earth."

The Duchess paused, with a sense of ultimate triumph. She had made the same observation at a drawing-room meeting, and it had been extremely well received.

"I wonder," said Reginald, "if you have ever walked down the Embankment on a winter night?"

"Gracious, no, child! Why do you ask?"

"I didn't; I only wondered. And even your philanthropy, practised in a world where everything is based on competition, must have a debit as well as a credit account. The young ravens cry for food."

"And are fed."

"Exactly. Which presupposes that something else is fed upon."

"Oh, you're simply exasperating. You've been reading Nietzsche till you haven't got any sense of moral proportion left. May I ask if you are governed by *any* laws of conduct whatever?"

"There are certain fixed rules that one observes for one's own comfort. For instance, never be flippantly rude to any inoffensive grey-bearded stranger that you may meet in pine forests or hotel smoking-rooms on the Continent. It always turns out to be the King of Sweden."

"The restraint must be dreadfully irksome to you. When I was younger, boys of your age used to be nice and innocent."

"Now we are only nice. One must specialise in these days. Which reminds me of the man I read of in some sacred book who was given a choice of what he most desired. And because he didn't ask for titles and honours and dignities, but only for immense wealth, these other things came to him also."

"I am sure you didn't read about him in any sacred book."

"Yes, I fancy you will find him in Debrett."

4. Reginald's Choir Treat

"Never," wrote Reginald to his most darling friend, "be a pioneer. It's the Early Christian that gets the fattest lion."

Reginald, in his way, was a pioneer.

None of the rest of his family had anything approaching Titian hair or a sense of humour, and they used primroses as a table decoration.

It follows that they never understood Reginald, who came down late to breakfast, and nibbled toast, and said disrespectful things about the universe. The family ate porridge, and believed in everything, even the weather forecast.

Therefore the family was relieved when the vicar's daughter undertook the reformation of Reginald. Her name was Amabel; it was the vicar's one extravagance. Amabel was accounted a beauty and intellectually gifted; she never played tennis, and was reputed to have read Maeterlinck's Life of the Bee. If you abstain from tennis *and* read Maeterlinck in a small country village, you are of necessity intellectual. Also she had been twice to Fecamp to pick up a good French accent from the Americans staying there; consequently she had a knowledge of the world which might be considered useful in dealings with a worldling.

Hence the congratulations in the family when Amabel undertook the reformation of its wayward member.

Amabel commenced operations by asking her unsuspecting pupil to tea in the vicarage garden; she believed in the healthy influence of natural surroundings, never having been in Sicily, where things are different.

And like every woman who has ever preached repentance to unregenerate youth, she dwelt on the sin of an empty life, which always seems so much more scandalous in the country, where people rise early to see if a new strawberry has happened during the night.

Reginald recalled the lilies of the field, "which simply sat and looked beautiful, and defied competition."

"But that is not an example for us to follow," gasped Amabel.

"Unfortunately, we can't afford to. You don't know what a world of trouble I take in trying to rival the lilies in their artistic simplicity."

"You are really indecently vain of your appearance. A good life is infinitely preferable to good looks."

"You agree with me that the two are incompatible. I always say beauty is only sin deep."

Amabel began to realise that the battle is not always to the strong-minded. With the immemorial resource of her sex, she abandoned the frontal attack, and laid stress on her unassisted labours in parish work, her mental loneliness, her discouragements – and at the right moment she produced strawberries and cream. Reginald was obviously affected by the latter, and when his preceptress suggested that he might begin the strenuous life by helping her to supervise the annual outing of the bucolic infants who composed the local choir, his eyes shone with the dangerous enthusiasm of a convert.

Reginald entered on the strenuous life alone, as far as Amabel was concerned. The most virtuous women are not proof against damp grass, and Amabel kept her bed with a cold. Reginald called it a dispensation; it had been the dream of his life to stage-manage a choir outing. With strategic insight, he led his shy, bullet-headed charges to the nearest woodland stream and allowed them to bathe; then he seated himself on their discarded garments and discoursed on their immediate future, which, he decreed, was to embrace a Bacchanalian procession through the village. Forethought had provided the occasion with a supply of tin whistles, but the introduction of a he-goat from a neighbouring orchard was a brilliant afterthought. Properly, Reginald explained, there should have been an outfit of panther skins; as it was, those who had spotted handkerchiefs were allowed to wear them, which they did with thankfulness. Reginald recognised the impossibility, in the time at his disposal, of teaching his shivering neophytes a chant in honour of Bacchus, so he started them off with a more familiar, if less appropriate, temperance hymn. After all, he said, it is the spirit of the thing that counts. Following the etiquette of dramatic authors on first nights, he remained discreetly in the background while the procession, with extreme diffidence and the goat, wound its way lugubriously towards the village. The singing had died down long before the main street was reached, but the miserable wailing of pipes brought the inhabitants to their doors. Reginald said he had seen something like it in pictures; the villagers had seen nothing like it in their lives, and remarked as much freely.

Reginald's family never forgave him. They had no sense of humour.

5. Reginald On House-Parties

The drawback is, one never really *knows* one's hosts and hostesses. One gets to know their fox-terriers and their chrysanthemums, and whether the story about the go-cart can be turned loose in the drawing-room, or must be told privately to each member of the party, for fear of shocking public opinion; but one's host and hostess are a sort of human hinterland that one never has the time to explore.

There was a fellow I stayed with once in Warwickshire who farmed his own land, but was otherwise quite steady. Should never have suspected him of having a soul, yet not very long afterwards he eloped with a lion-tamer's widow and set up as a golf-instructor somewhere on the Persian Gulf; dreadfully immoral, of course, because he was only an indifferent player, but still, it showed imagination. His wife was really to be pitied, because he had been the only person in the house who understood how to manage the cook's temper, and now she has to put "D.V." on her dinner invitations. Still, that's better than a domestic scandal; a woman who leaves her cook never wholly recovers her position in Society.

I suppose the same thing holds good with the hosts; they seldom have more than a superficial acquaintance with their guests, and so often just when they do get to know you a bit better, they leave off knowing you altogether. There was rather a breath of winter in the air when I left those Dorsetshire people. You see, they had asked me down to shoot, and I'm not particularly immense at that sort of thing. There's such a deadly sameness about partridges; when you've missed one, you've missed the lot – at least, that's been my experience. And they tried to rag me in the smoking-room about not being able to hit a bird at five yards, a sort of bovine ragging that suggested cows buzzing round a gadfly and thinking they were teasing it. So I got up the next morning at early dawn – I know it was dawn, because there were lark-noises in the sky, and the grass looked as if it had been left out all night – and hunted up the most conspicuous thing in the bird line that I could find, and measured the distance, as nearly as it would let me, and shot away all I knew. They said afterwards that it was a tame bird; that's simply *silly*, because it was awfully wild at the first few shots. Afterwards it quieted down a bit, and when its legs had stopped waving farewells to the landscape I got a gardener-boy to drag it into the hall, where everybody must see it on their way to the breakfast-room. I breakfasted upstairs myself. I gathered afterwards that the meal was tinged with a very unchristian spirit. I suppose it's unlucky to bring peacock's feathers into a house; anyway, there was a blue-pencilly look in my hostess's eye when I took my departure.

Some hostesses, of course, will forgive anything, even unto pavonicide (is there such a word?), as long as one is nice-looking and sufficiently unusual to counterbalance some of the others; and there *are* others – the girl, for instance, who reads Meredith, and appears at meals with unnatural punctuality in a frock that's made at home and repented at leisure. She eventually finds her way to India and gets married, and comes home to admire the Royal Academy, and to imagine that an indifferent prawn curry is for ever an effective substitute for all that we have been taught to believe is luncheon. It's then that she is really dangerous; but at her worst she is never quite so bad as the woman who fires Exchange and Mart questions at you without the least provocation. Imagine the other day, just when I was doing my best to understand half the things I was saying, being asked by one of those seekers after country home truths how many fowls she could keep in a run ten feet by six, or whatever it was! I told her whole crowds, as long as she kept the door shut, and the idea didn't seem to have struck her before; at least, she brooded over it for the rest of dinner.

Of course, as I say, one never really *knows* one's ground, and one may make mistakes occasionally. But then one's mistakes sometimes turn out assets in the long-run: if we had never bungled away our American colonies we might never have had the boy from the States to teach us how to wear our hair and cut our clothes, and we must get our ideas from somewhere, I suppose. Even the Hooligan was probably invented in China centuries before we thought of him. England must wake up, as the Duke of Devonshire said the other day; wasn't it? Oh, well, it was someone else. Not that I ever indulge in despair about the Future; there always have been men who have gone about despairing of the Future, and when the Future arrives it says nice, superior things about their having acted according to their lights. It is dreadful to think that other people's grandchildren may one day rise up and call one amiable.

There are moments when one sympathises with Herod.

6. Reginald At The Carlton

"A most variable climate," said the Duchess; "and how unfortunate that we should have had that very cold weather at a time when coal was so dear! So distressing for the poor."

"Someone has observed that Providence is always on the side of the big dividends," remarked Reginald.

The Duchess ate an anchovy in a shocked manner; she was sufficiently old-fashioned to dislike irreverence towards dividends.

Reginald had left the selection of a feeding-ground to her womanly intuition, but he chose the wine himself, knowing that womanly intuition stops short at claret. A woman will cheerfully choose husbands for her less attractive friends, or take sides in a political controversy without the least knowledge of the issues involved – but no woman ever cheerfully chose a claret.

"*Hors d'oeuvres* have always a pathetic interest for me," said Reginald: "they remind me of one's childhood that one goes through, wondering what the next course is going to be like – and during the rest of the menu one wishes one had eaten more of the *hors d'oeuvres*. Don't you love watching the different ways people have of entering a restaurant? There is the woman who races in as though her whole scheme of life were held together by a one-pin despotism which might abdicate its functions at any moment; it's really a relief to see her reach her chair in safety. Then there are the people who troop in with an-unpleasant-duty-to-perform air, as if they were angels of Death entering a plague city. You see that type of Briton very much in hotels abroad. And nowadays there are always the Johannesbourgeois, who bring a

Cape-to-Cairo atmosphere with them – what may be called the Rand Manner, I suppose."

"Talking about hotels abroad," said the Duchess, "I am preparing notes for a lecture at the Club on the educational effects of modern travel, dealing chiefly with the moral side of the question. I was talking to Lady Beauwhistle's aunt the other day – she's just come back from Paris, you know. Such a sweet woman –"

"And so silly. In these days of the over-education of women she's quite refreshing. They say some people went through the siege of Paris without knowing that France and Germany were at war; but the Beauwhistle aunt is credited with having passed the whole winter in Paris under the impression that the Humberts were a kind of bicycle… Isn't there a bishop or somebody who believes we shall meet all the animals we have known on earth in another world? How frightfully embarrassing to meet a whole shoal of whitebait you had last known at Prince's! I'm sure in my nervousness I should talk of nothing but lemons. Still, I daresay they would be quite as offended if one hadn't eaten them. I know if I were served up at a cannibal feast I should be dreadfully annoyed if anyone found fault with me for not being tender enough, or having been kept too long."

"My idea about the lecture," resumed the Duchess hurriedly, "is to inquire whether promiscuous Continental travel doesn't tend to weaken the moral fibre of the social conscience. There are people one knows, quite nice people when they are in England, who are so *different* when they are anywhere the other side of the Channel."

"The people with what I call Tauchnitz morals," observed Reginald. "On the whole, I think they get the best of two very desirable worlds. And, after all, they charge so much for excess luggage on some of those foreign lines that it's really an economy to leave one's reputation behind one occasionally."

"A scandal, my dear Reginald, is as much to be avoided at Monaco or any of those places as at Exeter, let us say."

"Scandal, my dear Irene – I may call you Irene, mayn't I?"

"I don't know that you have known me long enough for that."

"I've known you longer than your god-parents had when they took the liberty of calling you that name. Scandal is merely the compassionate allowance which the gay make to the humdrum. Think how many blameless lives are brightened by the blazing indiscretions of other people. Tell me, who is the woman with the old lace at the table on our left? Oh, THAT doesn't matter; it's quite the thing nowadays to stare at people as if they were yearlings at Tattersall's."

"Mrs. Spelvexit? Quite a charming woman; separated from her husband"

"Incompatibility of income?"

"Oh, nothing of that sort. By miles of frozen ocean, I was going to say. He explores ice-floes and studies the movements of herrings, and has written a most interesting book on the home-life of the Esquimaux; but naturally he has very little home-life of his own."

"A husband who comes home with the Gulf Stream *would* be rather a tied-up asset."

"His wife is exceedingly sensible about it. She collects postage-stamps. Such a resource. Those people with her are the Whimples, very old acquaintances of mine; they're always having trouble, poor things."

"Trouble is not one of those fancies you can take up and drop at any moment; it's like a grouse-moor or the opium-habit – once you start it you've got to keep it up."

"Their eldest son was such a disappointment to them; they wanted him to be a linguist, and spent no end of money on having him taught to speak – oh, dozens of languages! – and then he became a Trappist monk. And the youngest, who was intended for the American marriage market, has developed political tendencies, and writes pamphlets about the housing of the poor. Of course it's a most important question, and I devote a good deal of time to it myself in the mornings; but, as Laura Whimple says, it's as well to have an establishment of one's own before agitating about other people's. She feels it very keenly, but she always maintains a cheerful appetite, which I think is so unselfish of her."

"There are different ways of taking disappointment. There was a girl I knew who nursed a wealthy uncle through a long illness, borne by her with Christian fortitude, and then he died and left his money to a swine-fever hospital. She found she'd about cleared stock in fortitude by that time, and now she gives drawing-room recitations. That's what I call being vindictive."

"Life is full of its disappointments," observed the Duchess, "and I suppose the art of being happy is to disguise them as illusions. But that, my dear Reginald, becomes more difficult as one grows older."

"I think it's more generally practised than you imagine. The young have aspirations that never come to pass, the old have reminiscences of what never happened. It's only the middle-aged who are really conscious of their limitations – that is why one should be so patient with them. But one never is."

"After all," said the Duchess, "the disillusions of life may depend on our way of assessing it. In the minds of those who come after us we may be remembered for qualities and successes which we quite left out of the reckoning."

"It's not always safe to depend on the commemorative tendencies of those who come after us. There may have been disillusionments in the lives of the mediaeval saints, but they would scarcely have been better pleased if they could have foreseen that their names would be associated nowadays chiefly with racehorses and the cheaper clarets. And now, if you can tear yourself away from the salted almonds, we'll go and have coffee under the palms that are so necessary for our discomfort."

7. Reginald On Besetting Sins – The Woman Who Told The Truth

There was once (said Reginald) a woman who told the truth. Not all at once, of course, but the habit grew upon her gradually, like lichen on an apparently healthy tree. She had no children – otherwise it might have been different. It began with little things, for no particular reason except that her life was a rather empty one, and it is so easy to slip into the habit of telling the truth in little matters. And then it became difficult to draw the line at more important things, until at last she took to telling the truth about her age; she said she was forty-two and five months – by that time, you see, she was veracious even to months. It may have been pleasing to the angels, but her elder sister was not gratified. On the Woman's birthday, instead of the opera-tickets which she had hoped for, her sister gave her a view of Jerusalem from the Mount of Olives, which is not quite the same thing. The revenge of an elder sister may be long in coming, but, like a South-Eastern express, it arrives in its own good time.

The friends of the Woman tried to dissuade her from over-indulgence in the practice, but she said she was wedded to the truth; whereupon it was remarked that it was scarcely logical to be so much together in public. (No really provident woman lunches regularly with her husband if she wishes to burst upon him as a revelation at dinner. He must have time to forget; an afternoon is not enough.) And after a while her friends began to thin out in patches. Her passion for the truth was not compatible with a large visiting-list. For instance, she told Miriam Klopstock *exactly* how she looked at the Ilexes' ball.

Certainly Miriam had asked for her candid opinion, but the Woman prayed in church every Sunday for peace in our time, and it was not consistent.

It was unfortunate, everyone agreed, that she had no family; with a child or two in the house, there is an unconscious check upon too free an indulgence in the truth. Children are given us to discourage our better emotions. That is why the stage, with all its efforts, can never be as artificial as life; even in an Ibsen drama one must reveal to the audience things that one would suppress before the children or servants.

Fate may have ordained the truth-telling from the commencement and should justly bear some of the blame; but in having no children the Woman was guilty, at least, of contributory negligence.

Little by little she felt she was becoming a slave to what had once been merely an idle propensity; and one day she knew. Every woman tells ninety percent, of the truth to her dressmaker; the other ten per cent, is the irreducible minimum of deception beyond which no self-respecting client trespasses. Madame Draga's establishment was a meeting ground for naked truths and overdressed fictions, and it was here, the Woman felt, that she might make a final effort to recall the artless mendacity of past days. Madame herself was in an inspiring mood, with the air of a sphinx who knew all things and preferred to forget most of them. As a War Minister she might have been celebrated, but she was content to be merely rich.

"If I take it in here, and – Miss Howard, one moment, if you please – and there, and round like this – so – I really think you will find it quite easy."

The Woman hesitated; it seemed to require such a small effort to simply acquiesce in Madame's views. But habit had become too strong. "I'm afraid," she faltered, "it's just the least little bit in the world too..."

And by that least little bit she measured the deeps and eternities of her thralldom to fact. Madame was not best pleased at being contradicted on a professional matter, and when Madame lost her temper you usually found it afterwards in the bill.

And at last the dreadful thing came, as the Woman had foreseen all along that it must; it was one of those paltry little truths with which she harried her waking hours. On a raw Wednesday morning, in a few ill-chosen words, she told the cook that she drank. She remembered the scene afterwards as vividly as though it had been painted in her mind by Abbey. The cook was a good cook, as cooks go; and as cooks go she went.

Miriam Klopstock came to lunch the next day. Women and elephants never forget an injury.

8. Reginald's Drama

Reginald closed his eyes with the elaborate weariness of one who has rather nice eyelashes and thinks it useless to conceal the fact.

"One of these days," he said, "I shall write a really great drama. No one will understand the drift of it, but everyone will go back to their homes with a vague feeling of dissatisfaction with their lives and surroundings. Then they will put up new wall-papers and forget."

"But how about those that have oak panelling all over the house?" said the Other.

"They can always put down new stair-carpets," pursued Reginald, "and, anyhow, I'm not responsible for the audience having a happy ending. The play would be quite sufficient strain on one's energies. I should get a bishop to say it was immoral and beautiful – no dramatist has thought of that before, and everyone would come to condemn the bishop, and they would stay on out of sheer nervousness. After all, it requires a great deal of moral courage to leave in a marked manner in the middle of the second act, when your carriage isn't ordered till twelve. And it would commence with wolves worrying something on a lonely waste – you wouldn't see them, of course; but you would hear them snarling and scrunching, and I should arrange to have a wolfy fragrance suggested across the footlights. It would look so well on the programmes, 'Wolves in the first act, by Jamrach.' And old Lady Whortleberry, who never misses a first night, would scream. She's always been nervous since she lost her first husband. He died quite abruptly while watching a county cricket match; two and a half inches of rain had fallen for seven runs, and it was supposed that the excitement killed him. Anyhow, it gave her quite a shock; it was the first husband she'd lost, you know, and now she always screams if anything thrilling happens too soon after dinner. And after the audience had heard the Whortleberry scream the thing would be fairly launched."

"And the plot?"

"The plot," said Reginald, "would be one of those little everyday tragedies that one sees going on all round one. In my mind's eye there is the case of the Mudge-Jervises, which in an unpretentious way has quite an Enoch Arden intensity underlying it. They'd only been married some eighteen months or so, and circumstances had prevented their seeing much of each other. With him there was always a foursome or something that had to be played and replayed in different parts of the country, and she went in for slumming quite as seriously as if it was a sport. With her, I suppose, it was. She belonged to the Guild of the Poor Dear Souls, and they hold the record for having nearly reformed a washerwoman. No one has ever really reformed a washerwoman, and that is why the competition is so keen. You can rescue charwomen by fifties with a little tea and personal magnetism, but with washerwomen it's different; wages are too high. This particular laundress, who came from Bermondsey or some such place, was really rather a hopeful venture, and they thought at last that she might be safely put in the window as a specimen of successful work. So they had her paraded at a drawing-room "At Home" at Agatha Camelford's; it was sheer bad luck that some liqueur chocolates had been turned loose by mistake among the refreshments – really liqueur chocolates, with very little chocolate. And of course the old soul found them out, and cornered the entire stock. It was like finding a whelk-stall in a desert, as she afterwards partially expressed herself. When the liqueurs began to take effect, she started to give them imitations of farmyard animals as they know them in Bermondsey. She began with a dancing bear, and you know Agatha doesn't approve of dancing, except at Buckingham Palace under proper supervision. And then she got up on the piano and gave them an organ monkey; I gather she went in for realism rather than a Maeterlinckian treatment of the subject Finally, she fell into the piano and said she was a parrot in a cage, and for an impromptu performance I believe she was very word-perfect; no one had heard anything like it, except Baroness Boobelstein who has attended sittings of the Austrian Reichsrath. Agatha is trying the Rest-cure at Buxton."

"But the tragedy?"

"Oh, the Mudge-Jervises. Well, they were getting along quite happily, and their married life was one continuous exchange of picture-postcards; and then one day they were thrown together on some neutral ground where foursomes and washerwomen overlapped, and discovered that they were hopelessly divided on the Fiscal Question. They have thought it best to separate, and she is to have the custody of the Persian kittens for nine months in the year – they go back to him for the winter, when she is abroad. There you have the material for a tragedy drawn straight from life – and the piece could be called 'The Price They Paid for Empire.' And of course one would have to work in studies of the struggle of hereditary tendency against environment and all that sort of thing. The woman's father could have been an Envoy to some of the smaller German Courts; that's where she'd get her passion for visiting the poor, in spite of the most careful upbringing. *C'est le premier pas qui compte,* as the cuckoo said when it swallowed its foster-parent. That, I think, is quite clever."

"And the wolves?"

"Oh, the wolves would be a sort of elusive undercurrent in the background that would never be satisfactorily explained. After all, life teems with things that have no earthly reason. And whenever the characters could think of nothing brilliant to say about marriage or the War Office, they could open a window and listen to the howling of the wolves. But that would be very seldom."

9. Reginald's Rubaiyat

The other day (confided Reginald), when I was killing time in the bathroom and making bad resolutions for the New Year, it occurred to me that I would like to be a poet. The chief qualification, I understand, is that you must be born. Well, I hunted up my birth certificate, and found that I was all right on that score, and then I got to work on a Hymn to the New Year, which struck me as having possibilities. It suggested extremely unusual things to absolutely unlikely people, which I believe is the art of first-class catering in any department. Quite the best verse in it went something like this –

"Have you heard the groan of a gravelled grouse, Or the snarl of a snaffled snail (Husband or mother, like me, or spouse), Have you lain a-creep in the darkened house, Where the wounded wombats wail?"

It was quite improbable that anyone had, you know, and that's where it stimulated the imagination and took people out of their narrow, humdrum selves. No one has ever called me narrow or humdrum, but even I felt worked up now and then at the thought of that house with the stricken wombats in it. It simply wasn't nice. But the editors were unanimous in leaving it alone; they said the thing had been done before and done worse, and that the market for that sort of work was extremely limited.

It was just on the top of that discouragement that the Duchess wanted me to write something in her album – something Persian, you know, and just a little bit decadent – and I thought a quatrain on an unwholesome egg would meet the requirements of the case. So I started in with –"Cackle, cackle, little hen, How

I wonder if and when Once you laid the egg that I Met, alas! too late. Amen."

The Duchess objected to the Amen, which I thought gave an air of forgiveness and chose jugée to the whole thing; also she said it wasn't Persian enough, as though I were trying to sell her a kitten whose mother had married for love rather than pedigree. So I recast it entirely, and the new version read –

"The hen that laid thee moons ago, who knows In what Dead Yesterday her shades repose; To some election turn thy waning span, And rain thy rottenness on fiscal foes."

I thought there was enough suggestion of decay in that to satisfy a jackal, and to me there was something infinitely pathetic and appealing in the idea of the egg having a sort of St. Luke's summer of commercial usefulness. But the Duchess begged me to leave out any political allusions; she's the president of a Women's Something or other, and she said it might be taken as an endorsement of deplorable, methods. I never can remember which Party Irene discourages with her support, but I shan't forget an occasion when I was staying at her place and she gave me a pamphlet to leave at the house of a doubtful voter, and some grapes and things for a woman who was suffering from a chill on the top of a patent medicine. I thought it much cleverer to give the grapes to the former and the political literature to the sick woman, and the Duchess was quite absurdly annoyed about it afterwards. It seems the leaflet was addressed "To those about to wobble"– I wasn't responsible for the silly title of the thing – and the woman never recovered; anyway, the voter was completely won over by the grapes and jellies, and I think that should have balanced matters. The Duchess called it bribery, and said it might have compromised the candidate she was supporting; he was expected to subscribe to church funds and chapel funds, and football and cricket clubs and regattas, and bazaars and beanfeasts and bellringers, and poultry shows and ploughing matches, and reading-rooms and choir outings, and shooting trophies and testimonials, and anything of that sort; but bribery would not have been tolerated.

I fancy I have perhaps more talent for electioneering than for poetry, and I was really getting extended over this quatrain business. The egg began to be unmanageable, and the Duchess suggested something with a French literary ring about it. I hunted back in my mind for the most familiar French classic that I could take liberties with, and after a little exercise of memory I turned out the following:-

"Hast thou the pen that once the gardener had? I have it not; and know, these pears are had. Oh, larger than the horses of the Prince Are those the general drives in Kaikobad."

Even that didn't altogether satisfy Irene; I fancy the geography of it puzzled her. She probably thought Kaikobad was an unfashionable German spa, where you'd meet matrimonial bargain-hunters and emergency Servian kings. My temper was beginning to slip its moorings by that time I look rather nice when I lose my temper. (I hoped you would say I lose it very often. I mustn't monopolise the conversation.)

"Of course, if you want something really Persian and passionate, with red wine and bulbuls in it," I went on to suggest; but she grabbed the book away from me.

"Not for worlds. Nothing with red wine or passion in it. Dear Agatha gave me the album, and she would be mortified to the quick –"

I said I didn't believe Agatha had a quick, and we got quite heated in arguing the matter. Finally, the Duchess declared I shouldn't write anything nasty in her book, and I said I wouldn't write anything in her nasty book, so there wasn't a very wide point of difference between us. For the rest of the afternoon I pretended to be sulking, but I was really working back to that quatrain, like a fox-terrier that's buried a deferred lunch in a private flower-bed. When I got an opportunity I hunted up Agatha's autograph, which had the front page all to itself, and, copying her prim handwriting as well as I could, I inserted above it the following Tibetan fragment:-

"With Thee, oh, my Beloved, to do a *dak* (a *dak* I believe is a sort of uncomfortable post-journey) On the pack-saddle of a grunting yak, With never room for chilling chaperone, Twere better than a Panhard in the Park."

That Agatha would get on to a yak in company with a lover even in the comparative seclusion of Tibet is unthinkable. I very much doubt if she'd do it with her own husband in the privacy of the Simplon tunnel. But poetry, as I've remarked before, should always stimulate the imagination.

By the way, when you asked me the other day to dine with you on the 14th, I said I was dining with the Duchess. Well, I'm not. I'm dining with you.

10. The Innocence Of Reginald

Reginald slid a carnation of the newest shade into the buttonhole of his latest lounge coat, and surveyed the result with approval. "I am just in the mood," he observed, "to have my portrait painted by someone with an unmistakable future. So comforting to go down to posterity as 'Youth with a Pink Carnation' in catalogue – company with 'Child with Bunch of Primroses,' and all that crowd."

"Youth," said the Other, "should suggest innocence."

"But never act on the suggestion. I don't believe the two ever really go together. People talk vaguely about the innocence of a little child, but they take mighty good care not to let it out of their sight for twenty minutes. The watched pot never boils over. I knew a boy once who really was innocent; his parents were in Society, but they never gave him a moment's anxiety from his infancy. He believed in company prospectuses, and in the purity of elections, and in women marrying for love, and even in a system for winning at roulette. He never quite lost his faith in it, but he dropped more money than his employers could afford to lose. When last I heard of him, he was believing in his innocence; the jury weren't. All the same, I really am innocent just now of something everyone accuses me of having done, and so far as I can see, their accusations will remain unfounded."

"Rather an unexpected attitude for you."

"I love people who do unexpected things. Didn't you always adore the man who slew a lion in a pit on a snowy day? But about this unfortunate innocence. Well, quite long ago, when I'd been quarrelling with more people than usual, you among the number – it must have been in November, I never quarrel with you too near Christmas – I had an idea that I'd like to write a book. It was to be a book of personal reminiscences, and was to leave out nothing."

"Reginald!"

"Exactly what the Duchess said when I mentioned it to her. I was provoking and said nothing, and the next thing, of course, was that everyone heard that I'd written the book and got it in the press. After that, I might have been a goldfish in a glass bowl for all the privacy I got. People attacked me about it in the most unexpected places, and implored or commanded me to leave out things that I'd forgotten had ever happened. I sat behind Miriam Klopstock one night in the dress circle at His Majesty's, and she began at once about the incident of the Chow dog in the bathroom, which she insisted must be struck out. We had to argue it in a disjointed fashion, because some of the people wanted to listen to the play, and Miriam takes nines in voices. They had to stop her playing in the 'Macaws' Hockey Club because you could hear what she thought when her shins got mixed up in a scrimmage for half a mile on a still day. They are called the Macaws because of their blue-and-yellow costumes, but I understand there was nothing yellow about Miriam's language. I agreed to make one alteration, as I pretended I had got it a Spitz instead of a Chow, but beyond that I was firm. She megaphoned back two minutes later, 'You promised you would never mention it; don't you ever keep a promise?' When people had stopped glaring in our direction, I replied that I'd as soon think of keeping white mice. I saw her tearing little bits out of her programme for a minute or two, and then she leaned back and snorted, 'You're not the boy I took you for,' as though she were an eagle arriving at Olympus with the wrong Ganymede. That was her last audible remark, but she went on tearing up her programme and scattering the pieces around her, till one of her neighbours asked with immense dignity whether she should send for a wastepaper basket. I didn't stay for the last act."

"Then there is Mrs. – oh, I never can remember her name; she lives in a street that the cabmen have never heard of, and is at home on Wednesdays. She frightened me horribly once at a private view by saying mysteriously, 'I oughtn't to be here, you know; this is one of my days.' I thought she meant that she was subject to periodical outbreaks and was expecting an attack at any moment. So embarrassing if she had suddenly taken it into her head that she was Cesar Borgia or St. Elizabeth of Hungary. That sort of thing would make one unpleasantly conspicuous even at a private view. However, she merely meant to say that it was Wednesday, which at the moment was incontrovertible. Well, she's on quite a different tack to the Klopstock. She doesn't visit anywhere very extensively, and, of course, she's awfully keen for me to drag in an incident that occurred at one of the Beauwhistle garden-parties, when she says she accidentally hit the shins of a Serene Somebody or other with a croquet mallet and that he swore at her in German. As a matter of fact, he went on discoursing on the Gordon-Bennett affair in French. (I never can remember if it's a new submarine or a divorce. Of course, how stupid of me!) To be disagreeably exact, I fancy she missed him by about two inches – over-anxiousness, probably – but she likes to think she hit him. I've felt that way with a partridge which I always imagine keeps on flying strong, out of false pride, till it's the other side of the hedge. She said she could tell me everything she was wearing on the occasion. I said I didn't want my book to read like a laundry list, but she explained that she didn't mean those sort of things."

"And there's the Chilworth boy, who can be charming as long as he's content to be stupid and wear what he's told to; but he gets the idea now and then that he'd like to be epigrammatic, and the result is like watching a rook trying to build a nest in a gale. Since he got wind of the book, he's been persecuting me to work in something of his about the Russians and the Yalu Peril, and is quite sulky because I won't do it."

"Altogether, I think it would be rather a brilliant inspiration if you were to suggest a fortnight in Paris."

11. Reginald In Russia

Reginald sat in a corner of the Princess's salon and tried to forgive the furniture, which started out with an obvious intention of being Louis Quinze, but relapsed at frequent intervals into Wilhelm II.

He classified the Princess with that distinct type of woman that looks as if it habitually went out to feed hens in the rain.

Her name was Olga; she kept what she hoped and believed to be a fox-terrier, and professed what she thought were Socialist opinions. It is not necessary to be called Olga if you are a Russian Princess; in fact, Reginald knew quite a number who were called Vera; but the fox-terrier and the Socialism are essential.

"The Countess Lomshen keeps a bulldog," said the Princess suddenly. "In England is it more chic to have a bull-dog than a fox-terrier?"

Reginald threw his mind back over the canine fashions of the last ten years and gave an evasive answer.

"Do you think her handsome, the Countess Lomshen?" asked the Princess.

Reginald thought the Countess's complexion suggested an exclusive diet of macaroons and pale sherry. He said so.

"But that cannot be possible," said the Princess triumphantly; "I've seen her eating fish-soup at Donon's."

The Princess always defended a friend's complexion if it was really bad. With her, as with a great many of her sex, charity began at homeliness and did not generally progress much farther.

Reginald withdrew his macaroon and sherry theory, and became interested in a case of miniatures.

"That?" said the Princess; "that is the old Princess Lorikoff. She lived in Millionaya Street, near the Winter Palace, and was one of the Court ladies of the old Russian school. Her knowledge of people and events was extremely limited; but she used to patronise every one who came in contact with her. There was a story that when she died and left the Millionaya for Heaven she addressed St. Peter in her formal staccato French: '*Je suis la Princesse Lorikoff. Il me donne grand plaisir de faire votre connaissance. Je vous en prie de me presenter au Bon Dieu.*' St. Peter made the desired introduction, and the Princess addressed le Bon Dieu: '*Je suis la Princesse Lorikoff. Il me donne grand plaisir de faire votre connaissance. On a souvent parlé de vous à l'église de la rue Million.*'"

"Only the old and the clergy of Established churches know how to be flippant gracefully," commented Reginald; "which reminds me that in the Anglican Church in a certain foreign capital, which shall be nameless, I was present the other day when one of the junior chaplains was preaching in aid of distressed somethings or other, and he brought a really eloquent passage to a close with the remark, 'The tears of the afflicted, to what shall I liken them – to diamonds?' The other junior chaplain, who had been dozing out of professional jealousy, awoke with a start and asked hurriedly, 'Shall I play to diamonds, partner?' It didn't improve matters when the senior chaplain remarked dreamily but with painful distinctness, 'Double diamonds.' Every one looked at the preacher, half expecting him to redouble, but he contented himself with scoring what points he could under the circumstances."

"You English are always so frivolous," said the Princess. "In Russia we have too many troubles to permit of our being lighthearted."

Reginald gave a delicate shiver, such as an Italian greyhound might give in contemplating the approach of an ice age of which he personally disapproved, and resigned himself to the inevitable political discussion.

"Nothing that you hear about us in England is true," was the Princess's hopeful beginning.

"I always refused to learn Russian geography at school," observed Reginald; "I was certain some of the names must be wrong."

"Everything is wrong with our system of government," continued the Princess placidly. "The Bureaucrats think only of their pockets, and the people are exploited and plundered in every direction, and everything is mismanaged."

"With us," said Reginald, "a Cabinet usually gets the credit of being depraved and worthless beyond the bounds of human conception by the time it has been in office about four years."

"But if it is a bad Government you can turn it out at the elections," argued the Princess.

"As far as I remember, we generally do," said Reginald.

"But here it is dreadful, every one goes to such extremes. In England you never go to extremes."

"We go to the Albert Hall," explained Reginald.

"There is always a see-saw with us between repression and violence," continued the Princess; "and the pity of it is the people are really not in the least inclined to be anything but peaceable. Nowhere will you find people more good-natured, or family circles where there is more affection."

"There I agree with you," said Reginald. "I know a boy who lives somewhere on the French Quay who is a case in point. His hair curls naturally, especially on Sundays, and he plays bridge well, even for a Russian, which is saying much. I don't think he has any other accomplishments, but his family affection is really of a very high order. When his maternal grandmother died he didn't go as far as to give up bridge altogether, but he declared on nothing but black suits for the next three months. That, I think, was really beautiful."

The Princess was not impressed.

"I think you must be very self-indulgent and live only for amusement," she said, "a life of pleasure-seeking and card-playing and dissipation brings only dissatisfaction. You will find that out some day."

"Oh, I know it turns out that way sometimes," assented Reginald. "Forbidden fizz is often the sweetest."

But the remark was wasted on the Princess, who preferred champagne that had at least a suggestion of dissolved barley-sugar.

"I hope you will come and see me again," she said, in a tone that prevented the hope from becoming too infectious; adding as a happy afterthought, "you must come to stay with us in the country."

Her particular part of the country was a few hundred versts the other side of Tamboff, with some fifteen miles of agrarian disturbance between her and the nearest neighbour. Reginald felt that there is some privacy which should be sacred from intrusion.

12. The Lost Sanjak

The prison Chaplain entered the condemned's cell for the last time, to give such consolation as he might.

"The only consolation I crave for," said the condemned, "is to tell my story in its entirety to some one who will at least give it a respectful hearing."

"We must not be too long over it," said the Chaplain, looking at his watch.

The condemned repressed a shiver and commenced.

"Most people will be of opinion that I am paying the penalty of my own violent deeds. In reality I am a victim to a lack of specialisation in my education and character."

"Lack of specialisation!" said the Chaplain.

"Yes. If I had been known as one of the few men in England familiar with the fauna of the Outer Hebrides, or able to repeat stanzas of Camoens' poetry in the original, I should have had no difficulty in proving my identity in the crisis when my identity became a matter of life and death for me. But my education was merely a moderately good one, and my temperament was of the general order that avoids specialisation. I know a little in a general way about gardening and history and old masters, but I could never tell you off-hand whether 'Stella van der Loopen' was a chrysanthemum or a heroine of the American War of Independence, or something by Romney in the Louvre."

The Chaplain shifted uneasily in his seat. Now that the alternatives had been suggested they all seemed dreadfully possible.

"I fell in love, or thought I did, with the local doctor's wife," continued the condemned. "Why I should have done so, I cannot say, for I do not remember that she possessed any particular attractions of mind or body. On looking back at past events if seems to me that she must have been distinctly ordinary, but I suppose the doctor had fallen in love with her once, and what man had done man can do. She appeared to be pleased with the attentions which I paid her, and to that extent I suppose I might say she encouraged me, but I think she was honestly unaware that I meant anything more than a little neighbourly interest. When one is face to face with Death one wishes to be just."

The Chaplain murmured approval. "At any rate, she was genuinely horrified when I took advantage of the doctor's absence one evening to declare what I believed to be my passion. She begged me to pass out of her life, and I could scarcely do otherwise than agree, though I hadn't the dimmest idea of how it was to be done. In novels and plays I knew it was a regular occurrence, and if you mistook a lady's sentiments or intentions you went off to India and did things on the frontier as a matter of course. As I stumbled along the doctor's carriage-drive I had no very clear idea as to what my line of action was to be, but I had a vague feeling that I must look at the Times Atlas before going to bed. Then, on the dark and lonely highway, I came suddenly on a dead body."

The Chaplain's interest in the story visibly quickened.

"Judging by the clothes it wore, the corpse was that of a Salvation Army captain. Some shocking accident seemed to have struck him down, and the head was crushed and battered out of all human semblance. Probably, I thought, a motor-car fatality; and then, with a sudden overmastering insistence, came another thought, that here was a remarkable opportunity for losing my identity and passing out of the life of the doctor's wife for ever. No tiresome and risky voyage to distant lands, but a mere exchange of clothes and identity with the unknown victim of an unwitnessed accident. With considerable difficulty I undressed the corpse, and clothed it anew in my own garments. Any one who has valeted a dead Salvation Army captain in an uncertain light will appreciate the difficulty. With the idea, presumably, of inducing the doctor's wife to leave her husband's roof-tree for some habitation which would be run at my expense, I had crammed my pockets with a store of banknotes, which represented a good deal of my immediate worldly wealth. When, therefore, I stole away into the world in the guise of a nameless Salvationist, I was not without resources which would easily support so humble a role for a considerable period. I tramped to a neighbouring market-town, and, late as the hour was, the production of a few shillings procured me supper and a night's lodging in a cheap coffee-house. The next day I started forth on an aimless course of wandering from one small town to another. I was already somewhat disgusted with the upshot of my sudden freak; in a few hours' time I was considerably more so. In the contents-bill of a local news sheet I read the announcement of my own murder at the hands of some person unknown; on buying a copy of the paper for a detailed account of the tragedy, which at first had aroused in me a certain grim amusement, I found that the deed ascribed to a wandering Salvationist of doubtful antecedents, who had been seen lurking in the roadway near the scene of the crime. I was no longer amused.

The matter promised to be embarrassing. What I had mistaken for a motor accident was evidently a case of savage assault and murder, and, until the real culprit was found, I should have much difficulty in explaining my intrusion into the affair. Of course I could establish my own identity; but how, without disagreeably involving the doctor's wife, could I give any adequate reason for changing clothes with the murdered man? While my brain worked feverishly at this problem, I subconsciously obeyed a secondary instinct – to get as far away as possible from the scene of the crime, and to get rid at all costs of my incriminating uniform. There I found a difficulty. I tried two or three obscure clothes shops, but my entrance invariably aroused an attitude of hostile suspicion in the proprietors, and on one excuse or another they avoided serving me with the now ardently desired change of clothing. The uniform that I had so thoughtlessly donned seemed as difficult to get out of as the fatal shirt of – You know, I forget the creature's name."

"Yes, yes," said the Chaplain hurriedly. "Go on with your story."

"Somehow, until I could get out of those compromising garments, I felt it would not be safe to surrender myself to the police. The thing that puzzled me was why no attempt was made to arrest me, since there was no question as to the suspicion which followed me, like an inseparable shadow, wherever I went. Stares, nudgings, whisperings, and even loud-spoken remarks of 'that's 'im' greeted my every appearance, and the meanest and most deserted eating-house that I patronised soon became filled with a crowd of furtively watching customers. I began to sympathise with the feeling of Royal personages trying to do a little private shopping under the unsparing scrutiny of an irrepressible public. And still, with all this inarticulate shadowing, which weighed on my nerves almost worse than open hostility would have done, no attempt was made to interfere with my liberty. Later on I discovered the reason. At the time of the murder on the lonely highway a series of important bloodhound trials had been taking place in the near neighbourhood, and some dozen and a half couples of trained animals had been put on the track of the supposed murderer – on my track. One of our most public-spirited London dailies had offered a princely prize to the owner of the pair that should first track me down, and betting on the chances of the respective competitors became rife throughout the land. The dogs ranged far and wide over about thirteen counties, and though my own movements had become by this time perfectly well-known to police and public alike, the sporting instincts of the nation stepped in to prevent my premature arrest. "Give the dogs a chance," was the prevailing sentiment, whenever some ambitious local constable wished to put an end to my drawn-out evasion of justice. My final capture by the winning pair was not a very dramatic episode, in fact, I'm not sure that they would have taken any notice of me if I hadn't spoken to them and patted them, but the event gave rise to an extraordinary amount of partisan excitement. The owner of the pair who were next nearest up at the finish was an American, and he lodged a protest on the ground that an otterhound had married into the family of the winning pair six generations ago, and that the prize had been offered to the first pair of bloodhounds to capture the murderer, and that a dog that had 1/64th part of otterhound blood in it couldn't technically be considered a bloodhound. I forget how the matter was ultimately settled, but it aroused a tremendous amount of acrimonious discussion on both sides of the Atlantic. My own contribution to the controversy consisted in pointing out that the whole dispute was beside the mark, as the actual murderer had not yet been captured; but I soon discovered that on this point there was not the least divergence of public or expert opinion. I had looked forward apprehensively to the proving of my identity and the establishment of my motives as a disagreeable necessity; I speedily found out that the most disagreeable part of the business was that it couldn't be done. When I saw in the glass the haggard and hunted expression which the experiences of the past few weeks had stamped on my erstwhile placid countenance, I could scarcely feel surprised that the few friends and relations I possessed refused to recognise me in my altered guise, and persisted in their obstinate but widely shared belief that it was I who had been done to death on the highway. To make matters worse, infinitely worse, an aunt of the really murdered man, an appalling female of an obviously low order of intelligence, identified me as her nephew, and gave the authorities a lurid account of my depraved youth and of her laudable but unavailing efforts to spank me into a better way. I believe it was even proposed to search me for fingerprints."

"But," said the Chaplain, "surely your educational attainments –"

"That was just the crucial point," said the condemned; "that was where my lack of specialisation told so fatally against me. The dead Salvationist, whose identity I had so lightly and so disastrously adopted, had possessed a veneer of cheap modern education. It should have been easy to demonstrate that my learning was on altogether another plane to his, but in my nervousness I bungled miserably over test after test that was put to me. The little French I had ever known deserted me; I could not render a simple phrase about the gooseberry of the gardener into that language, because I had forgotten the French for gooseberry."

The Chaplain again wriggled uneasily in his seat. "And then," resumed the condemned, "came the final discomfiture. In our village we had a modest little debating club, and I remembered having promised, chiefly, I suppose, to please and impress the doctor's wife, to give a sketchy kind of lecture on the Balkan Crisis. I had relied on being able to get up my facts from one or two standard works, and the back-numbers of certain periodicals. The prosecution had made a careful note of the circumstance that the man whom I claimed to be – and actually was – had posed locally as some sort of second-hand authority on Balkan affairs, and, in the midst of a string of questions on indifferent topics, the examining counsel asked me with a diabolical suddenness if I could tell the Court the whereabouts of Novibazar. I felt the question to be a crucial one; something told me that the answer was St. Petersburg or Baker Street. I hesitated, looked helplessly round at the sea of tensely expectant faces, pulled myself together, and chose Baker Street. And then I knew that everything was lost. The prosecution had no difficulty in demonstrating that an individual, even moderately versed in the affairs of the Near East, could never have so unceremoniously dislocated Novibazar from its accustomed corner of the map. It was an answer which the Salvation Army captain might conceivably have made – and I made it. The circumstantial evidence connecting the Salvationist with the crime was overwhelmingly convincing, and I had inextricably identified myself with the Salvationist. And thus it comes to pass that in ten minutes' time I shall be hanged by the neck until I am dead in expiation of the murder of myself, which murder never took place, and of which, in any case, I am innocent."

~

When the Chaplain returned to his quarters some fifteen minutes later, the black flag was floating over the prison tower. Breakfast was waiting for him in the dining-room, but he first passed into his library, and, taking up the Times Atlas, consulted a map of the Balkan Peninsula. "A thing like that," he observed, closing the volume with a snap, "might happen to any one."

13. The Sex That Doesn't Shop

The opening of a large new centre for West End shopping, particularly feminine shopping, suggests the reflection, Do women ever really shop? Of course, it is a well-attested fact that they go forth shopping as assiduously as a bee goes flower-visiting, but do they shop in the practical sense of the word? Granted the money, time, and energy, a resolute course of shopping transactions would naturally result in having one's ordinary domestic needs unfailingly supplied, whereas it is notorious that women servants (and housewives of all classes) make it almost a point of honour not to be supplied with everyday necessities. "We shall be out of starch by Thursday," they say with fatalistic foreboding, and by Thursday they are out of starch. They have predicted almost to a minute the moment when their supply would give out and if Thursday happens to be early closing day their triumph is complete. A shop where starch is stored for retail purposes possibly stands at their very door, but the feminine mind has rejected such an obvious source for replenishing a dwindling stock. "We don't deal there" places it at once beyond the pale of human resort. And it is noteworthy that, just as a sheep-worrying dog seldom molests the flocks in his near neighbourhood, so a woman rarely deals with shops in her immediate vicinity. The more remote the source of supply the more fixed seems to be the resolve to run short of the commodity. The Ark had probably not quitted its last moorings five minutes before some feminine voice gloatingly recorded a shortage of bird-seed. A few days ago two lady acquaintances of mine were confessing to some mental uneasiness because a friend had called just before lunchtime, and they had been unable to ask her to stop and share their meal, as (with a touch of legitimate pride) "there was nothing in the house." I pointed out that they lived in a street that bristled with provision shops and that it would have been easy to mobilise a very passable luncheon in less than five minutes. "That," they said with quiet dignity, "would not have occurred to us," and I felt that I had suggested something bordering on the indecent.

But it is in catering for her literary wants that a woman's shopping capacity breaks down most completely. If you have perchance produced a book which has met with some little measure of success, you are certain to get a letter from some lady whom you scarcely known to bow to, asking you "how it can be got." She knows the name of the book, its author, and who published it, but how to get into actual contact with it is still an unsolved problem to her. You write back pointing out that to have recourse to an ironmonger or a corn-dealer will only entail delay and disappointment, and suggest an application to a bookseller as the most hopeful thing you can think of. In a day or two she writes again: "It is all right; I have borrowed it from your aunt." Here, of course, we have an example of the Beyond-Shopper, one who has learned the Better Way, but the helplessness exists even when such bypaths of relief are closed. A lady who lives in the West End was expressing to me the other day her interest in West Highland terriers, and her desire to know more about the breed, so when, a few days later, I came across an exhaustive article on that subject in the current number of one of our best known outdoor-life weeklies, I mentioned that circumstance in a letter, giving the date of that number. "I cannot get the paper," was her telephoned response. And she couldn't. She lived in a city where newsagents are numbered, I suppose, by the thousand, and she must have passed dozens of such shops in her daily shopping excursions, but as far as she was concerned that article on West Highland terriers might as well have been written in a missal stored away in some Buddhist monastery in Eastern Tibet.

The brutal directness of the masculine shopper arouses a certain combative derision in the feminine onlooker. A cat that spreads one shrew-mouse over the greater part of a long summer afternoon, and then possibly loses him, doubtless feels the same contempt for the terrier who compresses his rat into ten seconds of the strenuous life. I was finishing off a short list of purchases a few afternoons ago when I was discovered by a lady of my acquaintance whom, swerving aside from the lead given us by her godparents thirty years ago, we will call Agatha.

"You're surely not buying blotting-paper *here*?" she exclaimed in an agitated whisper, and she seemed so genuinely concerned that I stayed my hand.

"Let me take you to Winks and Pinks," she said as soon as we were out of the building: "they've got such lovely shades of blotting-paper – pearl and heliotrope and momie and crushed –"

"But I want ordinary white blotting-paper," I said.

"Never mind. They know me at Winks and Pinks," she replied inconsequently. Agatha apparently has an idea that blotting-paper is only sold in small quantities to persons of known reputation, who may be trusted not to put it to dangerous or improper uses. After walking some two hundred yards she began to feel that her tea was of more immediate importance than my blotting-paper.

"What do you want blotting-paper for?" she asked suddenly. I explained patiently.

"I use it to dry up the ink of wet manuscript without smudging the writing. Probably a Chinese invention of the second century before Christ, but I'm not sure. The only other use for it that I can think of is to roll it into a ball for a kitten to play with."

"But you haven't got a kitten," said Agatha, with a feminine desire for stating the entire truth on most occasions.

"A stray one might come in at any moment," I replied.

Anyway, I didn't get the blotting-paper.

14. A Young Turkish Catastrophe – In Two Scenes

The Minister for Fine Arts (to whose Department had been lately added the new sub-section of Electoral Engineering) paid a business visit to the Grand Vizier. According to Eastern etiquette they discoursed for a while on indifferent subjects. The minister only checked himself in time from making a passing reference to the Marathon Race, remembering that the Vizier had a Persian grandmother and might consider any allusion to Marathon as somewhat tactless. Presently the Minister broached the subject of his interview.

"Under the new Constitution are women to have votes?" he asked suddenly.

"To have votes? Women?" exclaimed the Vizier in some astonishment. "My dear Pasha, the New Departure has a flavour of the absurd as it is; don't let's try and make it altogether ridiculous. Women have no souls and no intelligence; why on earth should they have votes?"

"I know it sounds absurd," said the Minister, "but they are seriously considering the idea in the West."

"Then they must have a larger equipment of seriousness than I gave them credit for. After a lifetime of specialised effort in maintaining my gravity I can scarcely restrain an inclination to smile at the suggestion. Why, out womenfolk in most cases don't know how to read or write. How could they perform the operation of voting?"

"They could be shown the names of the candidates and where to make their cross."

"I beg your pardon?" interrupted the Vizier.

"Their crescent, I mean," corrected the Minister. "It would be to the liking of the Young Turkish Party," he added.

"Oh, well," said the Vizier, "if we are to do the thing at all we may as well go the whole h –" he pulled up just as he was uttering the name of an unclean animal, and continued, "the complete camel. I will issue instructions that womenfolk are to have votes."

~

The poll was drawing to a close in the Lakoumistan division. The candidate of the Young Turkish Party was known to be three or four hundred votes ahead, and he was already drafting his address, returning thanks to the electors. His victory had been almost a foregone conclusion, for he had set in motion all the approved electioneering machinery of the West. He had even employed motorcars. Few of his supporters had gone to the poll in these vehicles, but, thanks to the intelligent driving of his chauffeurs, many of his opponents had gone to their graves or to the local hospitals, or otherwise abstained from voting. And then something unlooked-for happened. The rival candidate, Ali the Blest, arrived on the scene with his wives and womenfolk, who numbered, roughly, six hundred. Ali had wasted little effort on election literature, but had been heard to remark that every vote given to his opponent meant another sack thrown into the Bosphorus. The Young Turkish candidate, who had conformed to the Western custom of one wife and hardly any mistresses, stood by helplessly while his adversary's poll swelled to a triumphant majority.

"Cristabel Columbus!" he exclaimed, invoking in some confusion the name of a distinguished pioneer; "who would have thought it?"

"Strange," mused Ali, "that one who harangued so clamorously about the Secret Ballot should have overlooked the Veiled Vote."

And, walking homeward with his constituents, he murmured in his beard an improvisation on the heretic poet of Persia:

"One, rich in metaphors, his Cause contrives To urge with edged words, like Kabul knives; And I, who worst him in this sorry game, Was never rich in anything but – wives."

15. GABRIEL-ERNEST

"There is a wild beast in your woods," said the artist Cunningham, as he was being driven to the station. It was the only remark he had made during the drive, but as Van Cheele had talked incessantly his companion's silence had not been noticeable.

"A stray fox or two and some resident weasels. Nothing more formidable," said Van Cheele. The artist said nothing.

"What did you mean about a wild beast?" said Van Cheele later, when they were on the platform.

"Nothing. My imagination. Here is the train," said Cunningham.

That afternoon Van Cheele went for one of his frequent rambles through his woodland property. He had a stuffed bittern in his study, and knew the names of quite a number of wild flowers, so his aunt had possibly some justification in describing him as a great naturalist. At any rate, he was a great walker. It was his custom to take mental notes of everything he saw during his walks, not so much for the purpose of assisting contemporary science as to provide topics for conversation afterwards. When the bluebells began to show themselves in flower he made a point of informing every one of the fact; the season of the year might have warned his hearers of the likelihood of such an occurrence, but at least they felt that he was being absolutely frank with them.

What Van Cheele saw on this particular afternoon was, however, something far removed from his ordinary range of experience. On a shelf of smooth stone overhanging a deep pool in the hollow of an oak coppice a boy of about sixteen lay asprawl, drying his wet brown limbs luxuriously in the sun. His wet hair, parted by a recent dive, lay close to his head, and his light-brown eyes, so light that there was an almost tigerish gleam in them, were turned towards Van Cheele with a certain lazy watchfulness. It was an unexpected apparition, and Van Cheele found himself engaged in the novel process of thinking before he spoke. Where on earth could this wild-looking boy hail from? The miller's wife had lost a child some two months ago, supposed to have been swept away by the mill-race, but that had been a mere baby, not a half-grown lad.

"What are you doing there?" he demanded.

"Obviously, sunning myself," replied the boy.

"Where do you live?"

"Here, in these woods."

"You can't live in the woods," said Van Cheele.

"They are very nice woods," said the boy, with a touch of patronage in his voice.

"But where do you sleep at night?"

"I don't sleep at night; that's my busiest time."

Van Cheele began to have an irritated feeling that he was grappling with a problem that was eluding him.

"What do you feed on?" he asked.

"Flesh," said the boy, and he pronounced the word with slow relish, as though he were tasting it.

"Flesh! What Flesh?"

"Since it interests you, rabbits, wild-fowl, hares, poultry, lambs in their season, children when I can get any; they're usually too well locked in at night, when I do most of my hunting. It's quite two months since I tasted child-flesh."

Ignoring the chaffing nature of the last remark Van Cheele tried to draw the boy on the subject of possible poaching operations.

"You're talking rather through your hat when you speak of feeding on hares." (Considering the nature of the boy's toilet the simile was hardly an apt one.) "Our hillside hares aren't easily caught."

"At night I hunt on four feet," was the somewhat cryptic response.

"I suppose you mean that you hunt with a dog?" hazarded Van Cheele.

The boy rolled slowly over on to his back, and laughed a weird low laugh, that was pleasantly like a chuckle and disagreeably like a snarl.

"I don't fancy any dog would be very anxious for my company, especially at night."

Van Cheele began to feel that there was something positively uncanny about the strange-eyed, strange-tongued youngster.

"I can't have you staying in these woods," he declared authoritatively.

"I fancy you'd rather have me here than in your house," said the boy.

The prospect of this wild, nude animal in Van Cheele's primly ordered house was certainly an alarming one.

"If you don't go. I shall have to make you," said Van Cheele.

The boy turned like a flash, plunged into the pool, and in a moment had flung his wet and glistening body half-way up the bank where Van Cheele was standing. In an otter the movement would not have been remarkable; in a boy Van Cheele found it sufficiently startling. His foot slipped as he made an involuntarily backward movement, and he found himself almost prostrate on the slippery weed-grown bank, with those tigerish yellow eyes not very far from his own. Almost instinctively he half raised his hand to his throat. They boy laughed again, a laugh in which the snarl had nearly driven out the chuckle, and then, with another of his astonishing lightning movements, plunged out of view into a yielding tangle of weed and fern.

"What an extraordinary wild animal!" said Van Cheele as he picked himself up. And then he recalled Cunningham's remark "There is a wild beast in your woods."

Walking slowly homeward, Van Cheele began to turn over in his mind various local occurrences which might be traceable to the existence of this astonishing young savage.

Something had been thinning the game in the woods lately, poultry had been missing from the farms, hares were growing unaccountably scarcer, and complaints had reached him of lambs being carried off bodily from the hills. Was it possible that this wild boy was really hunting the countryside in company with some clever poacher dogs? He had spoken of hunting "four-footed" by night, but then, again, he had hinted strangely at no dog caring to come near him, "especially at night." It was certainly puzzling. And then, as Van Cheele ran his mind over the various depredations that had been committed during the last month or two, he came suddenly to a dead stop, alike in his walk and his speculations. The child missing from the mill two months ago – the accepted theory was that it had tumbled into the mill-race and been swept away; but the mother had always declared she had heard a shriek on the hill side of the house, in the opposite direction from the water. It was unthinkable, of course, but he wished that the boy had not made that uncanny remark about child-flesh eaten two months ago. Such dreadful things should not be said even in fun.

Van Cheele, contrary to his usual wont, did not feel disposed to be communicative about his discovery in the wood. His position as a parish councillor and justice of the peace seemed somehow compromised by the fact that he was harbouring a personality of such doubtful repute on his property; there was even a possibility that a heavy bill of damages for raided lambs and poultry might be laid at his door. At dinner that night he was quite unusually silent.

"Where's your voice gone to?" said his aunt. "One would think you had seen a wolf."

Van Cheele, who was not familiar with the old saying, thought the remark rather foolish; if he *had* seen a wolf on his property his tongue would have been extraordinarily busy with the subject.

At breakfast next morning Van Cheele was conscious that his feeling of uneasiness regarding yesterday's episode had not wholly disappeared, and he resolved to go by train to the neighbouring cathedral town, hunt up Cunningham, and learn from him what he had really seen that had prompted the remark about a wild beast in the woods. With this resolution taken, his usual cheerfulness partially returned, and he hummed a bright little melody as he sauntered to the morning-room for his customary cigarette. As he entered the room the melody made way abruptly for a pious invocation. Gracefully asprawl on the ottoman, in an attitude of almost exaggerated repose, was the boy of the woods. He was drier than when Van Cheele had last seen him, but no other alteration was noticeable in his toilet.

"How dare you come here?" asked Van Cheele furiously.

"You told me I was not to stay in the woods," said the boy calmly.

"But not to come here. Supposing my aunt should see you!"

And with a view to minimising that catastrophe, Van Cheele hastily obscured as much of his unwelcome guest as possible under the folds of a *Morning Post*. At that moment his aunt entered the room.

"This is a poor boy who has lost his way – and lost his memory. He doesn't know who he is or where he comes from," explained Van Cheele desperately, glancing apprehensively at the waif's face to see whether he was going to add inconvenient candour to his other savage propensities.

Miss Van Cheele was enormously interested.

"Perhaps his underlinen is marked," she suggested.

"He seems to have lost most of that, too," said Van Cheele, making frantic little grabs at the *Morning Post* to keep it in its place.

A naked homeless child appealed to Miss Van Cheele as warmly as a stray kitten or derelict puppy would have done.

"We must do all we can for him," she decided, and in a very short time a messenger, dispatched to the rectory, where a page-boy was kept, had returned with a suit of pantry clothes, and the necessary accessories of shirt, shoes, collar, etc. Clothed, clean, and groomed, the boy lost none of his uncanniness in Van Cheele's eyes, but his aunt found him sweet.

"We must call him something till we know who he really is," she said. "Gabriel-Ernest, I think; those are nice suitable names."

Van Cheele agreed, but he privately doubted whether they were being grafted on to a nice suitable child. His misgivings were not diminished by the fact that his staid and elderly spaniel had bolted out of the house at the first incoming of the boy, and now obstinately remained shivering and yapping at the farther end of the orchard, while the canary, usually as vocally industrious as Van Cheele himself, had put itself on an allowance of frightened cheeps. More than ever he was resolved to consult Cunningham without loss of time.

As he drove off to the station his aunt was arranging that Gabriel-Ernest should help her to entertain the infant members of her Sunday-school class at tea that afternoon.

Cunningham was not at first disposed to be communicative.

"My mother died of some brain trouble," he explained, "so you will understand why I am averse to dwelling on anything of an impossibly fantastic nature that I may see or think that I have seen."

"But what *did* you see?" persisted Van Cheele.

"What I thought I saw was something so extraordinary that no really sane man could dignify it with the credit of having actually happened. I was standing, the last evening I was with you, half-hidden in the hedge-growth by the orchard gate, watching the dying glow of the sunset. Suddenly I became aware of a naked boy, a bather from some neighbouring pool, I took him to be, who was standing out on the bare hillside also watching the sunset. His pose was so suggestive of some wild faun of Pagan myth that I instantly wanted to engage him as a model, and in another moment I think I should have hailed him. But just then the sun dipped out of view, and all the orange and pink slid out of the landscape, leaving it cold and grey. And at the same moment an astounding thing happened – the boy vanished too!"

"What! vanished away into nothing?" asked Van Cheele excitedly.

"No; that is the dreadful part of it," answered the artist; "on the open hillside where the boy had been standing a second ago, stood a large wolf, blackish in colour, with gleaming fangs and cruel, yellow eyes. You may think –"

But Van Cheele did not stop for anything as futile as thought. Already he was tearing at top speed towards the station. He dismissed the idea of a telegram. "Gabriel-Ernest is a werewolf" was a hopelessly inadequate effort at conveying the situation, and his aunt would think it was a code message to which he had omitted to give her the key. His one hope was that he might reach home before sundown. The cab which he chartered at the other end of the railway journey bore him with what seemed exasperating slowness along the country roads, which were pink and mauve with the flush of the sinking sun. His aunt was putting away some unfinished jams and cake when he arrived.

"Where is Gabriel-Ernest?" he almost screamed.

"He is taking the little Toop child home," said his aunt. "It was getting so late, I thought it wasn't safe to let it go back alone. What a lovely sunset, isn't it?"

But Van Cheele, although not oblivious of the glow in the western sky, did not stay to discuss its beauties. At a speed for which he was scarcely geared he raced along the narrow lane that led to the home of the Toops. On one side ran the swift current of the mill-stream, on the other rose the stretch of bare hillside. A dwindling rim of red sun showed still on the skyline, and the next turning must bring him in view of the ill-assorted couple he was pursuing. Then the colour went suddenly out of things, and a grey light settled itself with a quick shiver over the landscape. Van Cheele heard a shrill wail of fear, and stopped running.

Nothing was ever seen again of the Toop child or Gabriel-Ernest, but the latter's discarded garments were found lying in the road so it was assumed that the child had fallen into the water, and that the boy had stripped and jumped in, in a vain endeavour to save it. Van Cheele and some workmen who were near by at the time testified to having heard a child scream loudly just near the spot where the clothes were found. Mrs. Toop, who had eleven other children, was decently resigned to her bereavement, but Miss Van Cheele sincerely mourned her lost foundling. It was on her initiative that a memorial brass was put up in the parish church to "Gabriel-Ernest, an unknown boy, who bravely sacrificed his life for another."

Van Cheele gave way to his aunt in most things, but he flatly refused to subscribe to the Gabriel-Ernest memorial.

16. The Soul Of Laploshka

Laploshka was one of the meanest men I have ever met, and quite one of the most entertaining. He said horrid things about other people in such a charming way that one forgave him for the equally horrid things he said about oneself behind one's back. Hating anything in the way of ill-natured gossip ourselves, we are always grateful to those who do it for us and do it well. And Laploshka did it really well.

Naturally Laploshka had a large circle of acquaintances, and as he exercised some care in their selection it followed that an appreciable proportion were men whose bank balances enabled them to acquiesce indulgently in his rather one-sided views on hospitality. Thus, although possessed of only moderate means, he was able to live comfortably within his income, and still more comfortably within those of various tolerantly disposed associates.

But towards the poor or to those of the same limited resources as himself his attitude was one of watchful anxiety; he seemed to be haunted by a besetting fear lest some fraction of a shilling or Franc, or whatever the prevailing coinage might be, should be diverted from his pocket or service into that of a hard-up companion. A two-Franc cigar would be cheerfully offered to a wealthy patron, on the principle of doing evil that good may come, but I have known him indulge in agonies of perjury rather than admit the incriminating possession of a copper coin when change was needed to tip a waiter. The coin would have been duly returned at the earliest opportunity – he would have taken means to insure against forgetfulness on the part of the borrower – but accidents might happen, and even the temporary estrangement from his penny or sou was a calamity to be avoided.

The knowledge of this amiable weakness offered a perpetual temptation to play upon Laploshka's fears of involuntary generosity. To offer him a lift in a cab and pretend not to have enough money to pay the fair, to fluster him with a request for a sixpence when his hand was full of silver just received in change, these were a few of the petty torments that ingenuity prompted as occasion afforded. To do justice to Laploshka's resourcefulness it must be admitted that he always emerged somehow or other from the most embarrassing dilemma without in any way compromising his reputation for saying "No." But the gods send opportunities at some time to most men, and mine came one evening when Laploshka and I were supping together in a cheap boulevard restaurant. (Except when he was the bidden guest of some one with an irreproachable income, Laploshka was wont to curb his appetite for high living; on such fortunate occasions he let it go on an easy snaffle.) At the conclusion of the meal a somewhat urgent message called me away, and without heeding my companion's agitated protest, I called back cruelly, "Pay my share; I'll settle with you to-morrow." Early on the morrow Laploshka hunted me down by instinct as I walked along a side street that I hardly ever frequented. He had the air of a man who had not slept.

"You owe me two Francs from last night," was his breathless greeting.

I spoke evasively of the situation in Portugal, where more trouble seemed brewing. But Laploshka listened with the abstraction of the deaf adder, and quickly returned to the subject of the two Francs.

"I'm afraid I must owe it to you," I said lightly and brutally. "I haven't a sou in the world," and I added mendaciously, "I'm going away for six months or perhaps longer."

Laploshka said nothing, but his eyes bulged a little and his cheeks took on the mottled hues of an ethnographical map of the Balkan Peninsula. That same day, at sundown, he died. "Failure of the heart's action," was the doctor's verdict; but I, who knew better, knew that he died of grief.

There arose the problem of what to do with his two Francs. To have killed Laploshka was one thing; to have kept his beloved money would have argued a callousness of feeling of which I am not capable. The ordinary solution, of giving it to the poor, would by no means fit the present situation, for nothing would have distressed the dead man more than such a misuse of his property. On the other hand, the bestowal of two Francs on the rich was an operation which called for some tact. An easy way out of the difficulty seemed, however, to present itself the following Sunday, as I was wedged into the cosmopolitan crowd which filled the side-aisle of one of the most popular Paris churches. A collecting-bag, for "the poor of Monsieur le Cure," was buffeting its tortuous way across the seemingly impenetrable human sea, and a German in front of me, who evidently did not wish his appreciation of the magnificent music to be marred by a suggestion of payment, made audible criticisms to his companion on the claims of the said charity.

"They do not want money," he said; "they have too much money. They have no poor. They are all pampered."

If that were really the case my way seemed clear. I dropped Laploshka's two Francs into the bag with a murmured blessing on the rich of Monsieur le Cure.

Some three weeks later chance had taken me to Vienna, and I sat one evening regaling myself in a humble but excellent little Gasthaus up in the Wahringer quarter. The appointments were primitive, but the Schnitzel, the beer, and the cheese could not have been improved on. Good cheer brought good custom, and with the exception of one small table near the door every place was occupied. Half-way through my meal I happened to glance in the direction of that empty seat, and saw that it was no longer empty. Poring over the bill of fare with the absorbed scrutiny of one who seeks the cheapest among the cheap was Laploshka. Once he looked across at me, with a comprehensive glance at my repast, as though to say, "It is my two Francs you are eating," and then looked swiftly away. Evidently the poor of Monsieur le Cure had been genuine poor. The Schnitzel turned to leather in my mouth, the beer seemed tepid; I left the Emmenthaler untasted. My one idea was to get away from the room, away from the table where *that* was seated; and as I fled I felt Laploshka's reproachful eyes watching the amount that I gave to the piccolo – out of his two Francs. I lunched next day at an expensive restaurant which I felt sure that the living Laploshka would never have entered on his own account, and I hoped that the dead Laploshka would observe the same barriers. I was not mistaken, but as I came out I found him miserably studying the bill of fare stuck up on the portals. Then he slowly made his way over to a milk-hall. For the first time in my experience I missed the charm and gaiety of Vienna life.

After that, in Paris or London or wherever I happened to be, I continued to see a good deal of Laploshka. If I had a seat in a box at a theatre I was always conscious of his eyes furtively watching me from the dim recesses of the gallery. As I turned into my club on a rainy afternoon I would see him taking inadequate shelter in a doorway opposite. Even if I indulged in the modest luxury of a penny chair in the Park he generally confronted me from one of the free benches, never staring at me, but always elaborately conscious of my presence. My friends began to comment on my changed looks, and advised me to leave off heaps of things. I should have liked to have left off Laploshka.

On a certain Sunday – it was probably Easter, for the crush was worse than ever – I was again wedged into the crowd listening to the music in the fashionable Paris church, and again the collection-bag was buffeting its way across the human sea. An English lady behind me was making ineffectual efforts to convey a coin into the still distant bag, so I took the money at her request and helped it forward to its destination. It was a two-Franc piece. A swift inspiration came to me, and I merely dropped my own sou into the bag and slid the silver coin into my pocket. I had withdrawn Laploshka's two Francs from the poor, who should never have had the legacy. As I backed away from the crowd I heard a woman's voice say, "I don't believe he put my money in the bag. There are swarms of people in Paris like that!" But my mind was lighter that it had been for a long time.

The delicate mission of bestowing the retrieved sum on the deserving rich still confronted me. Again I trusted to the inspiration of accident, and again fortune favoured me. A shower drove me, two days later, into one of the historic churches on the left bank of the Seine, and there I found, peering at the old wood-carvings, the Baron R., one of the wealthiest and most shabbily dressed men in Paris. It was now or never. Putting a strong American inflection into the French which I usually talked with an unmistakable British accent, I catechised the Baron as to the date of the church's building, its dimensions, and other details which an American tourist would be certain to want to know. Having acquired such information as the Baron was able to impart on short notice, I solemnly placed the two-Franc piece in his hand, with the hearty assurance that it was "pour vous," and turned to go. The Baron was slightly taken aback, but accepted the situation with a good grace. Walking over to a small box fixed in the wall, he dropped Laploshka's two Francs into the slot. Over the box was the inscription, "Pour les pauvres de M. le Cure."

That evening, at the crowded corner by the Cafe de la Paix, I caught a fleeting glimpse of Laploshka. He smiled, slightly raised his hat, and vanished. I never saw him again. After all, the money had been *given* to the deserving rich, and the soul of Laploshka was at peace.

17. The Baker's Dozen

Characters –
MAJOR RICHARD DUMBARTON
MRS. CAREWE
MRS. PALY-PAGET

Scene – Deck of eastward-bound steamer. Major Dumbarton seated on deck-chair, another chair by his side, with the name "Mrs. Carewe" painted on it, a third near by.

(Enter R. Mrs. Carewe, seats herself leisurely in her deck-chair, the Major affecting to ignore her presence.)

Major (turning suddenly): Emily! After all these years! This is fate!

Em.: Fate! Nothing of the sort; it's only me. You men are always such fatalists. I deferred my departure three whole weeks, in order to come out in the same boat that I saw you were travelling by. I bribed the steward to put out chairs side by side in an unfrequented corner, and I took enormous pains to be looking particularly attractive this morning, and then you say "This is fate." I *am* looking particularly attractive, am I not?

Maj.: More than ever. Time has only added a ripeness to your charms.

Em.: I knew you'd put it exactly in those words. The phraseology of love-making is awfully limited, isn't it? After all, the chief charm is in the fact of being made love to. You ARE making love to me, aren't you?

Maj.: Emily dearest, I had already begun making advances, even before you sat down here. I also bribed the steward to put our seats together in a secluded corner. "You may consider it done, sir," was his reply. That was immediately after breakfast.

Em.: How like a man to have his breakfast first. I attended to the seat business as soon as I left my cabin.

Maj.: Don't be unreasonable. It was only at breakfast that I discovered your blessed presence on the boat. I paid violent and unusual attention to a flapper all through the meal in order to make you jealous. She's probably in her cabin writing reams about me to a fellow-flapper at this very moment.

Em.: You needn't have taken all that trouble to make me jealous, Dickie. You did that years ago, when you married another woman.

Maj.: Well, you had gone and married another man – a widower, too, at that.

Em.: Well, there's no particular harm in marrying a widower, I suppose. I'm ready to do it again, if I meet a really nice one.

Maj.: Look here, Emily, it's not fair to go at that rate. You're a lap ahead of me the whole time. It's my place to propose to you; all you've got to do is to say "Yes."

Em.: Well, I've practically said it already, so we needn't dawdle over that part.

Maj.: Oh, well –

(They look at each other, then suddenly embrace with considerable energy.)

Maj.: We dead-heated it that time. (Suddenly jumping to his feet) Oh, d— I'd forgotten!

Em.: Forgotten what?

Maj.: The children. I ought to have told you. Do you mind children?

Em.: Not in moderate quantities. How many have you got?

Maj. (counting hurriedly on his fingers): Five.

Em.: Five!

Maj. (anxiously): Is that too many?

Em.: It's rather a number. The worst of it is, I've some myself.

Maj.: Many?

Em.: Eight.

Maj.: Eight in six years! Oh, Emily!

Em.: Only four were my own. The other four were by my husband's first marriage. Still, that practically makes eight.

Maj.: And eight and five make thirteen. We can't start our married life with thirteen children; it would be most unlucky. (Walks up and down in agitation.) Some way must be found out of this. If we could only bring them down to twelve. Thirteen is so horribly unlucky.

Em.: Isn't there some way by which we could part with one or two? Don't the French want more children? I've often seen articles about it in the *Figaro*.

Maj.: I fancy they want French children. Mind don't even speak French.

Em.: There's always a chance that one of them might turn out depraved and vicious, and then you could disown him. I've heard of that being done.

Maj.: But, good gracious, you've got to educate him first. You can't expect a boy to be vicious till he's been to a good school.

Em.: Why couldn't he be naturally depraved. Lots of boys are.

Maj.: Only when they inherit it from depraved parents. You don't suppose there's any depravity in me, do you?

Em.: It sometimes skips a generation, you know. Weren't any of your family bad?

Maj.: There was an aunt who was never spoken of.

Em.: There you are!

Maj.: But one can't build too much on that. In mid-Victorian days they labelled all sorts of things as unspeakable that we should speak about quite tolerantly. I dare say this particular aunt had only married a Unitarian, or rode to hounds on both sides of her horse, or something of that sort. Anyhow, we can't wait indefinitely for one of the children to take after a doubtfully depraved great-aunt. Something else must be thought of.

Em.: Don't people ever adopt children from other families?

Maj.: I've heard of it being done by childless couples, and those sort of people –

Em.: Hush! Some one's coming. Who is it?

Maj.: Mrs. Paly-Paget.

Em.: The very person!

Maj.: What, to adopt a child? Hasn't she got any?

Em.: Only one miserable hen-baby.

Maj.: Let's sound her on the subject.

(Enter Mrs. Paly-Paget, R.)

Ah, good morning. Mrs. Paly-Paget. I was just wondering at breakfast where did we meet last?

Mrs. P.-P.: At the Criterion, wasn't it?

(Drops into vacant chair.)

Maj.: At the Criterion, of course.

Mrs. P.-P.: I was dining with Lord and Lady Slugford. Charming people, but so mean. They took us afterwards to the Velodrome, to see some dancer interpreting Mendelssohn's "song without clothes." We were all packed up in a little box near the roof, and you may imagine how hot it was. It was like a Turkish bath. And, of course, one couldn't see anything.

Maj.: Then it was not like a Turkish bath.

Mrs. P.-P.: Major!

Em.: We were just talking of you when you joined us.

Mrs. P.-P.: Really! Nothing very dreadful, I hope.

Em.: Oh dear, no! It's too early on the voyage for that sort of thing. We were feeling rather sorry for you.

Mrs. P.-P.: Sorry for me? Whatever for?

Maj.: Your childless hearth and all that, you know. No little pattering feet.

Mrs. P.-P.: Major! How dare you? I've got my little girl, I suppose you know. Her feet can patter as well as other children's.

Maj.: Only one pair of feet.

Mrs. P.-P.: Certainly. My child isn't a centipede. Considering the way they move us about in those horrid jungle stations, without a decent bungalow to set one's foot in, I consider I've got a hearthless child, rather than a childless hearth. Thank you for your sympathy all the same. I dare say it was well meant. Impertinence often is.

Em.: Dear Mrs. Paly-Paget, we were only feeling sorry for your sweet little girl when she grows older, you know. No little brothers and sisters to play with.

Mrs. P.-P.: Mrs. Carewe, this conversation strikes me as being indelicate, to say the least of it. I've only been married two and a half years, and my family is naturally a small one.

Maj.: Isn't it rather an exaggeration to talk of one little female child as a family? A family suggests numbers.

Mrs. P.-P.: Really, Major, you language is extraordinary. I dare say I've only got a little female child, as you call it, at present –

Maj.: Oh, it won't change into a boy later on, if that's what you're counting on. Take our word for it; we've had so much more experience in these affairs than you have. Once a female, always a female. Nature is not infallible, but she always abides by her mistakes.

Mrs. P.-P. (rising): Major Dumbarton, these boats are uncomfortably small, but I trust we shall find ample accommodation for avoiding each other's society during the rest of the voyage. The same wish applies to you, Mrs. Carewe.

(Exit Mrs. Paly-Paget, L.)

Maj.: What an unnatural mother! (Sinks into chair.)

Em.: I wouldn't trust a child with any one who had a temper like hers. Oh, Dickie, why did you go and have such a large family? You always said you wanted me to be the mother of your children.

Maj.: I wasn't going to wait while you were founding and fostering dynasties in other directions. Why you couldn't be content to have children of your own, without collecting them like batches of postage stamps I can't think. The idea of marrying a man with four children!

Em.: Well, you're asking me to marry one with five.

Maj.: Five! (Springing to his feet) Did I say five?

Em.: You certainly said five.

Maj.: Oh, Emily, supposing I've miscounted them! Listen now, keep count with me. Richard – that's after me, of course.

Em.: One.

Maj.: Albert-Victor – that must have been in Coronation year.

Em.: Two!

Maj.: Maud. She's called after –

Em.: Never mind who's she's called after. Three!

Maj.: And Gerald.

Em.: Four!

Maj.: That's the lot.

Em.: Are you sure?

Maj.: I swear that's the lot. I must have counted Albert-Victor as two.

Em.: Richard!

Maj.: Emily!

(They embrace.)

18. The Mouse

Theodoric Voler had been brought up, from infancy to the confines of middle age, by a fond mother whose chief solicitude had been to keep him screened from what she called the coarser realities of life. When she died she left Theodoric alone in a world that was as real as ever, and a good deal coarser than he considered it had any need to be. To a man of his temperament and upbringing even a simple railway journey was crammed with petty annoyances and minor discords, and as he settled himself down in a second class compartment one September morning he was conscious of ruffled feelings and general mental discomposure. He had been staying at a country vicarage, the inmates of which had been certainly neither brutal nor bacchanalian, but their supervision of the domestic establishment had been of that lax order which invites disaster. The pony carriage that was to take him to the station had never been properly ordered, and when the moment for his departure drew near the handy-man who should have produced the required article was nowhere to be found. In this emergency Theodoric, to his mute but very intense disgust, found himself obliged to collaborate with the vicar's daughter in the task of harnessing the pony, which necessitated groping about in an ill-lighted outhouse called a stable, and smelling very like one – except in patches where it smelt of mice. Without being actually afraid of mice, Theodoric classed them among the coarser incidents of life, and considered that Providence, with a little exercise of moral courage, might long ago have recognised that they were not indispensable, and have withdrawn them from circulation. As the train glided out of the station Theodoric's nervous imagination accused himself of exhaling a weak odour of stable-yard, and possibly of displaying a mouldy straw or two on his usually well-brushed garments. Fortunately the only other occupant of the compartment, a lady of about the same age as himself, seemed inclined for slumber rather than scrutiny; the train was not due to stop till the terminus was reached, in about an hour's time, and the carriage was of the old-fashioned sort, that held no communication with a corridor, therefore no further travelling companions were likely to intrude on Theodoric's semi-privacy. And yet the train had scarcely attained its normal speed before he became reluctantly but vividly aware that he was not alone with the slumbering lady; he was not even alone in his own clothes. A warm, creeping movement over his flesh betrayed the unwelcome and highly resented presence, unseen but poignant, of a strayed mouse, that had evidently dashed into its present retreat during the episode of the pony harnessing. Furtive stamps and shakes and wildly directed pinches failed to dislodge the intruder, whose motto, indeed, seemed to be Excelsior; and the lawful occupant of the clothes lay back against the cushions and endeavoured rapidly to evolve some means for putting an end to the dual ownership. It was unthinkable that he should continue for the space of a whole hour in the horrible position of a Rowton House for vagrant mice (already his imagination had at least doubled the numbers of the alien invasion). On the other hand, nothing less drastic than partial disrobing would ease him of his tormentor, and to undress in the presence of a lady, even for so laudable a purpose, was an idea that made his eartips tingle in a blush of abject shame. He had never been able to bring himself even to the mild exposure of open-work socks in the presence of the fair sex. And yet – the lady in this case was to all appearances soundly and securely asleep; the mouse, on the other hand, seemed to be trying to crowd a Wanderjahr into a few strenuous minutes. If there is any truth in the theory of transmigration, this particular mouse must certainly have been in a former state a member of the Alpine Club. Sometimes in its eagerness it lost its footing and slipped for half an inch or so; and then, in fright, or more probably temper, it bit. Theodoric was goaded into the most audacious undertaking of his life. Crimsoning to the hue of a beetroot and keeping an agonised watch on his slumbering fellow-traveller, he swiftly and noiselessly secured the ends of his railway-rug to the racks on either side of the carriage, so that a substantial curtain hung athwart the compartment. In the narrow dressing-room that he had thus improvised he proceeded with violent haste to extricate himself partially and the mouse entirely from the surrounding casings of tweed and half-wool. As the unravelled mouse gave a wild leap to the floor, the rug, slipping its fastening at either end, also came down with a heart-curdling flop, and almost simultaneously the awakened sleeper opened her eyes. With a movement almost quicker than the mouse's, Theodoric pounced on the rug, and hauled its ample folds chin-high over his dismantled person as he collapsed into the further corner of the carriage. The blood raced and beat in the veins of his neck and forehead, while he waited dumbly for the communication-cord to be pulled. The lady, however, contented herself with a silent stare at her strangely muffled companion. How much had she seen, Theodoric queried to himself, and in any case what on earth must she think of his present posture?

"I think I have caught a chill," he ventured desperately.

"Really, I'm sorry," she replied. "I was just going to ask you if you would open this window."

"I fancy it's malaria," he added, his teeth chattering slightly, as much from fright as from a desire to support his theory.

"I've got some brandy in my hold-all, if you'll kindly reach it down for me," said his companion.

"Not for worlds – I mean, I never take anything for it," he assured her earnestly.

"I suppose you caught it in the Tropics?"

Theodoric, whose acquaintance with the Tropics was limited to an annual present of a chest of tea from an uncle in Ceylon, felt that even the malaria was slipping from him. Would it be possible, he wondered, to disclose the real state of affairs to her in small instalments?

"Are you afraid of mice?" he ventured, growing, if possible, more scarlet in the face.

"Not unless they came in quantities, like those that ate up Bishop Hatto. Why do you ask?"

"I had one crawling inside my clothes just now," said Theodoric in a voice that hardly seemed his own. "It was a most awkward situation."

"It must have been, if you wear your clothes at all tight," she observed; "but mice have strange ideas of comfort."

"I had to get rid of it while you were asleep," he continued; then, with a gulp, he added, "it was getting rid of it that brought me to...to this."

"Surely leaving off one small mouse wouldn't bring on a chill," she exclaimed, with a levity that Theodoric accounted abominable.

Evidently she had detected something of his predicament, and was enjoying his confusion. All the blood in his body seemed to have mobilised in one concentrated blush, and an agony of abasement, worse than a myriad mice, crept up and down over his soul. And the, as reflection began to assert itself, sheer terror took the place of humiliation. With every minute that passed the train was rushing nearer to the crowded and bustling terminus where dozens of prying eyes would be exchanged for the one paralysing pair that watched him from the further corner of the carriage. There was one slender despairing chance, which the next few minutes must decide. His fellow-traveller might relapse into a blessed slumber. But as the minutes throbbed by that chance ebbed away. The furtive glance which Theodoric stole at her from time to time disclosed only an unwinking wakefulness.

"I think we must be getting near now," she presently observed.

Theodoric had already noted with growing terror the recurring stacks of small, ugly dwellings that heralded the journey's end. The words acted as a signal. Like a hunted beast breaking cover and dashing madly towards some other haven of momentary safety he threw aside his rug, and struggled frantically into his dishevelled garments. He was conscious of dull surburban stations racing past the window, of a choking, hammering sensation in his throat and heart, and of an icy silence in that corner towards which he dared not look. Then as he sank back in his seat, clothed and almost delirious, the train slowed down to a final crawl, and the woman spoke.

"Would you be so kind," she asked, "as to get me a porter to put me into a cab? It's a shame to trouble you when you're feeling unwell, but being blind makes one so helpless at a railway station."

19. Tobermory

It was a chill, rain-washed afternoon of a late August day, that indefinite season when partridges are still in security or cold storage, and there is nothing to hunt – unless one is bounded on the north by the Bristol Channel, in which case one may lawfully gallop after fat red stags. Lady Blemley's house-party was not bounded on the north by the Bristol Channel, hence there was a full gathering of her guests round the tea-table on this particular afternoon. And, in spite of the blankness of the season and the triteness of the occasion, there was no trace in the company of that fatigued restlessness which means a dread of the pianola and a subdued hankering for auction bridge. The undisguised open-mouthed attention of the entire party was fixed on the homely negative personality of Mr. Cornelius Appin. Of all her guests, he was the one who had come to Lady Blemley with the vaguest reputation. Some one had said he was "clever," and he had got his invitation in the moderate expectation, on the part of his hostess, that some portion at least of his cleverness would be contributed to the general entertainment. Until tea-time that day she had been unable to discover in what direction, if any, his cleverness lay. He was neither a wit nor a croquet champion, a hypnotic force nor a begetter of amateur theatricals. Neither did his exterior suggest the sort of man in whom women are willing to pardon a generous measure of mental deficiency. He had subsided into mere Mr. Appin, and the Cornelius seemed a piece of transparent baptismal bluff. And now he was claiming to have launched on the world a discovery beside which the invention of gunpowder, of the printing-press, and of steam locomotion were inconsiderable trifles. Science had made bewildering strides in many directions during recent decades, but this thing seemed to belong to the domain of miracle rather than to scientific achievement.

"And do you really ask us to believe," Sir Wilfrid was saying, "that you have discovered a means for instructing animals in the art of human speech, and that dear old Tobermory has proved your first successful pupil?"

"It is a problem at which I have worked for the last seventeen years," said Mr. Appin, " but only during the last eight or nine months have I been rewarded with glimmerings of success. Of course I have experimented with thousands of animals, but latterly only with cats, those wonderful creatures which have assimilated themselves so marvellously with our civilisation while retaining all their highly developed feral instincts. Here and there among cats one comes across an outstanding superior intellect, just as one does among the ruck of human beings, and when I made the acquaintance of Tobermory a week ago I saw at once that I was in contact with a 'Beyond-cat' of extraordinary intelligence. I had gone far along the road to success in recent experiments; with Tobermory, as you call him, I have reached the goal."

Mr. Appin concluded his remarkable statement in a voice which he strove to divest of a triumphant inflection. No one said "Rats," though Clovis's lips moved in a monosyllabic contortion which probably invoked those rodents of disbelief.

"And do you mean to say," asked Miss Resker, after a slight pause, "that you have taught Tobermory to say and understand easy sentences of one syllable?"

"My dear Miss Resker," said the wonderworker patiently, "one teaches little children and savages and backward adults in that piecemeal fashion; when one has once solved the problem of making a beginning with an animal of highly developed intelligence one has no need for those halting methods. Tobermory can speak our language with perfect correctness."

This time Clovis very distinctly said, "Beyond-rats!" Sir Wilfrid was more polite, but equally sceptical.

"Hadn't we better have the cat in and judge for ourselves?" suggested Lady Blemley.

Sir Wilfrid went in search of the animal, and the company settled themselves down to the languid expectation of witnessing some more or less adroit drawing-room ventriloquism.

In a minute Sir Wilfrid was back in the room, his face white beneath its tan and his eyes dilated with excitement.

"By Gad, it's true!"

His agitation was unmistakably genuine, and his hearers started forward in a thrill of awakened interest.

Collapsing into an armchair he continued breathlessly: "I found him dozing in the smoking-room, and called out to him to come for his tea. He blinked at me in his usual way, and I said, 'Come on, Toby; don't keep us waiting;' and, by Gad! he drawled out in a most horribly natural voice that he'd come when he dashed well pleased! I nearly jumped out of my skin!"

Appin had preached to absolutely incredulous hearers; Sir Wilfrid's statement carried instant conviction. A Babel-like chorus of startled exclamation arose, amid which the scientist sat mutely enjoying the first fruit of his stupendous discovery.

In tile midst of the clamour Tobermory entered the room and made his way with velvet tread and studied unconcern across to the group seated round the tea-table.

A sudden hush of awkwardness and constraint fell on the company. Somehow there seemed an element of embarrassment in addressing on equal terms a domestic cat of acknowledged dental ability.

"Will you have some milk, Tobermory?" asked Lady Blemley in a rather strained voice.

"I don't mind if I do," was the response, couched in a tone of even indifference. A shiver of suppressed excitement went through the listeners, and Lady Blemley might be excused for pouring out the saucerful of milk rather unsteadily.

"I'm afraid I've spilt a good deal of it," she said apologetically.

"After all, it's not my Axminster," was Tobermory's rejoinder.

Another silence fell on the group, and then Miss Resker, in her best district-visitor manner, asked if the human language had been difficult to learn. Tobermory looked squarely at her for a moment and then fixed his gaze serenely on the middle distance. It was obvious that boring questions lay outside his scheme of life.

"What do you think of human intelligence?" asked Mavis Pellington lamely.

"Of whose intelligence in particular?" asked Tobermory coldly.

"Oh, well, mine for instance," said Mavis, with a feeble laugh.

"You put me in an embarrassing position," said Tobermory, whose tone and attitude certainly did not suggest a shred of embarrassment. "When your inclusion in this house-party was suggested Sir Wilfrid protested that you were the most brainless woman of his acquaintance, and that there was a wide distinction between hospitality and the care of the feeble-minded. Lady Blemley replied that your lack of brain-power was the precise quality which had earned you your invitation, as you were the only person she could think of who might be idiotic enough to buy their old car. You know, the one they call 'The Envy of Sisyphus,' because it goes quite nicely up-hill if you push it."

Lady Blemley's protestations would have had greater effect if she had not casually suggested to Mavis only that morning that the car in question would be just the thing for her down at her Devonshire home.

Major Barfield plunged in heavily to effect a diversion.

"How about your carryings-on with the tortoiseshell puss up at the stables, eh?"

The moment he had said it every one realised the blunder.

"One does not usually discuss these matters in public," said Tobermory frigidly. "From a slight observation of your ways since you've been in this house I should imagine you'd find it inconvenient if I were to shift the conversation on to your own little affairs."

The panic which ensued was not confined to the Major.

"Would you like to go and see if cook has got your dinner ready?" suggested Lady Blemley hurriedly, affecting to ignore the fact that it wanted at least two hours to Tobermory's dinner-time.

"Thanks," said Tobermory, "not quite so soon after my tea. I don't want to die of indigestion."

"Cats have nine lives, you know," said Sir Wilfrid heartily.

"Possibly," answered Tobermory; "but only one liver."

"Adelaide!" said Mrs. Cornett, "do you mean to encourage that cat to go out and gossip about us in the servants' hall?"

The panic had indeed become general. A narrow ornamental balustrade ran in front of most of the bedroom windows at the Towers, and it was recalled with dismay that this had formed a favourite promenade for Tobermory at all hours, whence he could watch the pigeons – and heaven knew what else besides. If he intended to become reminiscent in his present outspoken strain the effect would be something more than disconcerting. Mrs. Cornett, who spent much time at her toilet table, and whose complexion was reputed to be of a nomadic though punctual disposition, looked as ill at ease as the Major. Miss Scrawen, who wrote fiercely sensuous poetry and led a blameless life, merely displayed irritation; if you are methodical and virtuous in private you don't necessarily want every one to know it. Bertie van Tahn, who was so depraved at seventeen that he had long ago given up trying to be any worse, turned a dull shade of gardenia white, but he did not commit the error of dashing out of the room like Odo Finsberry, a young gentleman who was understood to be reading for the Church and who was possibly disturbed at the thought of scandals he might hear concerning other people. Clovis had the presence of mind to maintain a composed exterior; privately he was calculating how long it would take to procure a box of fancy mice through the agency of the Exchange and Mart as a species of hush-money.

Even in a delicate situation like the present, Agnes Resker could not endure to remain too long in the-background.

"Why did I ever come down here she asked dramatically.

Tobermory immediately accepted the opening.

"Judging by what you said to Mrs. Cornett on the croquet-lawn yesterday, you were out for food. You described the Blemleys as the dullest people to stay with that you knew, but said they were clever enough to employ a first-rate cook; otherwise they'd find it difficult to get anyone to come down a second time."

"There's not a word of truth in it! I appeal to Mrs. Cornett –" exclaimed the discomfited Agnes.

"Mrs. Cornett repeated your remark afterwards to Bertie van Tahn," continued Tobermory, "and said, 'That woman is a regular Hunger Marcher; she'd go anywhere for four square meals a day,' and Bertie van Tahn said –"

At this point the chronicle mercifully ceased. Tobermory had caught a glimpse of the big yellow Tom from the Rectory working his way through the shrubbery towards the stable wing. In a flash he had vanished through the open French window.

With the disappearance of his too brilliant pupil Cornelius Appin found himself beset by a hurricane of bitter upbraiding, anxious inquiry, and frightened entreaty. The responsibility for the situation lay with him, and he must prevent matters from becoming worse. Could Tobermory impart his dangerous gift to other cats? was the first question he had to answer. It was possible, he replied, that he might have initiated his intimate friend the stable puss into his new accomplishment, but it was unlikely that his teaching could have taken a wider range as yet.

"Then," said Mrs. Cornett, "Tobermory may be a valuable cat and a great pet; but I'm sure you'll agree, Adelaide, that both he and the stable cat must be done away with without delay."

"You don't suppose I've enjoyed the last quarter of an hour, do you?" said Lady Blemley bitterly. "My husband and I are very fond of Tobermory – at least, we were before this horrible accomplishment was infused into him; but now, of course, the only thing is to have him destroyed as soon as possible."

"We can put some strychnine in the scraps he always gets at dinner-time," said Sir Wilfrid, "and I will go and drown the stable cat myself. The coachman will be very sore at losing his pet, but I'll say a very catching form of mange has broken out in both cats and we're afraid of it spreading to the kennels."

"But my great discovery!" expostulated Mr. Appin; "after all my years of research and experiment –"

"You can go and experiment on the shorthorns at the farm, who are under proper control," said Mrs. Cornett, "or the elephants at the Zoological Gardens. They're said to be highly intelligent, and they have this recommendation, that they don't come creeping about our bedrooms and under chairs, and so forth."

An archangel ecstatically proclaiming the Millennium, and then finding that it clashed unpardonably with Henley and would have to be indefinitely postponed, could hardly have felt more crestfallen than Cornelius Appin at the reception of his wonderful achievement. Public opinion, however, was against him – in fact, had the general voice been consulted on the subject it is probable that a strong minority vote would have been in favour of including him in the strychnine diet.

Defective train arrangements and a nervous desire to see matters brought to a finish prevented an immediate dispersal of the party, but dinner that evening was not a social success. Sir Wilfrid had had rather a trying time with the stable cat and subsequently with the coachman. Agnes Resker ostentatiously limited her repast to a morsel of dry toast, which she bit as though it were a personal enemy; while Mavis Pellington maintained a vindictive silence throughout the meal. Lady Blemley kept up a flow of what she hoped was conversation, but her attention was fixed on the doorway. A plateful of carefully dosed fish scraps was in readiness on the sideboard, but sweets and savoury and dessert went their way, and no Tobermory appeared either in the dining-room or kitchen.

The sepulchral dinner was cheerful compared with the subsequent vigil in the smoking-room. Eating and drinking had at least supplied a distraction and cloak to the prevailing embarrassment. Bridge was out of the question in the general tension of nerves and tempers, and after Odo Finsberry had given a lugubrious rendering of "Melisande in the Wood" to a frigid audience, music was tacitly avoided. At eleven the servants went to bed, announcing that the small window in the pantry had been left open as usual for Tobermory's private use. The guests read steadily through the current batch of magazines, and fell back gradually, on the "Badminton Library" and bound volumes of *Punch*. Lady Blemley made periodic visits to the pantry, returning each time with an expression of listless depression which forestalled questioning.

At two o'clock Clovis broke the dominating silence.

"He won't turn up tonight. He's probably in the local newspaper office at the present moment, dictating the first installment of his reminiscences. Lady What's-her-name's book won't be in it. It will be the event of the day."

Having made this contribution to the general cheerfulness, Clovis went to bed. At long intervals the various members of the house-party followed his example.

The servants taking round the early tea made a uniform announcement in reply to a uniform question. Tobermory had not returned.

Breakfast was, if anything, a more unpleasant function than dinner had been, but before its conclusion the situation was relieved. Tobermory's corpse was brought in from the shrubbery, where a gardener had just discovered it. From the bites on his throat and the yellow fur which coated his claws it was evident that he had fallen in unequal combat with the big Tom from the Rectory.

By midday most of the guests had quit the Towers, and after lunch Lady Blemley had sufficiently recovered her spirits to write an extremely nasty letter to the Rectory about the loss of her valuable pet.

Tobermory had been Appin's one successful pupil, and he was destined to have no successor. A few weeks later an elephant in the Dresden Zoological Garden, which had shown no previous signs of irritability, broke loose and killed an Englishman who had apparently been teasing it. The victim's name was variously reported in the papers as Oppin and Eppelin, but his front name was faithfully rendered Cornelius.

"If he was trying German irregular verbs on the poor beast," said Clovis, "he deserved all he got."

20. A Matter Of Sentiment

It was the eve of the great race, and scarcely a member of Lady Susan's house-party had as yet a single bet on. It was one of those unsatisfactory years when one horse held a commanding market position, not by reason of any general belief in its crushing superiority, but because it was extremely difficult to pitch on any other candidate to whom to pin ones faith. Peradventure II was the favourite, not in the sense of being a popular fancy, but by virtue of a lack of confidence in any one of his rather undistinguished rivals. The brains of clubland were much exercised in seeking out possible merit where none was very obvious to the naked intelligence, and the house-party at Lady Susan's was possessed by the same uncertainty and irresolution that infected wider circles.

"It is just the time for bringing off a good coup," said Bertie van Tahn.

"Undoubtedly. But with what?" demanded Clovis for the twentieth time.

The women of the party were just as keenly interested in the matter, and just as helplessly perplexed; even the mother of Clovis, who usually got good racing information from her dressmaker, confessed herself fancy free on this occasion. Colonel Drake, who was professor of military history at a minor cramming establishment, was the only person who had a definite selection for the event, but as his choice varied every three hours he was worse than useless as an inspired guide. The crowning difficulty of the problem was that it could only be fitfully and furtively discussed. Lady Susan disapproved of racing. She disapproved of many things; some people went as far as to say that she disapproved of most things. Disapproval was to her what neuralgia and fancy needlework are to many other women. She disapproved of early morning tea and auction bridge, of skiing and the two-step, of the Russian ballet and the Chelsea Arts Club ball, of the French policy in Morocco and the British policy everywhere. It was not that she was particularly strict or narrow in her views of life, but she had been the eldest sister of a large family of self-indulgent children, and her particular form of indulgence had consisted in openly disapproving of the foibles of the others. Unfortunately the hobby had grown up with her. As she was rich, influential, and very, very kind, most people were content to count their early tea as well lost on her behalf. Still, the necessity for hurriedly dropping the discussion of an enthralling topic, and suppressing all mention of it during her presence on the scene, was an affliction at a moment like the present, when time was slipping away and indecision was the prevailing note.

After a lunch-time of rather strangled and uneasy conversation, Clovis managed to get most of the party together at the further end of the kitchen gardens, on the pretext of admiring the Himalayan pheasants. He had made an important discovery. Motkin, the butler, who (as Clovis expressed it) had grown prematurely grey in Lady Susan's service, added to his other excellent qualities an intelligent interest in matters connected with the Turf. On the subject of the forthcoming race he was not illuminating, except in so far that he shared the prevailing unwillingness to see a winner in Peradventure II. But where he outshone all the members of the house-party was in the fact that he had a second cousin who was head stable-lad at a neighbouring racing establishment, and usually gifted with much inside information as to private form and possibilities. Only the fact of her ladyship having taken it into her head to invite a house-party for the last week of May had prevented Mr. Motkin from paying a visit of consultation to his relative with respect to the big race; there was still time to cycle over if he could get leave of absence for the afternoon on some specious excuse.

"Let's jolly well hope he does," said Bertie van Tahn; "under the circumstances a second cousin is almost as useful as second sight."

"That stable ought to know something, if knowledge is to be found anywhere," said Mrs. Packletide hopefully.

"I expect you'll find he'll echo my fancy for Motorboat," said Colonel Drake.

At this moment the subject had to be hastily dropped. Lady Susan bore down upon them, leaning on the arm of Clovis's mother, to whom she was confiding the fact that she disapproved of the craze for Pekingese spaniels. It was the third thing she had found time to disapprove of since lunch, without counting her silent and permanent disapproval of the way Clovis's mother did her hair.

"We have been admiring the Himalayan pheasants," said Mrs. Packletide suavely.

"They went off to a bird-show at Nottingham early this morning," said Lady Susan, with the air of one who disapproves of hasty and ill-considered lying.

"Their house, I mean; such perfect roosting arrangements, and all so clean," resumed Mrs. Packletide, with an increased glow of enthusiasm. The odious Bertie van Tahn was murmuring audible prayers for Mrs. Packletide's ultimate estrangement from the paths of falsehood.

"I hope you don't mind dinner being a quarter of an hour late to-night," said Lady Susan; "Motkin has had an urgent summons to go and see a sick relative this afternoon. He wanted to bicycle there, but I am sending him in the motor."

"How very kind of you! Of course we don't mind dinner being put off." The assurances came with unanimous and hearty sincerity.

At the dinner-table that night an undercurrent of furtive curiosity directed itself towards Motkin's impassive countenance. One or two of the guests almost expected to find a slip of paper concealed in their napkins, bearing the name of the second cousin's selection. They had not long to wait. As the butler went round with the murmured question, "Sherry?" he added in an even lower tone the cryptic words, "Better not." Mrs. Packletide gave a start of alarm, and refused the sherry; there seemed some sinister suggestion in the butler's warning, as though her hostess had suddenly become addicted to the Borgia habit. A moment later the explanation flashed on her that "Better Not" was the name of one of the runners in the big race. Clovis was already pencilling it on his cuff, and Colonel Drake, in his turn, was signalling to every one in hoarse whispers and dumb-show the fact that he had all along fancied "B.N."

Early next morning a sheaf of telegrams went Townward, representing the market commands of the house-party and servants' hall.

It was a wet afternoon, and most of Lady Susan's guests hung about the hall, waiting apparently for the appearance of tea, though it was scarcely yet due. The advent of a telegram quickened every one into a flutter of expectancy; the page who brought the telegram to Clovis waited with unusual alertness to know if there might be an answer.

Clovis read the message and gave an exclamation of annoyance.

"No bad news, I hope," said Lady Susan. Every one else knew that the news was not good.

"It's only the result of the Derby," he blurted out; "Sadowa won; an utter outsider."

"Sadowa!" exclaimed Lady Susan; "you don't say so! How remarkable! It's the first time I've ever backed a horse; in fact I disapprove of horse-racing, but just for once in a way I put money on this horse, and it's gone and won."

"May I ask," said Mrs. Packletide, amid the general silence, "why you put your money on this particular horse. None of the sporting prophets mentioned it as having an outside chance."

"Well," said Lady Susan, "you may laugh at me, but it was the name that attracted me. You see, I was always mixed up with the Franco-German war; I was married on the day that the war was declared, and my eldest child was born the day that peace was signed, so anything connected with the war has always interested me. And when I saw there was a horse running in the Derby called after one of the battles in the Franco-German war, I said I *must* put some money on it, for once in a way, though I disapprove of racing. And it's actually won."

There was a general groan. No one groaned more deeply than the professor of military history.

21. The Recessional

Clovis sat in the hottest zone but two of a Turkish bath, alternately inert in statuesque contemplation and rapidly manoeuvring a fountain-pen over the pages of a note-book.

"Don't interrupt me with your childish prattle," he observed to Bertie van Tahn, who had slung himself languidly into a neighbouring chair and looked conversationally inclined; "I'm writing deathless verse."

Bertie looked interested.

"I say, what a boon you would be to portrait painters if you really got to be notorious as a poetry writer. If they couldn't get your likeness hung in the Academy as 'Clovis Sangrail, Esq., at work on his latest poem,' they could slip you in as a Study of the Nude or Orpheus descending into Jermyn Street. They always complain that modern dress handicaps them, whereas a towel and a fountain-pen –"

"It was Mrs. Packletide's suggestion that I should write this thing," said Clovis, ignoring the bypaths to fame that Bertie van Tahn was pointing out to him. "You see, Loona Bimberton had a Coronation Ode accepted by the *New Infancy,* a paper that has been started with the idea of making the *New Age* seem elderly and hidebound. 'So clever of you, dear Loona,' the Packletide remarked when she had read it; 'of course, anyone could write a Coronation Ode, but no one else would have thought of doing it.' Loona protested that these things were extremely difficult to do, and gave us to understand that they were more or less the province of a gifted few. Now the Packletide has been rather decent to me in many ways, a sort of financial ambulance, you know, that carries you off the field when you're hard hit, which is a frequent occurrence with me, and I've no use whatever for Loona Bimberton, so I chipped in and said I could turn out that sort of stuff by the square yard if I gave my mind to it. Loona said I couldn't, and we got bets on, and between you and me I think the money's fairly safe. Of course, one of the conditions of the wager is that the thing has to be published in something or other, local newspapers barred; but Mrs. Packletide has endeared herself by many little acts of thoughtfulness to the editor of the *Smoky Chimney*, so if I can hammer out anything at all approaching the level of the usual Ode output we ought to be all right. So far I'm getting along so comfortably that I begin to be afraid that I must he one of the gifted few."

"It's rather late in the day for a Coronation Ode, isn't it?" said Bertie.

"Of course," said Clovis; "this is going to be a Durbar Recessional, the sort of thing that you can keep by you for all time if you want to."

"Now I understand your choice of a place to write it in," said Bertie van Tahn, with the air of one who has suddenly unravelled a hitherto obscure problem; "you want to get the local temperature."

"I came here to get freedom from the inane interruptions of the mentally deficient," said Clovis, "but it seems I asked too much of fate."

Bertie van Tahn prepared to use his towel as a weapon of precision, but reflecting that he had a good deal of unprotected coast-line himself, and that Clovis was equipped with a fountain-pen as well as a towel, he relapsed pacifically into the depths of his chair.

"May one hear extracts from the immortal work?" he asked. "I promise that nothing that I hear now shall prejudice me against borrowing a copy of the *Smoky Chimney* at the right moment."

"It's rather like casting pearls into a trough," remarked Clovis pleasantly, "but I don't mind reading you bits of it. It begins with a general dispersal of the Durbar participants:

'Back to their homes in Himalayan heights
The stale pale elephants of Cutch Behar
Roll like great galleons on a tideless sea –'

"I don't believe Cutch Behar is anywhere near the Himalayan region," interrupted Bertie. "You ought to have an atlas on hand when you do this sort of thing; and why stale and pale?"

"After the late hours and the excitement, of course," said Clovis; "and I said their *homes* were in the Himalayas. You can have Himalayan elephants in Cutch Behar, I suppose, just as you have Irish-bred horses running at Ascot."

"You said they were going back to the Himalayas," objected Bertie.

"Well, they would naturally be sent home to recuperate. It's the usual thing out there to turn elephants loose in the hills, just as we put horses out to grass in this country."

Clovis could at least flatter himself that he had infused some of the reckless splendour of the East into his mendacity.

"Is it all going to be in blank verse?" asked the critic.

"Of course not; 'Durbar' comes at the end of the fourth line."

"That seems so cowardly; however, it explains why you pitched on Cutch Behar."

"There is more connection between geographical place-names and poetical inspiration than is generally recognised; one of the chief reasons why there are so few really great poems about Russia in our language is that you can't possibly get a rhyme to names like Smolensk and Tobolsk and Minsk."

Clovis spoke with the authority of one who has tried.

"Of course, you could rhyme Omsk with Tomsk," he continued; "in fact, they seem to be there for that purpose, but the public wouldn't stand that sort of thing indefinitely."

"The public will stand a good deal," said Bertie malevolently, "and so small a proportion of it knows Russian that you could always have an explanatory footnote asserting that the last three letters in Smolensk are not pronounced. It's quite as believable as your statement about putting elephants out to grass in the Himalayan range."

"I've got rather a nice bit," resumed Clovis with unruffled serenity, "giving an evening scene on the outskirts of a jungle village:

'Where the coiled cobra in the gloaming gloats,
And prowling panthers stalk the wary goats.'

"There is practically no gloaming in tropical countries," said Bertie indulgently; "but I like the masterly reticence with which you treat the cobra's motive for gloating. The unknown is proverbially the uncanny. I can picture nervous readers of the *Smoky Chimney* keeping the light turned on in their bedrooms all night out of sheer sickening uncertainty as to *what* the cobra might have been gloating about."

"Cobras gloat naturally," said Clovis, "just as wolves are always ravening from mere force of habit, even after they've hopelessly overeaten themselves. I've got a fine bit of colour painting later on," he added, "where I describe the dawn coming up over the Brahmaputra river:

'The amber dawn-drenched East with sun-shafts kissed,
Stained sanguine apricot and amethyst,
O'er the washed emerald of the mango groves
Hangs in a mist of opalescent mauves,
While painted parrot-flights impinge the haze
With scarlet, chalcedon and chrysoprase.'

"I've never seen the dawn come up over the Brahmaputra river," said Bertie, "so I can't say if it's a good description of the event, but it sounds more like an account of an extensive jewel robbery. Anyhow, the parrots give a good useful touch of local colour. I suppose you've introduced some tigers into the scenery? An Indian landscape would have rather a bare, unfinished look without a tiger or two in the middle distance."

"I've got a hen-tiger somewhere in the poem," said Clovis, hunting through his notes. "Here she is:

'The tawny tigress 'mid the tangled teak
Drags to her purring cubs' enraptured ears
The harsh death-rattle in the pea-fowl's beak,
A jungle lullaby of blood and tears.'

Bertie van Tahn rose hurriedly from his recumbent position and made for the glass door leading into the next compartment.

"I think your idea of home life in the jungle is perfectly horrid," he said. "The cobra was sinister enough, but the improvised rattle in the tiger-nursery is the limit. If you're going to make me turn hot and cold all over I may as well go into the steam room at once."

"Just listen to this line," said Clovis; "it would make the reputation of any ordinary poet:

'and overhead
The pendulum-patient Punkah, parent of stillborn breeze.'

"Most of your readers will think 'punkah' is a kind of iced drink or half-time at polo," said Bertie, and disappeared into the steam.

~

The *Smoky Chimney* published the "Recessional," but it proved to be its swan song, for the paper never attained to another issue.

Loona Bimberton gave up her intention of attending the Durbar and went into a nursing-home on the Sussex Downs. Nervous breakdown after a particularly strenuous season was the usually accepted explanation, but there are three or four people who know that she never really recovered from the dawn breaking over the Brahmaputra river.

22. The Unrest-Cure

On the rack in the railway carriage immediately opposite Clovis was a solidly wrought travelling-bag, with a carefully written label, on which was inscribed, "J. P. Huddle, The Warren, Tilfield, near Slowborough." Immediately below the rack sit the human embodiment of the label, a solid, sedate individual, sedately dressed, sedately conversational. Even without his conversation (which was addressed to a friend seated by his side, and touched chiefly on such topics as the backwardness of Roman hyacinths and the prevalence of measles at the Rectory), one could have gauged fairly accurately the temperament and mental outlook of the travelling bag's owner. But he seemed unwilling to leave anything to the imagination of a casual observer, and his talk grew presently personal and introspective.

"I don't know how it is," he told his friend, "I'm not much over forty, but I seem to have settled down into a deep groove of elderly middle-age. My sister shows the same tendency. We like everything to be exactly in its accustomed place; we like things to happen exactly at their appointed times; we like everything to be usual, orderly, punctual, methodical, to a hair's breadth, to a minute. It distresses and upsets us if it is not so. For instance, to take a very trifling matter, a thrush has built its nest year after year in the catkin-tree on the lawn; this year, for no obvious reason, it is building in the ivy on the garden wall. We have said very little about it, but I think we both feel that the change is unnecessary, and just a little irritating."

"Perhaps," said the friend, "it is a different thrush."

"We have suspected that," said J. P. Huddle, "and I think it gives us even more cause for annoyance. We don't feel that we want a change of thrush at our time of life; and yet, as I have said, we have scarcely reached an age when these things should make themselves seriously felt."

"What you want," said the friend, "is an Unrest-cure."

"An Unrest-cure? I've never heard of such a thing."

"You've heard of Rest-cures for people who've broken down under stress of too much worry and strenuous living; well, you're suffering from overmuch repose and placidity, and you need the opposite kind of treatment."

"But where would one go for such a thing?"

"Well, you might stand as an Orange candidate for Kilkenny, or do a course of district visiting in one of the Apache quarters of Paris, or give lectures in Berlin to prove that most of Wagner's music was written by Gambetta; and there's always the interior of Morocco to travel in. But, to be really effective, the Unrest-cure ought to be tried in the home. How you would do it I haven't the faintest idea."

It was at this point in the conversation that Clovis became galvanised into alert attention. After all, his two days' visit to an elderly relative at Slowborough did not promise much excitement. Before the train had stopped he had decorated his sinister shirt-cuff with the inscription, "J. P. Huddle, The Warren, Tilfield, near Slowborough."

~

Two mornings later Mr. Huddle broke in on his sister's privacy as she sat reading Country Life in the morning room. It was her day and hour and place for reading Country Life, and the intrusion was absolutely irregular; but he bore in his hand a telegram, and in that household telegrams were recognised as happening by the hand of God. This particular telegram partook of the nature of a thunderbolt. "Bishop examining confirmation class in neighbourhood unable stay rectory on account measles invokes your hospitality sending secretary arrange."

"I scarcely know the Bishop; I've only spoken to him once," exclaimed J. P. Huddle, with the exculpating air of one who realises too late the indiscretion of speaking to strange Bishops. Miss Huddle was the first to rally; she disliked thunderbolts as fervently as her brother did, but the womanly instinct in her told her that thunderbolts must be fed.

"We can curry the cold duck," she said. It was not the appointed day for curry, but the little orange envelope involved a certain departure from rule and custom. Her brother said nothing, but his eyes thanked her for being brave.

"A young gentleman to see you," announced the parlour-maid.

"The secretary!" murmured the Huddles in unison; they instantly stiffened into a demeanour which proclaimed that, though they held all strangers to be guilty, they were willing to hear anything they might have to say in their defence. The young gentleman, who came into the room with a certain elegant haughtiness, was not at all Huddle's idea of a bishop's secretary; he had not supposed that the episcopal establishment could have afforded such an expensively upholstered article when there were so many other claims on its resources. The face was fleetingly familiar; if he had bestowed more attention on the fellow-traveller sitting opposite him in the railway carriage two days before he might have recognised Clovis in his present visitor.

"You are the Bishop's secretary?" asked Huddle, becoming consciously deferential.

"His confidential secretary," answered Clovis. You may call me Stanislaus; my other name doesn't matter. The Bishop and Colonel Alberti may be here to lunch. I shall be here in any case."

It sounded rather like the programme of a Royal visit.

"The Bishop is examining a confirmation class in the neighbourhood, isn't he?" asked Miss Huddle.

"Ostensibly," was the dark reply, followed by a request for a large-scale map of the locality.

Clovis was still immersed in a seemingly profound study of the map when another telegram arrived. It was addressed to

"Prince Stanislaus, care of Huddle, The Warren, etc." Clovis glanced at the contents and announced: "The Bishop and Alberti won't be here till late in the afternoon." Then he returned to his scrutiny of the map.

The luncheon was not a very festive function. The princely secretary ate and drank with fair appetite, but severely discouraged conversation. At the finish of the meal he broke suddenly into a radiant smile, thanked his hostess for a charming repast, and kissed her hand with deferential rapture.

Miss Huddle was unable to decide in her mind whether the action savoured of Louis Quatorzian courtliness or the reprehensible Roman attitude towards the Sabine women. It was not her day for having a headache, but she felt that the circumstances excused her, and retired to her room to have as much headache as was possible before the Bishop's arrival. Clovis, having asked the way to the nearest telegraph office, disappeared presently down the carriage drive. Mr. Huddle met him in the hall some two hours later, and asked when the Bishop would arrive.

"He is in the library with Alberti," was the reply.

"But why wasn't I told? I never knew he had come!" exclaimed Huddle.

"No one knows he is here," said Clovis; "the quieter we can keep matters the better. And on no account disturb him in the library. Those are his orders."

"But what is all this mystery about? And who is Alberti? And isn't the Bishop going to have tea?"

"The Bishop is out for blood, not tea."

"Blood!" gasped Huddle, who did not find that the thunderbolt improved on acquaintance.

"To-night is going to be a great night in the history of Christendom," said Clovis. "We are going to massacre every Jew in the neighbourhood."

"To massacre the Jews!" said Huddle indignantly. "Do you mean to tell me there's a general rising against them?"

"No, it's the Bishop's own idea. He's in there arranging all the details now."

"But – the Bishop is such a tolerant, humane man."

"That is precisely what will heighten the effect of his action. The sensation will be enormous."

That at least Huddle could believe.

"He will be hanged!" he exclaimed with conviction.

"A motor is waiting to carry him to the coast, where a steam yacht is in readiness."

"But there aren't thirty Jews in the whole neighbourhood," protested Huddle, whose brain, under the repeated shocks of the day, was operating with the uncertainty of a telegraph wire during earthquake disturbances.

"We have twenty-six on our list," said Clovis, referring to a bundle of notes. "We shall be able to deal with them all the more thoroughly."

"Do you mean to tell me that you are meditating violence against a man like Sir Leon Birberry," stammered Huddle; "he's one of the most respected men in the country."

"He's down on our list," said Clovis carelessly; "after all, we've got men we can trust to do our job, so we shan't have to rely on local assistance. And we've got some Boy-scouts helping us as auxiliaries."

"Boy-scouts!"

"Yes; when they understood there was real killing to be done they were even keener than the men."

"This thing will be a blot on the Twentieth Century!"

"And your house will be the blotting-pad. Have you realised that half the papers of Europe and the United States will publish pictures of it? By the way, I've sent some photographs of you and your sister, that I found in the library, to the MATIN and DIE WOCHE; I hope you don't mind. Also a sketch of the staircase; most of the killing will probably be done on the staircase."

The emotions that were surging in J. P. Huddle's brain were almost too intense to be disclosed in speech, but he managed to gasp out: "There aren't any Jews in this house."

"Not at present," said Clovis.

"I shall go to the police," shouted Huddle with sudden energy.

"In the shrubbery," said Clovis, "are posted ten men who have orders to fire on anyone who leaves the house without my signal of permission. Another armed picquet is in ambush near the front gate. The Boy-scouts watch the back premises."

At this moment the cheerful hoot of a motor-horn was heard from the drive. Huddle rushed to the hall door with the feeling of a man half awakened from a nightmare, and beheld Sir Leon Birberry, who had driven himself over in his car. "I got your telegram," he said what's up?"

Telegram? It seemed to be a day of telegrams.

"Come here at once. Urgent. James Huddle," was the purport of the message displayed before Huddle's bewildered eyes.

"I see it all!" he exclaimed suddenly in a voice shaken with agitation, and with a look of agony in the direction of the shrubbery he hauled the astonished Birberry into the house. Tea had just been laid in the hall, but the now thoroughly panic-stricken Huddle dragged his protesting guest upstairs, and in a few minutes' time the entire household had been summoned to that region of momentary safety. Clovis alone graced the tea-table with his presence; the fanatics in the library were evidently too immersed in their monstrous machinations to dally with the solace of teacup and hot toast. Once the youth rose, in answer to the summons of the front-door bell, and admitted Mr. Paul Isaacs, shoemaker and parish councillor, who had also received a pressing invitation to The Warren. With an atrocious assumption of courtesy, which a Borgia could hardly have outdone, the secretary escorted this new captive of his net to the head of the stairway, where his involuntary host awaited him.

And then ensued a long ghastly vigil of watching and waiting. Once or twice Clovis left the house to stroll across to the shrubbery, returning always to the library, for the purpose evidently of making a brief report. Once he took in the letters from the evening postman, and brought them to the top of the stairs with punctilious politeness. After his next absence he came half-way up the stairs to make an announcement.

"The Boy-scouts mistook my signal, and have killed the postman. I've had very little practice in this sort of thing, you see. Another time I shall do better."

The housemaid, who was engaged to be married to the evening postman, gave way to clamorous grief.

"Remember that your mistress has a headache," said J. P. Huddle. (Miss Huddle's headache was worse.)

Clovis hastened downstairs, and after a short visit to the library returned with another message:

"The Bishop is sorry to hear that Miss Huddle has a headache. He is issuing orders that as far as possible no firearms shall be used near the house; any killing that is necessary on the premises will be done with cold steel. The Bishop does not see why a man should not be a gentleman as well as a Christian."

That was the last they saw of Clovis; it was nearly seven o'clock, and his elderly relative liked him to dress for dinner. But, though he had left them for ever, the lurking suggestion of his presence haunted the lower regions of the house during the long hours of the wakeful night, and every creak of the stairway, every rustle of wind through the shrubbery, was fraught with horrible meaning. At about seven next morning the gardener's boy and the early postman finally convinced the watchers that the Twentieth Century was still unblotted.

"I don't suppose," mused Clovis, as an early train bore him townwards, "that they will be in the least grateful for the Unrest-cure."

23. Sredni Vashtar

Conradin was ten years old, and the doctor had pronounced his professional opinion that the boy would not live another five years. The doctor was silky and effete, and counted for little, but his opinion was endorsed by Mrs. de Ropp, who counted for nearly everything. Mrs. De Ropp was Conradin's cousin and guardian, and in his eyes she represented those three-fifths of the world that are necessary and disagreeable and real; the other two-fifths, in perpetual antagonism to the foregoing, were summed up in himself and his imagination. One of these days Conradin supposed he would succumb to the mastering pressure of wearisome necessary things—such as illnesses and coddling restrictions and drawn-out dullness. Without his imagination, which was rampant under the spur of loneliness, he would have succumbed long ago.

Mrs. de Ropp would never, in her honestest moments, have confessed to herself that she disliked Conradin, though she might have been dimly aware that thwarting him "for his good" was a duty which she did not find particularly irksome. Conradin hated her with a desperate sincerity which he was perfectly able to mask. Such few pleasures as he could contrive for himself gained an added relish from the likelihood that they would be displeasing to his guardian, and from the realm of his imagination she was locked out – an unclean thing, which should find no entrance.

In the dull, cheerless garden, overlooked by so many windows that were ready to open with a message not to do this or that, or a reminder that medicines were due, he found little attraction. The few fruit-trees that it contained were set jealously apart from his plucking, as though they were rare specimens of their kind blooming in an arid waste; it would probably have been difficult to find a market-gardener who would have offered ten shillings for their entire yearly produce. In a forgotten corner, however, almost hidden behind a dismal shrubbery, was a disused tool-shed of respectable proportions, and within its walls Conradin found a haven, something that took on the varying aspects of a playroom and a cathedral. He had peopled it with a legion of familiar phantoms, evoked partly from fragments of history and partly from his own brain, but it also boasted two inmates of flesh and blood. In one corner lived a ragged-plumaged Houdan hen, on which the boy lavished an affection that had scarcely another outlet. Further back in the gloom stood a large hutch, divided into two compartments, one of which was fronted with close iron bars. This was the abode of a large polecat-ferret, which a friendly butcher-boy had once smuggled, cage and all, into its present quarters, in exchange for a long-secreted hoard of small silver. Conradin was dreadfully afraid of the lithe, sharp-fanged beast, but it was his most treasured possession. Its very presence in the tool-shed was a secret and fearful joy, to be kept scrupulously from the knowledge of the Woman, as he privately dubbed his cousin. And one day, out of Heaven knows what material, he spun the beast a wonderful name, and from that moment it grew into a god and a religion. The Woman indulged in religion once a week at a church near by, and took Conradin with her, but to him the church service was an alien rite in the House of Rimmon. Every Thursday, in the dim and musty silence of the tool-shed, he worshipped with mystic and elaborate ceremonial before the wooden hutch where dwelt Sredni Vashtar, the great ferret. Red flowers in their season and scarlet berries in the winter-time were offered at his shrine, for he was a god who laid some special stress on the fierce impatient side of things, as opposed to the Woman's religion, which, as far as Conradin could observe, went to great lengths in the contrary direction. And on great festivals powdered nutmeg was strewn in front of his hutch, an important feature of the offering being that the nutmeg had to be stolen. These festivals were of irregular occurrence, and were chiefly appointed to celebrate some passing event. On one occasion, when Mrs. de Ropp suffered from acute toothache for three days, Conradin kept up the festival during the entire three days, and almost succeeded in persuading himself that Sredni Vashtar was personally responsible for the toothache. If the malady had lasted for another day the supply of nutmeg would have given out.

The Houdan hen was never drawn into the cult of Sredni Vashtar. Conradin had long ago settled that she was an Anabaptist. He did not pretend to have the remotest knowledge as to what an Anabaptist was, but he privately hoped that it was dashing and not very respectable. Mrs. de Ropp was the ground plan on which he based and detested all respectability.

After a while Conradin's absorption in the tool-shed began to attract the notice of his guardian. "It is not good for him to be pottering down there in all weathers," she promptly decided, and at breakfast one morning she announced that the Houdan hen had been sold and taken away overnight. With her short-sighted eyes she peered at Conradin, waiting for an outbreak of rage and sorrow, which she was ready to rebuke with a flow of excellent precepts and reasoning. But Conradin said nothing: there was nothing to be said. Something perhaps in his white set face gave her a momentary qualm, for at tea that afternoon there was toast on the table, a delicacy which she usually banned on the ground that it was bad for him; also because the making of it "gave trouble," a deadly offence in the middle-class feminine eye.

"I thought you liked toast," she exclaimed, with an injured air, observing that he did not touch it.

"Sometimes," said Conradin.

In the shed that evening there was an innovation in the worship of the hutch-god. Conradin had been wont to chant his praises, tonight he asked a boon.

"Do one thing for me, Sredni Vashtar."

The thing was not specified. As Sredni Vashtar was a god he must be supposed to know. And choking back a sob as he looked at that other empty corner, Conradin went back to the world he so hated.

And every night, in the welcome darkness of his bedroom, and every evening in the dusk of the tool-shed, Conradin's bitter litany went up: "Do one thing for me, Sredni Vashtar."

Mrs. de Ropp noticed that the visits to the shed did not cease, and one day she made a further journey of inspection.

"What are you keeping in that locked hutch?" she asked. "I believe it's guinea-pigs. I'll have them all cleared away."

Conradin shut his lips tight, but the Woman ransacked his bedroom till she found the carefully hidden key, and forthwith marched down to the shed to complete her discovery. It was a cold afternoon, and Conradin had been bidden to keep to the house. From the furthest window of the dining-room the door of the shed could just be seen beyond the corner of the shrubbery, and there Conradin stationed himself. He saw the Woman enter, and then he imagined her opening the door of the sacred hutch and peering down with her short-sighted eyes into the thick straw bed where his god lay hidden. Perhaps she would prod at the straw in her clumsy impatience. And Conradin fervently breathed his prayer for the last time. But he knew as he prayed that he did not believe. He knew that the Woman would come out presently with that pursed smile he loathed so well on her face, and that in an hour or two the gardener would carry away his wonderful god, a god no longer, but a simple brown ferret in a hutch. And he knew that the Woman, would triumph always as she triumphed now, and that he would grow ever more sickly under her pestering and domineering and superior wisdom, till one day nothing would matter much more with him, and the doctor would be proved right. And in the sting and misery of his defeat, he began to chant loudly and defiantly the hymn of his threatened idol:

Sredni Vashtar went forth,
His thoughts were red thoughts and his teeth were white.
His enemies called for peace, but he brought them death.
Sredni Vashtar the Beautiful.

And then of a sudden he stopped his chanting and drew closer to the window-pane. The door of the shed still stood ajar as it had been left, and the minutes were slipping by. They were long minutes, but they slipped by nevertheless. He watched the starlings running and flying in little parties across the lawn; he counted them over and over again, with one eye always on that swinging door. A sour-faced maid came in to lay the table for tea, and still Conradin stood and waited and watched. Hope had crept by inches into his heart, and now a look of triumph began to blaze in his eyes that had only known the wistful patience of defeat. Under his breath, with a furtive exultation, he began once again the paean of victory and devastation. And presently his eyes were rewarded: out through that doorway came a long, low, yellow-and-brown beast, with eyes a-blink at the waning daylight, and dark wet stains around the fur of jaws and throat. Conradin dropped on his knees. The great polecat-ferret made its way down to a small brook at the foot of the garden, drank for a moment, then crossed a little plank bridge and was lost to sight in the bushes. Such was the passing of Sredni Vashtar.

"Tea is ready," said the sour-faced maid; "where is the mistress?"

"She went down to the shed some time ago," said Conradin.

And while the maid went to summon her mistress to tea, Conradin fished a toasting-fork out of the sideboard drawer and proceeded to toast himself a piece of bread. And during the toasting of it and the buttering of it with much butter and the slow enjoyment of eating it, Conradin listened to the noises and silences which fell in quick spasms beyond the dining-room door. The loud foolish screaming of the maid, the answering chorus of wondering ejaculations from the kitchen region, the scuttering footsteps and hurried embassies for outside help, and then, after a lull, the scared sobbings and the shuffling tread of those who bore a heavy burden into the house.

"Whoever will break it to the poor child? I couldn't for the life of me!" exclaimed a shrill voice. And while they debated the matter among themselves, Conradin made himself another piece of toast.

24. The Music On The Hill

Sylvia Seltoun ate her breakfast in the morning-room at Yessney with a pleasant sense of ultimate victory, such as a fervent Ironside might have permitted himself on the morrow of Worcester fight. She was scarcely pugnacious by temperament, but belonged to that more successful class of fighters who are pugnacious by circumstance. Fate had willed that her life should be occupied with a series of small struggles, usually with the odds slightly against her, and usually she had just managed to come through winning. And now she felt that she had brought her hardest and certainly her most important struggle to a successful issue. To have married Mortimer Seltoun, "Dead Mortimer" as his more intimate enemies called him, in the teeth of the cold hostility of his family, and in spite of his unaffected indifference to women, was indeed an achievement that had needed some determination and adroitness to carry through; yesterday she had brought her victory to its concluding stage by wrenching her husband away from Town and its group of satellite watering-places and "settling him down," in the vocabulary of her kind, in this remote wood-girt manor farm which was his country house.

"You will never get Mortimer to go," his mother had said carpingly, "but if he once goes he'll stay; Yessney throws almost as much a spell over him as Town does. One can understand what holds him to Town, but Yessney –" and the dowager had shrugged her shoulders.

There was a sombre almost savage wildness about Yessney that was certainly not likely to appeal to town-bred tastes, and Sylvia, notwithstanding her name, was accustomed to nothing much more sylvan than "leafy Kensington." She looked on the country as something excellent and wholesome in its way, which was apt to become, troublesome if you encouraged it overmuch. Distrust of town-life had been a new thing with her, born of her marriage with Mortimer, and she had watched with satisfaction the gradual fading of what she called "the Jermyn-street-look" in his eyes as the woods and heather of Yessney had closed in on them yesternight. Her will-power and strategy had prevailed; Mortimer would stay.

Outside the morning-room windows was a triangular slope of turf, which the indulgent might call a lawn, and beyond its low hedge of neglected fuchsia bushes a steeper slope of heather and bracken dropped down into cavernous combes overgrown with oak and yew. In its wild open savagery there seemed a stealthy linking of the joy of life with the terror of unseen things. Sylvia smiled complacently as she gazed with a School-of-Art appreciation at the landscape, and then of a sudden she almost shuddered.

"It is very wild," she said to Mortimer, who had joined her; "one could almost think that in such a place the worship of Pan had never quite died out."

"The worship of Pan never has died out," said Mortimer. "Other newer gods have drawn aside his votaries from time to time, but he is the Nature-God to whom all must come back at last. He has been called the Father of all the Gods, but most of his children have been stillborn."

Sylvia was religious in an honest vaguely devotional kind of way, and did not like to hear her beliefs spoken of as mere aftergrowths, but it was at least something new and hopeful to hear Dead Mortimer speak with such energy and conviction on any subject.

"You don't really believe in Pan?" she asked incredulously.

"I've been a fool in most things," said Mortimer quietly, "but I'm not such a fool as not to believe in Pan when I'm down here. And if you're wise you won't disbelieve in him too boastfully while you're in his country."

It was not till a week later, when Sylvia had exhausted the attractions of the woodland walks round Yessney, that she ventured on a tour of inspection of the farm buildings. A farmyard suggested in her mind a scene of cheerful bustle, with churns and flails and smiling dairymaids, and teams of horses drinking knee-deep in duck-crowded ponds. As she wandered among the gaunt grey buildings of Yessney manor farm her first impression was one of crushing stillness and desolation, as though she had happened on some lone deserted homestead long given over to owls and cobwebs; then came a sense of furtive watchful hostility, the same shadow of unseen things that seemed to lurk in the wooded combes and coppices. From behind heavy doors and shuttered windows came the restless stamp of hoof or rasp of chain halter, and at times a muffled bellow from some stalled beast. From a distant corner a shaggy dog watched her with intent unfriendly eyes; as she drew near it slipped quietly into its kennel, and slipped out again as noiselessly when she had passed by. A few hens, questing for food under a rick, stole away under a gate at her approach. Sylvia felt that if she had come across any human beings in this wilderness of barn and byre they would have fled wraith-like from her gaze. At last, turning a corner quickly, she came upon a living thing that did not fly from her. Astretch in a pool of mud was an enormous sow, gigantic beyond the town-woman's wildest computation of swine-flesh, and speedily alert to resent and if necessary repel the unwonted intrusion. It was Sylvia's turn to make an unobtrusive retreat. As she threaded her way past rickyards and cowsheds and long blank walls, she started suddenly at a strange sound – the echo of a boy's laughter, golden and equivocal. Jan, the only boy employed on the farm, a towheaded, wizen-faced yokel, was visibly at work on a potato clearing halfway up the nearest hill-side, and Mortimer, when questioned, knew of no other probable or possible begetter of the hidden mockery that had ambushed Sylvia's retreat. The memory of that untraceable echo was added to her other impressions of a furtive sinister "something " that hung around Yessney.

Of Mortimer she saw very little; farm and woods and trout-streams seemed to swallow him up from dawn till dusk. Once, following the direction she had seen him take in the morning, she came to an open space in a nut copse, further shut in by huge yew trees, in the centre of which stood a stone pedestal surmounted by a small bronze figure of a youthful Pan. It was a beautiful piece of workmanship, but her attention was chiefly held by the fact that a newly cut bunch of grapes had been placed as an offering at its feet. Grapes were none too plentiful at the manor house, and Sylvia snatched the bunch angrily from the pedestal. Contemptuous annoyance dominated her thoughts as she strolled slowly homeward, and then gave way to a sharp feeling of something that was very near fright; across a thick tangle of undergrowth a boy's face was scowling at her, brown and beautiful, with unutterably evil eyes. It was a lonely pathway, all pathways round Yessney were lonely for the matter of that, and she sped forward without waiting to give a closer scrutiny to this sudden apparition. It was not till she had reached the house that she discovered that she had dropped the bunch of grapes in her flight.

"I saw a youth in the wood to-day," she told Mortimer that evening, "brown-faced and rather handsome, but a scoundrel to look at. A gipsy lad, I suppose."

"A reasonable theory," said Mortimer, "only there aren't any gipsies in these parts at present."

"Then who was he?" asked Sylvia, and as Mortimer appeared to have no theory of his own, she passed on to recount her finding of the votive offering.

"I suppose it was your doing," she observed; "it's a harmless piece of lunacy, but people would think you dreadfully silly if they knew of it."

"Did you meddle with it in any way?" asked Mortimer.

"I – I threw the grapes away. It seemed so silly," said Sylvia, watching Mortimer's impassive face for a sign of annoyance.

"I don't think you were wise to do that," he said reflectively. "I've heard it said that the Wood Gods are rather horrible to those who molest them."

"Horrible perhaps to those that believe in them, but you see I don't," retorted Sylvia.

"All the same," said Mortimer in his even, dispassionate tone, "I should avoid the woods and orchards if I were you, and give a wide berth to the horned beasts on the farm."

It was all nonsense, of course, but in that lonely wood-girt spot nonsense seemed able to rear a bastard brood of uneasiness.

"Mortimer," said Sylvia suddenly, "I think we will go back to Town some time soon."

Her victory had not been so complete as she had supposed; it had carried her on to ground that she was already anxious to quit.

"I don't think you will ever go back to Town," said Mortimer. He seemed to be paraphrasing his mother's prediction as to himself.

Sylvia noted with dissatisfaction and some self-contempt that the course of her next afternoon's ramble took her instinctively clear of the network of woods. As to the horned cattle, Mortimer's warning was scarcely needed, for she had always regarded them as of doubtful neutrality at the best: her imagination unsexed the most matronly dairy cows and turned them into bulls liable to "see red" at any moment. The ram who fed in the narrow paddock below the orchards she had adjudged, after ample and cautious probation, to be of docile temper; today, however, she decided to leave his docility untested, for the usually tranquil beast was roaming with every sign of restlessness from corner to corner of his meadow. A low, fitful piping, as of some reedy flute, was coming from the depth of a neighbouring copse, and there seemed to be some subtle connection between the animal's restless pacing and the wild music from the wood. Sylvia turned her steps in an upward direction and climbed the heather-clad slopes that stretched in rolling shoulders high above Yessney. She had left the piping notes behind her, but across the wooded combes at her feet the wind brought her another kind of music, the straining bay of hounds in full chase. Yessney was just on the outskirts of the Devon-and-Somerset country, and the hunted deer sometimes came that way. Sylvia could presently see a dark body, breasting hill after hill, and sinking again and again out of sight as he crossed the combes, while behind him steadily swelled that relentless chorus, and she grew tense with the excited sympathy that one feels for any hunted thing in whose capture one is not directly interested. And at last he broke through the outermost line of oak scrub and fern and stood panting in the open, a fat September stag carrying a well-furnished head. His obvious course was to drop down to the brown pools of Undercombe, and thence make his way towards the red deer's favoured sanctuary, the sea. To Sylvia's surprise, however, he turned his head to the upland slope and came lumbering resolutely onward over the heather. "It will be dreadful," she thought, "the hounds will pull him down under my very eyes." But the music of the pack seemed to have died away for a moment, and in its place she heard again that wild piping, which rose now on this side, now on that, as though urging the failing stag to a final effort. Sylvia stood well aside from his path, half hidden in a thick growth of whortle bushes, and watched him swing stiffly upward, his flanks dark with sweat, the coarse hair on his neck showing light by contrast. The pipe music shrilled suddenly around her, seeming to come from the bushes at her very feet, and at the same moment the great beast slewed round and bore directly down upon her. In an instant her pity for the hunted animal was changed to wild terror at her own danger; the thick heather roots mocked her scrambling efforts at flight, and she looked frantically downward for a glimpse of oncoming hounds. The huge antler spikes were within a few yards of her, and in a flash of numbing fear she remembered Mortimer's warning, to beware of homed beasts on the farm. And then with a quick throb of joy she saw that she was not alone; a human figure stood a few paces aside, knee-deep in the whortle bushes.

"Drive it off she shrieked. But the figure made no answering movement.

The antlers drove straight at her breast, the acrid smell of the hunted animal was in her nostrils, but her eyes were filled with the horror of something she saw other than her oncoming death. And in her ears rang the echo of a boy's laughter, golden and equivocal.

25. THE PEACE OFFERING

"I want you to help me in getting up a dramatic entertainment of some sort," said the Baroness to Clovis. "You see, there's been an election petition down here, and a member unseated and no end of bitterness and ill-feeling, and the County is socially divided against itself. I thought a play of some kind would be an excellent opportunity for bringing people together again, and giving them something to think of besides tiresome political squabbles."

The Baroness was evidently ambitious of reproducing beneath her own roof the pacifying effects traditionally ascribed to the celebrated Reel of Tullochgorum.

"We might do something on the lines of Greek tragedy," said Clovis, after due reflection; "the Return of Agamemnon, for instance."

The Baroness frowned.

"It sounds rather reminiscent of an election result, doesn't it?"

"It wasn't that sort of return;" explained Clovis it was a homecoming."

"I thought you said it was a tragedy."

"Well, it was. He was killed in his bathroom, you know."

"Oh, now I know the story, of course. Do you want me to take the part of Charlotte Corday?"

"That's a different story and a different century," said Clovis; "the dramatic unities forbid one to lay a scene in more than one century at a time. The killing in this case has to be done by Clytemnestra."

"Rather a pretty name. I'll do that part. I suppose you want to be Aga – whatever his name is?"

"Dear no. Agamemnon was the father of grown-up children, and probably wore a beard and looked prematurely aged. I shall be his charioteer or bath-attendant, or something decorative of that kind. We must do everything in the Sumurun manner, you know."

"I don't know," said the Baroness; "at least, I should know better if you would explain exactly what you mean by the Sumurun manner."

Clovis obliged: "Weird music, and exotic skippings and flying leaps, and lots of drapery and undrapery. Particularly undrapery."

"I think I told you the County are coming. The County won't stand anything very Greek."

"You can get over any objection by calling it Hygiene, or limb-culture, or something of that sort. After all, every one exposes their insides to the public gaze and sympathy nowadays, so why not one's outside?"

"My dear boy, I can ask the County to a Greek play, or to a costume play, but to a Greek-costume play, never. It doesn't do to let the dramatic instinct carry one too far; one must consider one's environment. When one lives among greyhounds one should avoid giving life-like imitations of a rabbit, unless one want's one's head snapped off. Remember, I've got this place on a seven years' lease. And then," continued the Baroness, "as to skippings and flying leaps; I must ask Emily Dushford to take a part. She's a dear good thing, and will do anything she's told, or try to; but can you imagine her doing a flying leap under any circumstances?"

"She can be Cassandra, and she need only take flying leaps into the future, in a metaphorical sense."

"Cassandra; rather a pretty name. What kind of character is she?"

"She was a sort of advance-agent for calamities. To know her was to know the worst. Fortunately for the gaiety of the age she lived in, no one took her very seriously. Still, it must have been fairly galling to have her turning up after every catastrophe with a conscious air of 'perhaps another time you'll believe what I say.'"

"I should have wanted to kill her."

"As Clytemnestra I believe you gratify that very natural wish."

"Then it has a happy ending, in spite of it being a tragedy?"

"Well, hardly," said Clovis; "you see, the satisfaction of putting a violent end to Cassandra must have been considerably damped by the fact that she had foretold what was going to happen to her. She probably dies with an intensely irritating 'what-did-I-tell-you' smile on her lips. By the way, of course all the killing will be done in the Sumurun manner."

"Please explain again," said the Baroness, taking out a notebook and pencil.

"Little and often, you know, instead of one sweeping blow. You see, you are at your own home, so there's no need to hurry over the murdering as though it were some disagreeable but necessary duty."

"And what sort of end do I have? I mean, what curtain do I get?"

"I suppose you rush into your lover's arms. That is where one of the flying leaps will come in."

The getting-up and rehearsing of the play seemed likely to cause, in a restricted area, nearly as much heart-burning and ill-feeling as the election petition. Clovis, as adapter and stage-manager, insisted, as far as he was able, on the charioteer being quite the most prominent character in the play, and his panther-skin tunic caused almost as much trouble and discussion as Clytemnestra's spasmodic succession of lovers, who broke down on probation with alarming uniformity. When the cast was at length fixed beyond hope of reprieve matters went scarcely more smoothly. Clovis and the Baroness rather overdid the Sumurun manner, while the rest of the company could hardly be said to attempt it at all. As for Cassandra, who was expected to improvise her own prophecies, she appeared to be as incapable of taking flying leaps into futurity as of executing more than a severely plantigrade walk across the stage.

"Woe! Trojans, woe to Troy!" was the most inspired remark she could produce after several hours of conscientious study of all the available authorities.

"It's no earthly use foretelling the fall of Troy," expostulated Clovis, "because Troy has fallen before the action of the play begins. And you mustn't say too much about your own impending doom either, because that will give things away too much to the audience."

After several minutes of painful brain-searching, Cassandra smiled reassuringly.

"I know. I'll predict a long and happy reign for George the Fifth."

"My dear girl," protested Clovis, "have you reflected that Cassandra specialised in foretelling calamities?"

There was another prolonged pause and another triumphant issue.

"I know. I'll foretell a most disastrous season for the foxhounds."

"On no account," entreated Clovis; "do remember that all Cassandra's predictions came true. The M. F. H. and the Hunt Secretary are both awfully superstitious, and they are both going to be present."

Cassandra retreated hastily to her bedroom to, bathe her eyes before appearing at tea.

The Baroness and Clovis were by this time scarcely on speaking terms. Each sincerely wished their respective role to be the pivot round which the entire production should revolve, and each lost no opportunity for furthering the cause they had at heart. As fast as Clovis introduced some effective bit of business for the charioteer (and he introduced a great many), the Baroness would remorselessly cut it out, or more often dovetail it into her own part, while Clovis retaliated in a similar fashion whenever possible. The climax came when Clytemnestra annexed some highly complimentary lines, which were to have been addressed to the charioteer by a bevy of admiring Greek damsels, and put them into the mouth of her lover. Clovis stood by in apparent unconcern while the words:

"Oh, lovely stripling, radiant as the dawn," were transposed into:

"Oh, Clytemnestra, radiant as the dawn," but there was a dangerous glitter in his eye that might have given the Baroness warning. He had composed the verse himself, inspired and thoroughly carried away by his subject; he suffered, therefore, a double pang in beholding his tribute deflected from its destined object, and his words mutilated and twisted into what became an extravagant panegyric on the Baroness's personal charms. It was from this moment that he became gentle and assiduous in his private coaching of Cassandra.

The County, forgetting its dissensions, mustered in full strength to witness the much-talked-of production. The protective Providence that looks after little children and amateur theatricals made good its traditional promise that everything should be right on the night. The Baroness and Clovis seemed to have sunk their mutual differences, and between them dominated the scene to the partial eclipse of all the other characters, who, for the most part, seemed well content to remain in the shadow. Even Agamemnon, with ten years of strenuous life around Troy standing to his credit, appeared to be an unobtrusive personality compared with his flamboyant charioteer. But the moment came for Cassandra (who had been excused from any very definite outpourings during rehearsals) to support her role by delivering herself of a few well-chosen anticipations of pending misfortune. The musicians obliged with appropriately lugubrious wailings and thumpings, and the Baroness seized the opportunity to make a dash to the dressing-room to effect certain repairs in her make-up. Cassandra, nervous but resolute, came down to the footlights and, like one repeating a carefully learned lesson, flung her remarks straight at the audience:

"I see woe for this fair country if the brood of corrupt, self-seeking, unscrupulous, unprincipled politicians" (here she named one of the two rival parties in the State) "continue to infest and poison our local councils and undermine our Parliamentary representation; if they continue to snatch votes by nefarious and discreditable means –"

A humming as of a great hive of bewildered and affronted bees drowned her further remarks and wore down the droning of the musicians. The Baroness, who should have been greeted on her return to the stage with the pleasing invocation, "Oh, Clytemnestra, radiant as the dawn," heard instead the imperious voice of Lady Thistledale ordering her carriage, and something like a storm of open discord going on at the back of the room.

~

The social divisions in the County healed themselves after their own fashion; both parties found common ground in condemning the Baroness's outrageously bad taste and tactlessness.

She has been fortunate in sub-letting for the greater part of her seven years' lease.

26. THE TALKING-OUT OF TARRINGTON

"Heavens!" exclaimed the aunt of Clovis, "here's some one I know bearing down on us. I can't remember his name, but he lunched with us once in Town. Tarrington – yes, that's it. He's heard of the picnic I'm giving for the Princess, and he'll cling to me like a life-belt till I give him an invitation; then he'll ask if he may bring all his wives and mothers and sisters with him. That's the worst of these small watering-places; one can't escape from anybody."

"I'll fight a rearguard action for you if you like to do a bolt now," volunteered Clovis; "you've a clear ten yards start if you don't lose time."

The aunt of Clovis responded gamely to the suggestion, and churned away like a Nile steamer, with a long brown ripple of Pekingese spaniel trailing in her wake.

"Pretend you don't know him," was her parting advice, tinged with the reckless courage of the non-combatant.

The next moment the overtures of an affably disposed gentleman were being received by Clovis with a "silent-upon-a-peak-in-Darien" stare which denoted an absence of all previous acquaintance with the object scrutinised.

"I expect you don't know me with my moustache," said the newcomer; "I've only grown it during the last two months."

"On the contrary," said Clovis, "the moustache is the only thing about you that seemed familiar to me. I felt certain that I had met it somewhere before."

"My name is Tarrington," resumed the candidate for recognition.

"A very useful kind of name," said Clovis; "with a name of that sort no one would blame you if you did nothing in particular heroic or remarkable, would they? And yet if you were to raise a troop of light horse in a moment of national emergency, 'Tarrington's Light Horse' would sound quite appropriate and pulse-quickening; whereas if you were called Spoopin, for instance, the thing would be out of the question. No one, even in a moment of national emergency, could possibly belong to Spoopin's Horse."

The new-comer smiled weakly, as one who is not to be put off by mere flippancy, and began again with patient persistence:

"I think you ought to remember my name –"

"I shall," said Clovis, with an air of immense sincerity. "My aunt was asking me only this morning to suggest names for four young owls she's just had sent her as pets. I shall call them all Tarrington; then if one or two of them die or fly away, or leave us in any of the ways that pet owls are prone to, there will be always one or two left to carry on your name. And my aunt won't LET me forget it; she will always be asking 'Have the Tarringtons had their mice?' and questions of that sort. She says if you keep wild creatures in captivity you ought to see after their wants, and of course she's quite right there."

"I met you at luncheon at your aunt's house once –" broke in Mr. Tarrington, pale but still resolute.

"My aunt never lunches," said Clovis; "she belongs to the National Anti-Luncheon League, which is doing quite a lot of good work in a quiet, unobtrusive way. A subscription of half a crown per quarter entitles you to go without ninety-two luncheons."

"This must be something new," exclaimed Tarrington.

"It's the same aunt that I've always had," said Clovis coldly.

"I perfectly well remember meeting you at a luncheon-party given by your aunt," persisted Tarrington, who was beginning to flush an unhealthy shade of mottled pink.

"What was there for lunch?" asked Clovis.

"Oh, well, I don't remember that –"

"How nice of you to remember my aunt when you can no longer recall the names of the things you ate. Now my memory works quite differently. I can remember a menu long after I've forgotten the hostess that accompanied it. When I was seven years old I recollect being given a peach at a garden-party by some Duchess or other; I can't remember a thing about her, except that I imagine our acquaintance must have been of the slightest, as she called me a 'nice little boy,' but I have unfading memories of that peach. It was one of those exuberant peaches that meet you halfway, so to speak, and are all over you in a moment. It was a beautiful unspoiled product of a hothouse, and yet it managed quite successfully to give itself the airs of a compote. You had to bite it and imbibe it at the same time. To me there has always been something charming and mystic in the thought of that delicate velvet globe of fruit, slowly ripening and warming to perfection through the long summer days and perfumed nights, and then coming suddenly athwart my life in the supreme moment of its existence. I can never forget it, even if I wished to. And when I had devoured all that was edible of it, there still remained the stone, which a heedless, thoughtless child would doubtless have thrown away; I put it down the neck of a young friend who was wearing a very *décolleté* sailor suit. I told him it was a scorpion, and from the way he wriggled and screamed he evidently believed it, though where the silly kid imagined I could procure a live scorpion at a garden-party I don't know. Altogether, that peach is for me an unfading and happy memory –"

The defeated Tarrington had by this time retreated out of earshot, comforting himself as best he might with the reflection that a picnic which included the presence of Clovis might prove a doubtfully agreeable experience.

"I shall certainly go in for a Parliamentary career," said Clovis to himself as he turned complacently to rejoin his aunt. "As a talker-out of inconvenient bills I should be invaluable."

27. "Ministers Of Grace"

Although he was scarcely yet out of his teens, the Duke of Scaw was already marked out as a personality widely differing from others of his caste and period. Not in externals; therein he conformed correctly to type. His hair was faintly reminiscent of Houbigant, and at the other end of him his shoes exhaled the right soupçon of harness-room; his socks compelled one's attention without losing one's respect; and his attitude in repose had just that suggestion of Whistler's mother, so becoming in the really young. It was within that the trouble lay, if trouble it could be accounted, which marked him apart from his fellows. The Duke was religious. Not in any of the ordinary senses of the word; he took small heed of High Church or Evangelical standpoints, he stood outside of all the movements and missions and cults and crusades of the day, uncaring and uninterested. Yet in a mystical-practical way of his own, which had served him unscathed and unshaken through the fickle years of boyhood, he was intensely and intensively religious. His family were naturally, though unobtrusively, distressed about it. "I am so afraid it may affect his bridge," said his mother.

The Duke sat in a pennyworth of chair in St. James's Park, listening to the pessimisms of Belturbet, who reviewed the existing political situation from the gloomiest of standpoints.

"Where I think you political spade-workers are so silly," said the Duke, "is in the misdirection of your efforts. You spend thousands of pounds of money, and Heaven knows how much dynamic force of brain power and personal energy, in trying to elect or displace this or that man, whereas you could gain your ends so much more simply by making use of the men as you find them. If they don't suit your purpose as they are, transform them into something more satisfactory."

"Do you refer to hypnotic suggestion?" asked Belturbet, with the air of one who is being trifled with.

"Nothing of the sort. Do you understand what I mean by the verb to koepenick? That is to say, to replace an authority by a spurious imitation that would carry just as much weight for the moment as the displaced original; the advantage, of course, being that the koepenick replica would do what you wanted, whereas the original does what seems best in its own eyes."

"I suppose every public man has a double, if not two or three," said Belturbet; "but it would be a pretty hard task to koepenick a whole bunch of them and keep the originals out of the way."

"There have been instances in European history of highly successful koepenickery," said the Duke dreamily.

"Oh, of course, there have been False Dimitris and Perkin Warbecks, who imposed on the world for a time," assented Belturbet, "but they personated people who were dead or safely out of the way. That was a comparatively simple matter. It would be far easier to pass oneself of as dead Hannibal than as living Haldane, for instance."

"I was thinking," said the Duke, "of the most famous case of all, the angel who koepenicked King Robert of Sicily with such brilliant results. Just imagine what an advantage it would be to have angels deputising, to use a horrible but convenient word, for Quinston and Lord Hugo Sizzle, for example. How much smoother the Parliamentary machine would work than at present!"

"Now you're talking nonsense," said Belturbet; "angels don't exist nowadays, at least, not in that way, so what is the use of dragging them into a serious discussion? It's merely silly."

"If you talk to me like that I shall just DO it," said the Duke.

"Do what?" asked Belturbet. There were times when his young friend's uncanny remarks rather frightened him.

"I shall summon angelic forces to take over some of the more troublesome personalities of our public life, and I shall send the ousted originals into temporary retirement in suitable animal organisms. It's not every one who would have the knowledge or the power necessary to bring such a thing off –"

"Oh, stop that inane rubbish," said Belturbet angrily; "it's getting wearisome. Here's Quinston coming," he added, as there approached along the almost deserted path the well-known figure of a young Cabinet Minister, whose personality evoked a curious mixture of public interest and unpopularity.

"Hurry along, my dear man," said the young Duke to the Minister, who had given him a condescending nod; "your time is running short," he continued in a provocative strain; "the whole inept crowd of you will shortly be swept away into the world's wastepaper basket."

"You poor little strawberry-leafed nonentity," said the Minister, checking himself for a moment in his stride and rolling out his words spasmodically; "who is going to sweep us away, I should like to know? The voting masses are on our side, and all the ability and administrative talent is on our side too. No power of earth or Heaven is going to move us from our place till we choose to quit it. No power of earth or –"

Belturbet saw, with bulging eyes, a sudden void where a moment earlier had been a Cabinet Minister; a void emphasised rather than relieved by the presence of a puffed-out bewildered-looking sparrow, which hopped about for h moment in a dazed fashion and then fell to a violent cheeping and scolding.

"If we could understand sparrow-language," said the Duke serenely, "I fancy we should hear something infinitely worse than 'strawberry-leafed nonentity.'"

"But good Heavens, Eugene," said Belturbet hoarsely, "what has become of – Why, there he is! How on earth did he get there?" And he pointed with a shaking finger towards a semblance of the vanished Minister, which approached once more along the unfrequented path.

The Duke laughed.

"It is Quinston to all outward appearance," he said composedly, "but I fancy you will find, on closer investigation, that it is an angel understudy of the real article."

The Angel-Quinston greeted them with a friendly smile.

"How beastly happy you two look sitting there!" he said wistfully.

"I don't suppose you'd care to change places with poor little us," replied the Duke chaffingly.

"How about poor little me?" said the Angel modestly. "I've got to run about behind the wheels of popularity, like a spotted dog behind a carriage, getting all the dust and trying to look as if I was an important part of the machine. I must seem a perfect fool to you onlookers sometimes."

"I think you are a perfect angel," said the Duke.

The Angel-that-had-been-Quinston smiled and passed on his way, pursued across the breadth of the Horse Guards Parade by a tiresome little sparrow that cheeped incessantly and furiously at him.

"That's only the beginning," said the Duke complacently; "I've made it operative with all of them, irrespective of parties."

Belturbet made no coherent reply; he was engaged in feeling his pulse. The Duke fixed his attention with some interest on a black swan that was swimming with haughty, stiff-necked aloofness amid the crowd of lesser water-fowl that dotted the ornamental water. For all its pride of bearing, something was evidently ruffling and enraging it; in its way it seemed as angry and amazed as the sparrow had been.

At the same moment a human figure came along the pathway. Belturbet looked up apprehensively.

"Kedzon," he whispered briefly.

"An Angel-Kedzon, if I am not mistaken," said the Duke. "Look, he is talking affably to a human being. That settles it."

A shabbily dressed lounger had accosted the man who had been Viceroy in the splendid East, and who still reflected in his mien some of the cold dignity of the Himalayan snow-peaks.

"Could you tell me, sir, if them white birds is storks or halbatrosses? I had an argyment –"

The cold dignity thawed at once into genial friendliness.

"Those are pelicans, my dear sir. Are you interested in birds? If you would join me in a bun and a glass of milk at the stall yonder,

I could tell you some interesting things about Indian birds. Right oh! Now the hill-mynah, for instance –"

The two men disappeared in the direction of the bun stall, chatting volubly as they went, and shadowed from the other side of the railed enclosure by a black swan, whose temper seemed to have reached the limit of inarticulate rage.

Belturbet gazed in an open-mouthed wonder after the retreating couple, then transferred his attention to the infuriated swan, and finally turned with a look of scared comprehension at his young friend lolling unconcernedly in his chair. There was no longer any room to doubt what was happening. The "silly talk" had been translated into terrifying action.

"I think a prairie oyster on the top of a stiffish brandy-and-soda might save my reason," said Belturbet weakly, as he limped towards his club.

It was late in the day before he could steady his nerves sufficiently to glance at the evening papers. The Parliamentary report proved significant reading, and confirmed the fears that he had been trying to shake off. Mr. Ap Dave, the Chancellor, whose lively controversial style endeared him to his supporters and embittered him, politically speaking, to his opponents, had risen in his place to make an unprovoked apology for having alluded in a recent speech to certain protesting taxpayers as "skulkers." He had realised on reflection that they were in all probability perfectly honest in their inability to understand certain legal technicalities of the new finance laws. The House had scarcely recovered from this sensation when Lord Hugo Sizzle caused a further flutter of astonishment by going out of his way to indulge in an outspoken appreciation of the fairness, loyalty, and straightforwardness not only of the Chancellor, but of all the members of the Cabinet. A wit had gravely suggested moving the adjournment of the House in view of the unexpected circumstances that had arisen.

Belturbet anxiously skimmed over a further item of news printed immediately below the Parliamentary report: "Wild cat found in an exhausted condition in Palace Yard."

"Now I wonder which of them –" he mused, and then an appalling idea came to him. "Supposing he's put them both into the same beast!" He hurriedly ordered another prairie oyster.

Belturbet was known in his club as a strictly moderate drinker; his consumption of alcoholic stimulants that day gave rise to considerable comment.

The events of the next few days were piquantly bewildering to the world at large; to Belturbet, who knew dimly what was happening, the situation was fraught with recurring alarms. The old saying that in politics it's the unexpected that always happens received a justification that it had hitherto somewhat lacked, and the epidemic of startling personal changes of front was not wholly confined to the realm of actual politics. The eminent chocolate magnate, Sadbury, whose antipathy to the Turf and everything connected with it was a matter of general knowledge, had evidently been replaced by an Angel-Sadbury, who proceeded to electrify the public by blossoming forth as an owner of race-horses, giving as a reason his matured conviction that the sport was, after all, one which gave healthy open-air recreation to large numbers of people drawn from all classes of the community, and incidentally stimulated the important industry of horse-breeding. His colours, chocolate and cream hoops spangled with pink stars, promised to become as popular as any on the Turf. At the same time, in order to give effect to his condemnation of the evils resulting from the spread of the gambling habit among wage-earning classes, who lived for the most part from hand to mouth, he suppressed all betting news and tipsters' forecasts in the popular evening paper that was under his control. His action received instant recognition and support from the Angel-proprietor of the *Evening Views*, the principal rival evening halfpenny paper, who forthwith issued an ukase decreeing a similar ban on betting news, and in a short while the regular evening Press was purged of all mention of starting prices and probable winners. A considerable drop in the circulation of all these papers was the immediate result, accompanied, of course, by a falling-off in advertisement value, while a crop of special betting broadsheets sprang up to supply the newly-created want. Under their influence the betting habit became if anything rather wore widely diffused than before. The Duke had possibly overlooked the futility of koepenicking the leaders of the nation with excellently intentioned angel understudies, while leaving the mass of the people in its original condition.

Further sensation and dislocation was caused in the Press world by the sudden and dramatic *rapprochement* which took place between the Angel-Editor of the *Scrutator* and the Angel-Editor of the *Anglian Review*, who not only ceased to criticise and disparage the tone and tendencies of each other's publication, but agreed to exchange editorships for alternating periods. Here again public support was not on the side of the angels; constant readers of the *Scrutator* complained bitterly of the strong meat which was thrust upon them at fitful intervals in place of the almost vegetarian diet to which they had become confidently accustomed; even those who were not mentally averse to strong meat as a separate course were pardonably annoyed at being supplied with it in the pages of the *Scrutator*. To be suddenly confronted with a pungent herring salad when one had attuned oneself to tea and toast, or to discover a richly truffled segment of *pâté de foie* dissembled in a bowl of bread and milk, would he an experience that might upset the equanimity of the most placidly disposed mortal. An equally vehement outcry arose from the regular subscribers of the *Anglian Review* who protested against being served from time to time with literary fare which no young person of sixteen could possibly want to devour in secret. To take infinite precautions, they complained, against the juvenile perusal of such eminently innocuous literature was like reading the Riot Act on an uninhabited island. Both reviews suffered a serious falling-off in circulation and influence. Peace hath its devastations as well as war.

The wives of noted public men formed another element of discomfiture which the young Duke had almost entirely left out of his calculations. It is sufficiently embarrassing to keep abreast of the possible wobblings and veerrings-round of a human husband, who, from the strength or weakness of his personal character, may leap over or slip through the barriers which divide the parties; for this reason a merciful politician usually marries late in life, when he has definitely made up his mind on which side he wishes his wife to be socially valuable. But these trials were as nothing compared to the bewilderment caused by the Angel-husbands who seemed in some cases to have revolutionised their outlook on life in the interval between breakfast and dinner, without premonition or preparation of any kind, and apparently without realising the least need for subsequent explanation. The temporary peace which brooded over the Parliamentary situation was by no means reproduced in the home circles of the leading statesmen and politicians. It had been frequently and extensively remarked of Mrs. Exe that she would try the patience of an angel; now the tables were reversed, and she unwittingly had an opportunity for discovering that the capacity for exasperating behaviour was not all on one side.

And then, with the introduction of the Navy Estimates, Parliamentary peace suddenly dissolved. It was the old quarrel between Ministers and the Opposition as to the adequacy or the reverse of the Government's naval programme. The Angel-Quinston and the Angel-Hugo-Sizzle contrived to keep the debates free from personalities and pinpricks, but an enormous sensation was created when the elegant lackadaisical Halfan Halfour threatened to bring up fifty, thousand stalwarts to wreck the House if the Estimates were not forthwith revised on a Two-Power basis. It was a memorable scene when he rose in his place, in response to the scandalised shouts of his opponents, and thundered forth, "Gentlemen, I glory in the name of Apache."

Belturbet, who had made several fruitless attempts to ring up his young friend since the fateful morning in St. James's Park, ran him to earth one afternoon at his club, smooth and spruce and unruffled as ever.

"Tell me, what on earth have you turned Cocksley Coxon into?" Belturbet asked anxiously, mentioning the name of one of the pillars of unorthodoxy in the Anglican Church. "I don't fancy he *believes* in angels, and if he finds an angel preaching orthodox sermons from his pulpit while he's been turned into a fox-terrier, he'll develop rabies in less than no time."

"I rather think it was a fox-terrier," said the Duke lazily.

Belturbet groaned heavily, and sank into a chair.

"Look here, Eugene," he whispered hoarsely, having first looked well round to see that no one was within hearing range, "you've got to stop it. Consols are jumping up and down like bronchos, and that speech of Halfour's in the House last night has simply startled everybody out of their wits. And then on the top of it, Thistlebery –"

"What has he been saying?" asked the Duke quickly.

"Nothing. That's just what's so disturbing. Every one thought it was simply inevitable that he should come out with a great epoch-making speech at this juncture, and I've just seen on the tape that he has refused to address any meetings at present, giving as a reason his opinion that something more than mere speech-making was wanted."

The young Duke said nothing, but his eyes shone with quiet exultation.

"It's so unlike Thistlebery," continued Belturbet; "at least," he said suspiciously, "it's unlike the *real* Thistlebery –"

"The real Thistlebery is flying about somewhere as a vocally-industrious lapwing," said the Duke calmly; "I expect great things of the Angel-Thistlebery," he added.

At this moment there was a magnetic stampede of members towards the lobby, where the tape-machines were ticking out some news of more than ordinary import.

"*Coup d'état* in the North. Thistlebery seizes Edinburgh Castle. Threatens civil war unless Government expands naval programme."

In the babel which ensued Belturbet lost sight of his young friend. For the best part of the afternoon he searched one likely haunt after another, spurred on by the sensational posters which the evening papers were displaying broadcast over the West End. "General Baden-Baden mobilises Boy-Scouts. Another *coup d'etat* feared. Is Windsor Castle safe?" This was one of the earlier posters, and was followed by one of even more sinister purport: "Will the Test-match have to be postponed?" It was this disquietening question which brought home the real seriousness of the situation to the London public, and made people wonder whether one might not pay too high a price for the advantages of party government. Belturbet, questing round in the hope of finding the originator of the trouble, with a vague idea of being able to induce him to restore matters to their normal human footing, came across an elderly club acquaintance who dabbled extensively in some of the more sensitive market securities. He was pale with indignation, and his pallor deepened as a breathless newsboy dashed past with a poster inscribed: "Premier's constituency harried by moss-troopers. Halfour sends encouraging telegram to rioters. Letchworth Garden City threatens reprisals. Foreigners taking refuge in Embassies and National Liberal Club."

"This is devils' work!" he said angrily.

Belturbet knew otherwise.

At the bottom of St. James's Street a newspaper motor-cart, which had just come rapidly along Pall Mall, was surrounded by a knot of eagerly talking people, and for the first time that afternoon Belturbet heard expressions of relief and congratulation.

It displayed a placard with the welcome announcement: "Crisis ended. Government gives way. Important expansion of naval programme."

There seemed to be no immediate necessity for pursuing the quest of the errant Duke, and Belturbet turned to make his way homeward through St. James's Park. His mind, attuned to the alarums and excursions of the afternoon, became dimly aware that some excitement of a detached nature was going on around him. In spite of the political ferment which reigned in the streets, quite a large crowd had gathered to watch the unfolding of a tragedy that had taken place on the shore of the ornamental water. A large black swan, which had recently shown signs of a savage and dangerous disposition, had suddenly attacked a young gentleman who was walking by the water's edge, dragged him down under the surface, and drowned him before anyone could come to his assistance. At the moment when Belturbet arrived on the spot several park-keepers were engaged in lifting the corpse into a punt. Belturbet stooped to pick up a hat that lay near the scene of the struggle. It was a smart soft felt hat, faintly reminiscent of Houbigant.

More than a month elapsed before Belturbet had sufficiently recovered from his attack of nervous prostration to take an interest once more in what was going on in the world of politics. The Parliamentary Session was still in full swing, and a General Election was looming in the near future. He called for a batch of morning papers and skimmed rapidly through the speeches of the Chancellor, Quinston, and other Ministerial leaders, as well as those of the principal Opposition champions, and then sank back in his chair with a sigh of relief. Evidently the spell had ceased to act after the tragedy which had overtaken its invoker. There was no trace of angel anywhere.

28. The Remoulding Of Groby Lington

"A man is known by the company he keeps."

In the morning-room of his sister-in-law's house Groby Lington fidgeted away the passing minutes with the demure restlessness of advanced middle age. About a quarter of an hour would have to elapse before it would be time to say his good-byes and make his way across the village green to the station, with a selected escort of nephews and nieces. He was a good-natured, kindly dispositioned man, and in theory he was delighted to pay periodical visits to the wife and children of his dead brother William; in practice, he infinitely preferred the comfort and seclusion of his own house and garden, and the companionship of his books and his parrot to these rather meaningless and tiresome incursions into a family circle with which he had little in common. It was not so much the spur of his own conscience that drove him to make the occasional short journey by rail to visit his relatives, as an obedient concession to the more insistent but vicarious conscience of his brother, Colonel John, who was apt to accuse him of neglecting poor old William's family. Groby usually forgot or ignored the existence of his neighbour kinsfolk until such time as he was threatened with a visit from the Colonel, when he would put matters straight by a hurried pilgrimage across the few miles of intervening country to renew his acquaintance with the young people and assume a kindly if rather forced interest in the well-being of his sister-in-law. On this occasion he had cut matters so fine between the timing of his exculpatory visit and the coming of Colonel John, that he would scarcely be home before the latter was due to arrive. Anyhow, Groby had got it over, and six or seven months might decently elapse before he need again sacrifice his comforts and inclinations on the altar of family sociability. He was inclined to be distinctly cheerful as he hopped about the room, picking up first one object, then another, and subjecting each to a brief bird-like scrutiny.

Presently his cheerful listlessness changed sharply to an attitude of vexed attention. In a scrap-book of drawings and caricatures belonging to one of his nephews he had come across an unkindly clever sketch of himself and his parrot, solemnly confronting each other in postures of ridiculous gravity and repose, and bearing a likeness to one another that the artist had done his utmost to accentuate. After the first flush of annoyance had passed away, Groby laughed good-naturedly and admitted to himself the cleverness of the drawing. Then the feeling of resentment repossessed him, resentment not against the caricaturist who had embodied the idea in pen and ink, but against the possible truth that the idea represented. Was it really the case that people grew in time to resemble the animals they kept as pets, and had he unconsciously become more and more like the comically solemn bird that was his constant companion? Groby was unusually silent as he walked to the train with his escort of chattering nephews and nieces, and during the short railway journey his mind was more and more possessed with an introspective conviction that he had gradually settled down into a sort of parrot-like existence. What, after all, did his daily routine amount to but a sedate meandering and pecking and perching, in his garden, among his fruit trees, in his wicker chair on the lawn, or by the fireside in his library? And what was the sum total of his conversation with chance-encountered neighbours? "Quite a spring day, isn't it?" "It looks as though we should have some rain." "Glad to see you about again; you must take care of yourself." "How the young folk shoot up, don't they?" Strings of stupid, inevitable perfunctory remarks came to his mind, remarks that were certainly not the mental exchange of human intelligences, but mere empty parrot-talk. One might really just as well salute one's acquaintances with "Pretty polly. Puss, puss, miaow!" Groby began to fume against the picture of himself as a foolish feathered fowl which his nephew's sketch had first suggested, and which his own accusing imagination was filling in with such unflattering detail.

"I'll give the beastly bird away," he said resentfully; though he knew at the same time that he would do no such thing. It would look so absurd after all the years that he had kept the parrot and made much of it suddenly to try and find it a new home.

"Has my brother arrived?" he asked of the stable-boy, who had come with the pony-carriage to meet him.

"Yessir, came down by the two-fifteen. Your parrot's dead." The boy made the latter announcement with the relish which his class finds in proclaiming a catastrophe.

"My parrot dead?" said Groby. "What caused its death?"

"The ipe," said the boy briefly.

"The ipe?" queried Groby. "Whatever's that?"

"The ipe what the Colonel brought down with him," came the rather alarming answer.

"Do you mean to say my brother is ill?" asked Groby. "Is it something infectious?"

"Th' Colonel's so well as ever he was," said the boy; and as no further explanation was forthcoming Groby had to possess himself in mystified patience till he reached home. His brother was waiting for him at the hall door.

"Have you heard about the parrot?" he asked at once. "'Pon my soul I'm awfully sorry. The moment he saw the monkey I'd brought down as a surprise for you he squawked out 'Rats to you, sir!' and the blessed monkey made one spring at him, got him by the neck and whirled him round like a rattle. He was as dead as mutton by the time I'd got him out of the little beggar's paws. Always been such a friendly little beast, the monkey has, should never have thought he'd got it in him to see red like that. Can't tell you how sorry I feel about it, and now of course you'll hate the sight of the monkey."

"Not at all," said Groby sincerely. A few hours earlier the tragic end which had befallen his parrot would have presented itself to him as a calamity; now it arrived almost as a polite attention on the part of the Fates.

"The bird was getting old, you know," he went on, in explanation of his obvious lack of decent regret at the loss of his pet. "I was really beginning to wonder if it was an unmixed kindness to let him go on living till he succumbed to old age. What a charming little monkey!" he added, when he was introduced to the culprit.

The new-comer was a small, long-tailed monkey from the Western Hemisphere, with a gentle, half-shy, half-trusting manner that instantly captured Groby's confidence; a student of simian character might have seen in the fitful red light in its eyes some indication of the underlying temper which the parrot had so rashly put to the test with such dramatic consequences for itself. The servants, who had come to regard the defunct bird as a regular member of the household, and one who gave really very little trouble, were scandalised to find his bloodthirsty aggressor installed in his place as an honoured domestic pet.

"A nasty heathen ipe what don't never say nothing sensible and cheerful, same as pore Polly did," was the unfavourable verdict of the kitchen quarters.

~

One Sunday morning, some twelve or fourteen months after the visit of Colonel John and the parrot-tragedy, Miss Wepley sat decorously in her pew in the parish church, immediately in front of that occupied by Groby Lington. She was, comparatively speaking a newcomer in the neighbourhood, and was not personally acquainted with her fellow-worshipper in the seat behind, but for the past two years the Sunday morning service had brought them regularly within each other's sphere of consciousness. Without having paid particular attention to the subject, she could probably have given a correct rendering of the way in which he pronounced certain words occurring in the responses, while he was well aware of the trivial fact that, in addition to her prayer book and handkerchief, a small paper packet of throat lozenges always reposed on the seat beside her. Miss Wepley rarely had recourse to her lozenges, but in case she should be taken with a fit of coughing she wished to have the emergency duly provided for. On this particular Sunday the lozenges occasioned an unusual diversion in the even tenor of her devotions, far more disturbing to her personally than a prolonged attack of coughing would have been. As she rose to take part in the singing of the first hymn, she fancied that she saw the hand of her neighbour, who was alone in the pew behind her, make a furtive downward grab at the packet lying on the seat; on turning sharply round she found that the packet had certainly disappeared, but Mr. Lington was to all outward seeming serenely intent on his hymnbook. No amount of interrogatory glaring on the part of the despoiled lady could bring the least shade of conscious guilt to his face.

"Worse was to follow," as she remarked afterwards to a scandalised audience of friends and acquaintances. "I had scarcely knelt in prayer when a lozenge, one of my lozenges, came whizzing into the pew, just under my nose. I turned round and stared, but Mr. Lington had his eyes closed and his lips moving as though engaged in prayer. The moment I resumed my devotions another lozenge came rattling in, and then another. I took no notice for awhile, and then turned round suddenly just as the dreadful man was about to flip another one at me. He hastily pretended to be turning over the leaves of his book, but I was not to be taken in that time. He saw that he had been discovered and no more lozenges came. Of course I have changed my pew."

"No gentleman would have acted in such a disgraceful manner," said one of her listeners; "and yet Mr. Lington used to be so respected by everybody. He seems to have behaved like a little ill-bred schoolboy."

"He behaved like a monkey," said Miss Wepley.

Her unfavourable verdict was echoed in other quarters about the same time. Groby Lington had never been a hero in the eyes of his personal retainers, but he had shared the approval accorded to his defunct parrot as a cheerful, well-dispositioned body, who gave no particular trouble. Of late months, however, this character would hardly have been endorsed by the members of his domestic establishment. The stolid stable-boy, who had first announced to him the tragic end of his feathered pet, was one of the first to give voice to the murmurs of disapproval which became rampant and general in the servants' quarters, and he had fairly substantial grounds for his disaffection. In a burst of hot summer weather he had obtained permission to bathe in a modest-sized pond in the orchard, and thither one afternoon Groby had bent his steps, attracted by loud imprecations of anger mingled with the shriller chattering of monkey-language. He, beheld his plump diminutive servitor, clad only in a waistcoat and a pair of socks, storming ineffectually at the monkey which was seated on a low branch of an apple tree, abstractedly fingering the remainder of the boy's outfit, which he had removed just out of has reach.

"The ipe's been an' took my clothes;" whined the boy, with the passion of his kind for explaining the obvious. His incomplete toilet effect rather embarrassed him, but he hailed the arrival of Groby with relief, as promising moral and material support in his efforts to get back his raided garments. The monkey had ceased its defiant jabbering, and doubtless with a little coaxing from its master it would hand back the plunder.

"If I lift you up," suggested Groby, "you will just be able to reach the clothes."

The boy agreed, and Groby clutched him firmly by the waistcoat, which was about all there was to catch hold of, and lifted, him clear of the ground. Then, with a deft swing he sent him crashing into a clump of tall nettles, which closed receptively round him. The victim had not been brought up in a school which teaches one to repress one's emotions – if a fox had attempted to gnaw at his vitals he would have flown to complain to the nearest hunt committee rather than have affected an attitude of stoical indifference. On this occasion the volume of sound which he produced under the stimulus of pain and rage and astonishment was generous and sustained, but above his bellowings he could distinctly hear the triumphant chattering of his enemy in the tree, and a peal of shrill laughter from Groby.

When the boy had finished an improvised St. Vitus caracole, which would have brought him fame on the boards of the Coliseum, and which indeed met with ready appreciation and applause from the retreating figure of Groby Lington, he found that the monkey had also discreetly retired, while his clothes were scattered on the grass at the foot of the tree.

"They'm two ipes, that's what they be," he muttered angrily, and if his judgment was severe, at least he spoke under the sting of considerable provocation.

It was a week or two later that the parlour-maid gave notice, having been terrified almost to tears by an outbreak of sudden temper on the part of the master anent some underdone cutlets. "'E gnashed 'is teeth at me, 'e did reely," she informed a sympathetic kitchen audience.

"I'd like to see 'im talk like that to me, I would," said the cook defiantly, but her cooking from that moment showed a marked improvement.

It was seldom that Groby Lington so far detached himself from his accustomed habits as to go and form one of a house-party, and he was not a little piqued that Mrs. Glenduff should have stowed him away in the musty old Georgian wing of the house, in the next room, moreover, to Leonard Spabbink, the eminent pianist.

"He plays Liszt like an angel," had been the hostess's enthusiastic testimonial.

"He may play him like a trout for all I care," had been Groby's mental comment, "but I wouldn't mind betting that he snores. He's just the sort and shape that would. And if I hear him snoring through those ridiculous thin-panelled walls, there'll be trouble."

He did, and there was.

Groby stood it for about two and a quarter minutes, and then made his way through the corridor into Spabbink's room. Under

Groby's vigorous measures the musician's flabby, redundant figure sat up in bewildered semi-consciousness like an ice-cream that has been taught to beg. Groby prodded him into complete wakefulness, and then the pettish self-satisfied pianist fairly lost his temper and slapped his domineering visitant on the hand. In another moment Spabbink was being nearly stifled and very effectually gagged by a pillow-case tightly bound round his head, while his plump pyjama'd limbs were hauled out of bed and smacked, pinched, kicked, and bumped in a catch-as-catch-can progress across the floor, towards the flat shallow bath in whose utterly inadequate depths Groby perseveringly strove to drown him. For a few moments the room was almost in darkness: Groby's candle had overturned in an early stage of the scuffle, and its flicker scarcely reached to the spot where splashings, smacks, muffled cries, and splutterings, and a chatter of ape-like rage told of the struggle that was being waged round the shores of the bath. A few instants later the one-sided combat was brightly lit up by the flare of blazing curtains and rapidly kindling panelling.

When the hastily aroused members of the house-party stampeded out on to the lawn, the Georgian wing was well alight and belching forth masses of smoke, but some moments elapsed before Groby appeared with the half-drowned pianist in his arms, having just bethought him of the superior drowning facilities offered by the pond at the bottom of the lawn. The cool night air sobered his rage, and when he found that he was innocently acclaimed as the heroic rescuer of poor Leonard Spabbink, and loudly commended for his presence of mind in tying a wet cloth round his head to protect him from smoke suffocation, he accepted the situation, and subsequently gave a graphic account of his finding the musician asleep with an overturned candle by his side and the conflagration well started. Spabbink gave HIS version some days later, when he had partially recovered from the shock of his midnight castigation and immersion, but the gentle pitying smiles and evasive comments with which his story was greeted warned him that the public ear was not at his disposal.

He refused, however, to attend the ceremonial presentation of the Royal Humane Society's life-saving medal.

It was about this time that Groby's pet monkey fell a victim to the disease which attacks so many of its kind when brought under the influence of a northern climate. Its master appeared to be profoundly affected by its loss, and never quite recovered the level of spirits that he had recently attained. In company with the tortoise, which Colonel John presented to him on his last visit, he potters about his lawn and kitchen garden, with none of his erstwhile sprightliness; and his nephews and nieces are fairly well justified in alluding to him as "Old Uncle Groby."

29. Laura

"You are not really dying, are you?" asked Amanda.

"I have the doctor's permission to live till Tuesday," said Laura.

"But today is Saturday; this is serious!" gasped Amanda.

"I don't know about it being serious; it is certainly Saturday," said Laura.

"Death is always serious," said Amanda.

"I never said I was going to die. I am presumably going to leave off being Laura, but I shall go on being something. An animal of some kind, I suppose. You see, when one hasn't been very good in the life one has just lived, one reincarnates in some lower organism. And I haven't been very good, when one comes to think of it. I've been petty and mean and vindictive and all that sort of thing when circumstances have seemed to warrant it."

"Circumstances never warrant that sort of thing," said Amanda hastily.

"If you don't mind my saying so," observed Laura, "Egbert is a circumstance that would warrant any amount of that sort of thing. You're married to him – that's different; you've sworn to love, honour, and endure him: I haven't."

"I don't see what's wrong with Egbert," protested Amanda.

"Oh, I daresay the wrongness has been on my part," admitted Laura dispassionately; "he has merely been the extenuating circumstance. He made a thin, peevish kind of fuss, for instance, when I took the collie puppies from the farm out for a run the other day."

"They chased his young broods of speckled Sussex and drove two sitting hens off their nests, besides running all over the flower beds. You know how devoted he is to his poultry and garden."

"Anyhow, he needn't have gone on about it for the entire evening and then have said, `Let's say no more about it' just when I was beginning to enjoy the discussion. That's where one of my petty vindictive revenges came in," added Laura with an unrepentant chuckle; "I turned the entire family of speckled Sussex into his seedling shed the day after the puppy episode."

"How could you?" exclaimed Amanda.

"It came quite easy," said Laura; "two of the hens pretended to be laying at the time, but I was firm."

"And we thought it was an accident!"

"You see," resumed Laura, "I really *have* some grounds for supposing that my next incarnation will be in a lower organism. I shall be an animal of some kind. On the other hand, I haven't been a bad sort in my way, so I think I may count on being a nice animal, something elegant and lively, with a love of fun. An otter, perhaps."

"I can't imagine you as an otter," said Amanda.

"Well, I don't suppose you can imagine me as an angel, if it comes to that," said Laura.

Amanda was silent. She couldn't.

"Personally I think an otter life would be rather enjoyable," continued Laura; "salmon to eat all the year round, and the satisfaction of being able to fetch the trout in their own homes without having to wait for hours till they condescend to rise to the fly you've been dangling before them; and an elegant svelte figure –"

"Think of the otter hounds," interposed Amanda; "how dreadful to be hunted and harried and finally worried to death!"

"Rather fun with half the neighbourhood looking on, and anyhow not worse than this Saturday-to-Tuesday business of dying by inches; and then I should go on into something else. If I had been a moderately good otter I suppose I should get back into human shape of some sort; probably something rather primitive – a little brown, unclothed Nubian boy, I should think."

"I wish you would be serious," sighed Amanda; "you really ought to be if you're only going to live till Tuesday."

As a matter of fact Laura died on Monday.

"So dreadfully upsetting," Amanda complained to her uncle-in-law, Sir Lulworth Quayne. "I've asked quite a lot of people down for golf and fishing, and the rhododendrons are just looking their best."

"Laura always was inconsiderate," said Sir Lulworth; "she was born during Goodwood week, with an Ambassador staying in the house who hated babies."

"She had the maddest kind of ideas," said Amanda; "do you know if there was any insanity in her family?"

"Insanity? No, I never heard of any. Her father lives in West Kensington, but I believe he's sane on all other subjects."

"She had an idea that she was going to be reincarnated as an otter," said Amanda.

"One meets with those ideas of reincarnation so frequently, even in the West," said Sir Lulworth, "that one can hardly set them down as being mad. And Laura was such an unaccountable person in this life that I should not like to lay down definite rules as to what she might be doing in an after state."

"You think she really might have passed into some animal form?" asked Amanda. She was one of those who shape their opinions rather readily from the standpoint of those around them.

Just then Egbert entered the breakfast-room, wearing an air of bereavement that Laura's demise would have been insufficient, in itself, to account for.

"Four of my speckled Sussex have been killed," he exclaimed; "the very four that were to go to the show on Friday. One of them was dragged away and eaten right in the middle of that new carnation bed that I've been to such trouble and expense over. My best flower bed and my best fowls singled out for destruction; it almost seems as if the brute that did the deed had special knowledge how to be as devastating as possible in a short space of time."

"Was it a fox, do you think?" asked Amanda.

"Sounds more like a polecat," said Sir Lulworth.

"No," said Egbert, "there were marks of webbed feet all over the place, and we followed the tracks down to the stream at the bottom of the garden; evidently an otter."

Amanda looked quickly and furtively across at Sir Lulworth.

Egbert was too agitated to eat any breakfast, and went out to superintend the strengthening of the poultry yard defenses.

"I think she might at least have waited till the funeral was over," said Amanda in a scandalised voice.

"It's her own funeral, you know," said Sir Lulworth; "it's a nice point in etiquette how far one ought to show respect to one's own mortal remains."

Disregard for mortuary convention was carried to further lengths next day; during the absence of the family at the funeral ceremony the remaining survivors of the speckled Sussex were massacred. The marauder's line of retreat seemed to have embraced most of the flower beds on the lawn, but the strawberry beds in the lower garden had also suffered.

"I shall get the otter hounds to come here at the earliest possible moment," said Egbert savagely.

"On no account! You can't dream of such a thing!" exclaimed Amanda. "I mean, it wouldn't do, so soon after a funeral in the house."

"It's a case of necessity," said Egbert; "once an otter takes to that sort of thing it won't stop."

"Perhaps it will go elsewhere now there are no more fowls left," suggested Amanda.

"One would think you wanted to shield the beast," said Egbert.

"There's been so little water in the stream lately," objected Amanda; "it seems hardly sporting to hunt an animal when it has so little chance of taking refuge anywhere."

"Good gracious!" fumed Egbert, "I'm not thinking about sport. I want to have the animal killed as soon as possible."

Even Amanda's opposition weakened when, during church time on the following Sunday, the otter made its way into the house, raided half a salmon from the larder and worried it into scaly fragments on the Persian rug in Egbert's studio.

"We shall have it hiding under our beds and biting pieces out of our feet before long," said Egbert, and from what Amanda knew of this particular otter she felt that the possibility was not a remote one.

On the evening preceding the day fixed for the hunt Amanda spent a solitary hour walking by the banks of the stream, making what she imagined to be hound noises. It was charitably supposed by those who overheard her performance, that she was practicing for farmyard imitations at the forth-coming village entertainment.

It was her friend and neighbour, Aurora Burret, who brought her news of the day's sport.

"Pity you weren't out; we had quite a good day. We found at once, in the pool just below your garden."

"Did you – kill?" asked Amanda.

"Rather. A fine she-otter. Your husband got rather badly bitten in trying to 'tail it.' Poor beast, I felt quite sorry for it, it had such a human look in its eyes when it was killed. You'll call me silly, but do you know who the look reminded me of? My dear woman, what is the matter?"

When Amanda had recovered to a certain extent from her attack of nervous prostration Egbert took her to the Nile Valley to recuperate. Change of scene speedily brought about the desired recovery of health and mental balance. The escapades of an adventurous otter in search of a variation of diet were viewed in their proper light. Amanda's normally placid temperament reasserted itself. Even a hurricane of shouted curses, coming from her husband's dressing-room, in her husband's voice, but hardly in his usual vocabulary, failed to disturb her serenity as she made a leisurely toilet one evening in a Cairo hotel.

"What is the matter? What has happened?" she asked in amused curiosity.

"The little beast has thrown all my clean shirts into the bath! Wait till I catch you, you little –"

"What little beast?" asked Amanda, suppressing a desire to laugh; Egbert's language was so hopelessly inadequate to express his outraged feelings.

"A little beast of a naked brown Nubian boy," spluttered Egbert.

And now Amanda is seriously ill.

30. The Boar-Pig

"There is a back way on to the lawn," said Mrs. Philidore Stossen to her daughter, "through a small grass paddock and then through a walled fruit garden full of gooseberry bushes. I went all over the place last year when the family were away. There is a door that opens from the fruit garden into a shrubbery, and once we emerge from there we can mingle with the guests as if we had come in by the ordinary way. It's much safer than going in by the front entrance and running the risk of coming bang up against the hostess; that would be so awkward when she doesn't happen to have invited us."

"Isn't it a lot of trouble to take for getting admittance to a garden party?"

"To a garden party, yes; to THE garden party of the season, certainly not. Every one of any consequence in the county, with the exception of ourselves, has been asked to meet the Princess, and it would be far more troublesome to invent explanations as to why we weren't there than to get in by a roundabout way. I stopped Mrs. Cuvering in the road yesterday and talked very pointedly about the Princess. If she didn't choose to take the hint and send me an invitation it's not my fault, is it? Here we are: we just cut across the grass and through that little gate into the garden."

Mrs. Stossen and her daughter, suitably arrayed for a county garden party function with an infusion of Almanack de Gotha, sailed through the narrow grass paddock and the ensuing gooseberry garden with the air of state barges making an unofficial progress along a rural trout stream. There was a certain amount of furtive haste mingled with the stateliness of their advance, as though hostile search-lights might be turned on them at any moment; and, as a matter of fact, they were not unobserved. Matilda Cuvering, with the alert eyes of thirteen years old and the added advantage of an exalted position in the branches of a medlar tree, had enjoyed a good view of the Stossen flanking movement and had foreseen exactly where it would break down in execution.

"They'll find the door locked, and they'll jolly well have to go back the way they came," she remarked to herself. "Serves them right for not coming in by the proper entrance. What a pity Tarquin Superbus isn't loose in the paddock. After all, as every one else is enjoying themselves, I don't see why Tarquin shouldn't have an afternoon out."

Matilda was of an age when thought is action; she slid down from the branches of the medlar tree, and when she clambered back again Tarquin, the huge white Yorkshire boar-pig, had exchanged the narrow limits of his stye for the wider range of the grass paddock. The discomfited Stossen expedition, returning in recriminatory but otherwise orderly retreat from the unyielding obstacle of the locked door, came to a sudden halt at the gate dividing the paddock from the gooseberry garden.

"What a villainous-looking animal," exclaimed Mrs. Stossen; "it wasn't there when we came in."

"It's there now, anyhow," said her daughter. "What on earth are we to do? I wish we had never come."

The boar-pig had drawn nearer to the gate for a closer inspection of the human intruders, and stood champing his jaws and blinking his small red eyes in a manner that was doubtless intended to be disconcerting, and, as far as the Stossens were concerned, thoroughly achieved that result.

"Shoo! Hish! Hish! Shoo!" cried the ladies in chorus.

"If they think they're going to drive him away by reciting lists of the kings of Israel and Judah they're laying themselves out for disappointment," observed Matilda from her seat in the medlar tree. As she made the observation aloud Mrs. Stossen became for the first time aware of her presence. A moment or two earlier she would have been anything but pleased at the discovery that the garden was not as deserted as it looked, but now she hailed the fact of the child's presence on the scene with absolute relief.

"Little girl, can you find some one to drive away –" she began hopefully.

"*Comment? Comprends pas*," was the response.

"Oh, are you French? *Etes-vous Française*?"

"*Pas de tous. 'Suis Angalaise.*"

"Then why not talk English? I want to know if –"

"*Permettez-moi d'expliquer*. You see, I'm rather under a cloud," said Matilda. "I'm staying with my aunt, and I was told I must behave particularly well today, as lots of people were coming for a garden party, and I was told to imitate Claude, that's my young cousin, who never does anything wrong except by accident, and then is always apologetic about it. It seems they thought I ate too much raspberry trifle at lunch, and they said Claude never eats too much raspberry trifle. Well, Claude always goes to sleep for half an hour after lunch, because he's told to, and I waited till he was asleep, and tied his hands and started forcible feeding with a whole bucketful of raspberry trifle that they were keeping for the garden-party. Lots of it went on to his sailor-suit and some of it on to the bed, but a good deal went down Claude's throat, and they can't say again that he has never been known to eat too much raspberry trifle. That is why I am not allowed to go to the party, and as an additional punishment I must speak French all the afternoon. I've had to tell you all this in English, as there were words like forcible feeding that I didn't know the French for; of course I could have invented them, but if I had said *nourriture obligatoire* you wouldn't have had the least idea what I was talking about. *Mais maintenant, nous parlons Française.*"

"Oh, very well, *très bien*," said Mrs. Stossen reluctantly; in moments of flurry such French as she knew was not under very good control. "*Là, à L'autre côté de la porte, est un cochin* –"

"*Un cochon? Ah, le petit charmant!*" exclaimed Matilda with enthusiasm.

"Mais non, pas du tout petit, et pas du tout charmant; un bête feroce –"

"Une bête," corrected Matilda; "a pig is masculine as long as you call it a pig, but if you lose your temper with it and call it a ferocious beast it becomes one of us at once. French is a dreadfully unsexing language."

"For goodness' sake let us talk English then," said Mrs. Stossen. "Is there any way out of this garden except through the paddock where the pig is?"

"I always go over the wall, by way of the plum tree," said Matilda.

"Dressed as we are we could hardly do that," said Mrs. Stossen; it was difficult to imagine her doing it in any costume.

"Do you think you could go and get some one who would drive the pig away?" asked Miss Stossen.

"I promised my aunt I would stay here till five o'clock; it's not four yet."

"I am sure, under the circumstances, your aunt would permit –"

"My conscience would not permit," said Matilda with cold dignity.

"We can't stay here till five o'clock," exclaimed Mrs. Stossen with growing exasperation.

"Shall I recite to you to make the time pass quicker?" asked Matilda obligingly. " Belinda, the little Breadwinner,' is considered my best piece, or, perhaps, it ought to be something in French. Henri Quatre's address to his soldiers is the only thing I really know in that language."

"If you will go and fetch some one to drive that animal away I will give you something to buy yourself a nice present," said Mrs. Stossen.

Matilda came several inches lower down the medlar tree.

"That is the most practical suggestion you have made yet for getting out of the garden," she remarked cheerfully; "Claude and I are collecting money for the Children's Fresh Air Fund, and we are seeing which of us can collect the biggest sum."

"I shall be very glad to contribute half a crown, very glad indeed," said Mrs. Stossen, digging that coin out of the depths of a receptacle which formed a detached outwork of her toilet.

"Claude is a long way ahead of me at present," continued Matilda, taking no notice of the suggested offering; "you see, he's only eleven, and has golden hair, and those are enormous advantages when you're on the collecting job. Only the other day a Russian lady gave him ten shillings. Russians understand the art of giving far better than we do. I expect Claude will net quite twenty-five shillings this afternoon; he'll have the field to himself, and he'll be able to do the pale, fragile, not-long-for-this-world business to perfection after his raspberry trifle experience. Yes, he'll be *quite* two pounds ahead of me by now."

With much probing and plucking and many regretful murmurs the beleaguered ladies managed to produce seven-and-sixpence between them.

"I am afraid this is all we've got," said Mrs. Stossen.

Matilda showed no sign of coming down either to the earth or to their figure.

"I could not do violence to my conscience for anything less than ten shillings," she announced stiffly.

Mother and daughter muttered certain remarks under their breath, in which the word "beast" was prominent, and probably had no reference to Tarquin.

"I find I *have* got another half-crown," said Mrs. Stossen in a shaking voice; "here you are. Now please fetch some one quickly."

Matilda slipped down from the tree, took possession of the donation, and proceeded to pick up a handful of over-ripe medlars from the grass at her feet. Then she climbed over the gate and addressed herself affectionately to the boar-pig.

"Come, Tarquin, dear old boy; you know you can't resist medlars when they're rotten and squashy."

Tarquin couldn't. By dint of throwing the fruit in front of him at judicious intervals Matilda decoyed him back to his stye, while the delivered captives hurried across the paddock.

"Well, I never! The little minx!" exclaimed Mrs. Stossen when she was safely on the high road. "The animal wasn't savage at all, and as for the ten shillings, I don't believe the Fresh Air Fund will see a penny of it!"

There she was unwarrantably harsh in her judgment. If you examine the books of the fund you will find the acknowledgment: "Collected by Miss Matilda Cuvering, 2s. 6d."

31. The Open Window

"MY aunt will be down presently, Mr. Nuttel," said a very self-possessed young lady of fifteen; "in the meantime you must try and put up with me."

Framton Nuttel endeavored to say the correct something which should duly flatter the niece of the moment without unduly discounting the aunt that was to come. Privately he doubted more than ever whether these formal visits on a succession of total strangers would do much towards helping the nerve cure which he was supposed to be undergoing.

"I know how it will be," his sister had said when he was preparing to migrate to this rural retreat; "you will bury yourself down there and not speak to a living soul, and your nerves will be worse than ever from moping. I shall just give you letters of introduction to all the people I know there. Some of them, as far as I can remember, were quite nice."

Framton wondered whether Mrs. Sappleton, the lady to whom he was presenting one of the letters of introduction, came into the nice division.

"Do you know many of the people round here?" asked the niece, when she judged that they had had sufficient silent communion.

"Hardly a soul," said Framton. "My sister was staying here, at the rectory, you know, some four years ago, and she gave me letters of introduction to some of the people here."

He made the last statement in a tone of distinct regret.

"Then you know practically nothing about my aunt?" pursued the self-possessed young lady.

"Only her name and address," admitted the caller. He was wondering whether Mrs. Sappleton was in the married or widowed state. An undefinable something about the room seemed to suggest masculine habitation.

"Her great tragedy happened just three years ago," said the child; "that would be since your sister's time."

"Her tragedy?" asked Framton; somehow in this restful country spot tragedies seemed out of place.

"You may wonder why we keep that window wide open on an October afternoon," said the niece, indicating a large French window that opened on to a lawn.

"It is quite warm for the time of the year," said Framton; "but has that window got anything to do with the tragedy?"

"Out through that window, three years ago to a day, her husband and her two young brothers went off for their day's shooting. They never came back. In crossing the moor to their favourite snipe-shooting ground they were all three engulfed in a treacherous piece of bog. It had been that dreadful wet summer, you know, and places that were safe in other years gave way suddenly without warning. Their bodies were never recovered. That was the dreadful part of it." Here the child's voice lost its self-possessed note and became falteringly human. "Poor aunt always thinks that they will come back some day, they and the little brown spaniel that was lost with them, and walk in at that window just as they used to do. That is why the window is kept open every evening till it is quite dusk. Poor dear aunt, she has often told me how they went out, her husband with his white waterproof coat over his arm, and Ronnie, her youngest brother, singing 'Bertie, why do you bound?' as he always did to tease her, because she said it got on her nerves. Do you know, sometimes on still, quiet evenings like this, I almost get a creepy feeling that they will all walk in through that window –"

She broke off with a little shudder. It was a relief to Framton when the aunt bustled into the room with a whirl of apologies for being late in making her appearance.

"I hope Vera has been amusing you?" she said.

"She has been very interesting," said Framton.

"I hope you don't mind the open window," said Mrs. Sappleton briskly; "my husband and brothers will be home directly from shooting, and they always come in this way. They've been out for snipe in the marshes to-day, so they'll make a fine mess over my poor carpets. So like you men-folk, isn't it?"

She rattled on cheerfully about the shooting and the scarcity of birds, and the prospects for duck in the winter. To Framton it was all purely horrible. He made a desperate but only partially successful effort to turn the talk on to a less ghastly topic; he was conscious that his hostess was giving him only a fragment of her attention, and her eyes were constantly straying past him to the open window and the lawn beyond. It was certainly an unfortunate coincidence that he should have paid his visit on this tragic anniversary.

"The doctors agree in ordering me complete rest, an absence of mental excitement, and avoidance of anything in the nature of violent physical exercise," announced Framton, who laboured under the tolerably wide-spread delusion that total strangers and chance acquaintances are hungry for the least detail of one's ailments and infirmities, their cause and cure. "On the matter of diet they are not so much in agreement," he continued.

"No?" said Mrs. Sappleton, in a voice which only replaced a yawn at the last moment. Then she suddenly brightened into alert attention – but not to what Framton was saying.

"Here they are at last!" she cried. "Just in time for tea, and don't they look as if they were muddy up to the eyes!"

Framton shivered slightly and turned towards the niece with a look intended to convey sympathetic comprehension. The child was staring out through the open window with dazed horror in her eyes. In a chill shock of nameless fear Framton swung round in his seat and looked in the same direction.

In the deepening twilight three figures were walking across the lawn towards the window; they all carried guns under their arms, and one of them was additionally burdened with a white coat hung over his shoulders. A tired brown spaniel kept close at their heels. Noiselessly they neared the house, and then a hoarse young voice chanted out of the dusk: "I said, Bertie, why do you bound?"

Framton grabbed wildly at his stick and hat; the hall-door, the gravel-drive, and the front gate were dimly-noted stages in his headlong retreat. A cyclist coming along the road had to run into the hedge to avoid an imminent collision.

"Here we are, my dear," said the bearer of the white mackintosh, coming in through the window; "fairly muddy, but most of it's dry. Who was that who bolted out as we came up?"

"A most extraordinary man, a Mr. Nuttel," said Mrs. Sappleton; "could only talk about his illnesses, and dashed off without a word of good-bye or apology when you arrived. One would think he had seen a ghost."

"I expect it was the spaniel," said the niece calmly; "he told me he had a horror of dogs. He was once hunted into a cemetery somewhere on the banks of the Ganges by a pack of pariah dogs, and had to spend the night in a newly dug grave with the creatures snarling and grinning and foaming just above him. Enough to make anyone their nerve."

Romance at short notice was her specialty.

32. The Unkindest Blow

The season of strikes seemed to have run itself to a standstill. Almost every trade and industry and calling in which a dislocation could possibly be engineered had indulged in that luxury. The last and least successful convulsion had been the strike of the World's Union of Zoological Garden attendants, who, pending the settlement of certain demands, refused to minister further to the wants of the animals committed to their charge or to allow any other keepers to take their place. In this case the threat of the Zoological Gardens authorities that if the men "came out" the animals should come out also had intensified and precipitated the crisis. The imminent prospect of the larger carnivores, to say nothing of rhinoceroses and bull bison, roaming at large and unfed in the heart of London, was not one which permitted of prolonged conferences. The Government of the day, which from its tendency to be a few hours behind the course of events had been nicknamed the Government of the afternoon, was obliged to intervene with promptitude and decision. A strong force of Bluejackets was despatched to Regent's Park to take over the temporarily abandoned duties of the strikers. Bluejackets were chosen in preference to land forces, partly on account of the traditional readiness of the British Navy to go anywhere and do anything, partly by reason of the familiarity of the average sailor with monkeys, parrots, and other tropical fauna, but chiefly at the urgent request of the First Lord of the Admiralty, who was keenly desirous of an opportunity for performing some personal act of unobtrusive public service within the province of his department.

"If he insists on feeding the infant jaguar himself, in defiance of its mother's wishes, there may be another by-election in the north," said one of his colleagues, with a hopeful inflection in his voice. "By-elections are not very desirable at present, but we must not be selfish."

As a matter of fact the strike collapsed peacefully without any outside intervention. The majority of the keepers had become so attached to their charges that they returned to work of their own accord.

And then the nation and the newspapers turned with a sense of relief to happier things. It seemed as if a new era of contentment was about to dawn. Everybody had struck who could possibly want to strike or who could possibly be cajoled or bullied into striking, whether they wanted to or not. The lighter and brighter side of life might now claim some attention. And conspicuous among the other topics that sprang into sudden prominence was the pending Falvertoon divorce suit.

The Duke of Falvertoon was one of those human *hors d'oeuvres* that stimulate the public appetite for sensation without giving it much to feed on. As a mere child he had been precociously brilliant; he had declined the editorship of the *Anglian Review* at an age when most boys are content to have declined MENSA, a table, and though he could not claim to have originated the Futurist movement in literature, his "Letters to a possible Grandson," written at the age of fourteen, had attracted considerable notice. In later days his brilliancy had been less conspicuously displayed. During a debate in the House of Lords on affairs in Morocco, at a moment when that country, for the fifth time in seven years, had brought half Europe to the verge of war, he had interpolated the remark "a little Moor and how much it is," but in spite of the encouraging reception accorded to this one political utterance he was never tempted to a further display in that direction. It began to be generally understood that he did not intend to supplement his numerous town and country residences by living overmuch in the public eye.

And then had come the unlooked-for tidings of the imminent proceedings for divorce. And such a divorce! There were cross-suits and allegations and counter-allegations, charges of cruelty and desertion, everything in fact that was necessary to make the case one of the most complicated and sensational of its kind. And the number of distinguished people involved or cited as witnesses not only embraced both political parties in the realm and several Colonial governors, but included an exotic contingent from France, Hungary, the United States of North America, and the Grand Duchy of Baden. Hotel accommodation of the more expensive sort began to experience a strain on its resources. "It will be quite like the Durbar without the elephants," exclaimed an enthusiastic lady who, to do her justice, had never seen a Durbar. The general feeling was one of thankfulness that the last of the strikes had been got over before the date fixed for the hearing of the great suit.

As a reaction from the season of gloom and industrial strife that had just passed away the agencies that purvey and stage-manage sensations laid themselves out to do their level best on this momentous occasion. Men who had made their reputations as special descriptive writers were mobilised from distant corners of Europe and the further side of the Atlantic in order to enrich with their pens the daily printed records of the case; one word-painter, who specialised in descriptions of how witnesses turn pale under cross-examination, was summoned hurriedly back from a famous and prolonged murder trial in Sicily, where indeed his talents were being decidedly wasted. Thumbnail artists and expert kodak manipulators were retained at extravagant salaries, and special dress reporters were in high demand. An enterprising Paris firm of costume builders presented the defendant Duchess with three special creations, to be worn, marked, learned, and extensively reported at various critical stages of the trial; and as for the cinematograph agents, their industry and persistence was untiring. Films representing the Duke saying good-bye to his favourite canary on the eve of the trial were in readiness weeks before the event was due to take place; other films depicted the

Duchess holding imaginary consultations with fictitious lawyers or making a light repast off specially advertised vegetarian sandwiches during a supposed luncheon interval. As far as human foresight and human enterprise could go nothing was lacking to make the trial a success.

Two days before the case was down for hearing the advance reporter of an important syndicate obtained an interview with the Duke for the purpose of gleaning some final grains of information concerning his Grace's personal arrangements during the trial.

"I suppose I may say this will be one of the biggest affairs of its kind during the lifetime of a generation," began the reporter as an excuse for the unsparing minuteness of detail that he was about to make quest for.

"I suppose so – if it comes off," said the Duke lazily.

"If?" queried the reporter, in a voice that was something between a gasp and a scream.

"The Duchess and I are both thinking of going on strike," said the Duke.

"Strike!"

The baleful word flashed out in all its old hideous familiarity. Was there to be no end to its recurrence?

"Do you mean," faltered the reporter, "that you are contemplating a mutual withdrawal of the charges?"

"Precisely," said the Duke.

"But think of the arrangements that have been made, the special reporting, the cinematographs, the catering for the distinguished foreign witnesses, the prepared music-hall allusions; think of all the money that has been sunk –"

"Exactly," said the Duke coldly, "the Duchess and I have realised that it is we who provide the material out of which this great far-reaching industry has been built up. Widespread employment will be given and enormous profits made during the duration of the case, and we, on whom all the stress and racket falls, will get – what? An unenviable notoriety and the privilege of paying heavy legal expenses whichever way the verdict goes.

Hence our decision to strike. We don't wish to be reconciled; we fully realise that it is a grave step to take, but unless we get some reasonable consideration out of this vast stream of wealth and industry that we have called into being we intend coming out of court and staying out. Good afternoon."

The news of this latest strike spread universal dismay. Its inaccessibility to the ordinary methods of persuasion made it peculiarly formidable. If the Duke and Duchess persisted in being reconciled the Government could hardly be called on to interfere. Public opinion in the shape of social ostracism might be brought to bear on them, but that was as far as coercive measures could go. There was nothing for it but a conference, with powers to propose liberal terms. As it was, several of the foreign witnesses had already departed and others had telegraphed cancelling their hotel arrangements.

The conference, protracted, uncomfortable, and occasionally acrimonious, succeeded at last in arranging for a resumption of litigation, but it was a fruitless victory. The Duke, with a touch of his earlier precocity, died of premature decay a fortnight before the date fixed for the new trial.

33. The Byzantine Omelette

Sophie Chattel-Monkheim was a Socialist by conviction and a Chattel-Monkheim by marriage. The particular member of that wealthy family whom she had married was rich, even as his relatives counted riches. Sophie had very advanced and decided views as to the distribution of money: it was a pleasing and fortunate circumstance that she also had the money. When she inveighed eloquently against the evils of capitalism at drawing-room meetings and Fabian conferences she was conscious of a comfortable feeling that the system, with all its inequalities and iniquities, would probably last her time. It is one of the consolations of middle-aged reformers that the good they inculcate must live after them if it is to live at all.

On a certain spring evening, somewhere towards the dinner-hour, Sophie sat tranquilly between her mirror and her maid, undergoing the process of having her hair built into an elaborate reflection of the prevailing fashion. She was hedged round with a great peace, the peace of one who has attained a desired end with much effort and perseverance, and who has found it still eminently desirable in its attainment. The Duke of Syria had consented to come beneath her roof as a guest, was even now installed beneath her roof, and would shortly be sitting at her dining-table. As a good Socialist, Sophie disapproved of social distinctions, and derided the idea of a princely caste, but if there were to be these artificial gradations of rank and dignity she was pleased and anxious to have an exalted specimen of an exalted order included in her house-party. She was broad-minded enough to love the sinner while hating the sin – not that she entertained any warm feeling of personal affection for the Duke of Syria, who was a comparative stranger, but still, as Duke of Syria, he was very, very welcome beneath her roof. She could not have explained why, but no one was likely to ask her for an explanation, and most hostesses envied her.

"You must surpass yourself tonight, Richardson," she said complacently to her maid; "I must be looking my very best. We must all surpass ourselves."

The maid said nothing, but from the concentrated look in her eyes and the deft play of her fingers it was evident that she was beset with the ambition to surpass herself.

A knock came at the door, a quiet but peremptory knock, as of some one who would not be denied.

"Go and see who it is," said Sophie; "it may be something about the wine."

Richardson held a hurried conference with an invisible messenger at the door; when she returned there was noticeable a curious listlessness in place of her hitherto alert manner.

"What is it?" asked Sophie.

"The household servants have 'downed tools,' madame," said Richardson.

"Downed tools!" exclaimed Sophie; "do you mean to say they've gone on strike?"

"Yes, madame," said Richardson, adding the information: "It's Gaspare that the trouble is about."

"Gaspare?" said Sophie wanderingly; "the emergency chef! The omelette specialist!"

"Yes, madame. Before he became an omelette specialist he was a valet, and he was one of the strike-breakers in the great strike at Lord Grimford's two years ago. As soon as the household staff here learned that you had engaged him they resolved to 'down tools' as a protest. They haven't got any grievance against you personally, but they demand that Gaspare should be immediately dismissed."

"But," protested Sophie, "he is the only man in England who understands how to make a Byzantine omelette. I engaged him specially for the Duke of Syria's visit, and it would be impossible to replace him at short notice. I should have to send to Paris, and the Duke loves Byzantine omelettes. It was the one thing we talked about coming from the station."

"He was one of the strike-breakers at Lord Grimford's," reiterated Richardson.

"This is too awful," said Sophie; "a strike of servants at a moment like this, with the Duke of Syria staying in the house. Something must be done immediately. Quick, finish my hair and I'll go and see what I can do to bring them round."

"I can't finish your hair, madame," said Richardson quietly, but with immense decision. "I belong to the union and I can't do another half-minute's work till the strike is settled. I'm sorry to be disobliging."

"But this is inhuman!" exclaimed Sophie tragically; "I've always been a model mistress and I've refused to employ any but union servants, and this is the result. I can't finish my hair myself; I don't know how to. What am I to do? It's wicked!"

"Wicked is the word," said Richardson; "I'm a good Conservative and I've no patience with this Socialist foolery, asking your pardon. It's tyranny, that's what it is, all along the line, but I've my living to make, same as other people, and I've got to belong to the union. I couldn't touch another hair-pin without a strike permit, not if you was to double my wages."

The door burst open and Catherine Malsom raged into the room.

"Here's a nice affair," she screamed, "a strike of household servants without a moment's warning, and I'm left like this! I can't appear in public in this condition."

After a very hasty scrutiny Sophie assured her that she could not.

"Have they all struck?" she asked her maid.

"Not the kitchen staff," said Richardson, "they belong to a different union."

"Dinner at least will be assured," said Sophie, "that is something to be thankful for."

"Dinner!" snorted Catherine, "what on earth is the good of dinner when none of us will be able to appear at it? Look at your hair – and look at me! or rather, don't."

"I know it's difficult to manage without a maid; can't your husband be any help to you?" asked Sophie despairingly.

"Henry? He's in worse case than any of us. His man is the only person who really understands that ridiculous new-fangled Turkish bath that he insists on taking with him everywhere."

"Surely he could do without a Turkish bath for one evening," said Sophie; "I can't appear without hair, but a Turkish bath is a luxury."

"My good woman," said Catherine, speaking with a fearful intensity, "Henry was in the bath when the strike started. In it, do you understand? He's there now."

"Can't he get out?"

"He doesn't know how to. Every time he pulls the lever marked 'release' he only releases hot steam. There are two kinds of steam in the bath, 'bearable' and 'scarcely bearable'; he has released them both. By this time I'm probably a widow."

"I simply can't send away Gaspare," wailed Sophie; "I should never be able to secure another omelette specialist."

"Any difficulty that I may experience in securing another husband is of course a trifle beneath anyone's consideration," said Catherine bitterly.

Sophie capitulated. "Go," she said to Richardson, "and tell the Strike Committee, or whoever are directing this affair, that Gaspare is herewith dismissed. And ask Gaspare to see me presently in the library, when I will pay him what is due to him and make what excuses I can; and then fly back and finish my hair."

Some half an hour later Sophie marshalled her guests in the Grand Salon preparatory to the formal march to the dining-room. Except that Henry Malsom was of the ripe raspberry tint that one sometimes sees at private theatricals representing the human complexion, there was little outward sign among those assembled of the crisis that had just been encountered and surmounted. But the tension had been too stupefying while it lasted not to leave some mental effects behind it. Sophie talked at random to her illustrious guest, and found her eyes straying with increasing frequency towards the great doors through which would presently come the blessed announcement that dinner was served. Now and again she glanced mirror-ward at the reflection of her wonderfully coiffed hair, as an insurance underwriter might gaze thankfully at an overdue vessel that had ridden safely into harbour in the wake of a devastating hurricane. Then the doors opened and the welcome figure of the butler entered the room. But he made no general announcement of a banquet in readiness, and the doors closed behind him; his message was for Sophie alone.

"There is no dinner, madame," he said gravely; "the kitchen staff have 'downed tools.' Gaspare belongs to the Union of Cooks and Kitchen Employees, and as soon as they heard of his summary dismissal at a moment's notice they struck work. They demand his instant reinstatement and an apology to the union. I may add, madame, that they are very firm; I've been obliged even to hand back the dinner rolls that were already on the table."

After the lapse of eighteen months Sophie Chattel-Monkheim is beginning to go about again among her old haunts and associates, but she still has to be very careful. The doctors will not let her attend anything at all exciting, such as a drawing-room meeting or a Fabian conference; it is doubtful, indeed, whether she wants to.

34. The Feast Of Nemesis

"It's a good thing that Saint Valentine's Day has dropped out of vogue," said Mrs. Thackenbury; "what with Christmas and New Year and Easter, not to speak of birthdays, there are quite enough remembrance days as it is. I tried to save myself trouble at Christmas by just sending flowers to all my friends, but it wouldn't work; Gertrude has eleven hot-houses and about thirty gardeners, so it would have been ridiculous to send flowers to her, and Milly has just started a florist's shop, so it was equally out of the question there. The stress of having to decide in a hurry what to give to Gertrude and Milly just when I thought I'd got the whole question nicely off my mind completely ruined my Christmas, and then the awful monotony of the letters of thanks: 'Thank you so much for your lovely flowers. It was so good of you to think of me.' Of course in the majority of cases I hadn't thought about the recipients at all; their names were down in my list of 'people who must not be left out.' If I trusted to remembering them there would be some awful sins of omission."

"The trouble is," said Clovis to his aunt, "all these days of intrusive remembrance harp so persistently on one aspect of human nature and entirely ignore the other; that is why they become so perfunctory and artificial. At Christmas and New Year you are emboldened and encouraged by convention to send gushing messages of optimistic goodwill and servile affection to people whom you would scarcely ask to lunch unless some one else had failed you at the last moment; if you are supping at a restaurant on New Year's Eve you are permitted and expected to join hands and sing 'For Auld Lang Syne' with strangers whom you have never seen before and never want to see again. But no licence is allowed in the opposite direction."

"Opposite direction; what opposite direction?" queried Mrs. Thackenbury.

"There is no outlet for demonstrating your feelings towards people whom you simply loathe. That is really the crying need of our modern civilisation. Just think how jolly it would be if a recognised day were set apart for the paying off of old scores and grudges, a day when one could lay oneself out to be gracefully vindictive to a carefully treasured list of 'people who must not be let off.' I remember when I was at a private school we had one day, the last Monday of the term I think it was, consecrated to the settlement of feuds and grudges; of course we did not appreciate it as much as it deserved, because, after all, any day of the term could be used for that purpose. Still, if one had chastised a smaller boy for being cheeky weeks before, one was always permitted on that day to recall the episode to his memory by chastising him again. That is what the French call reconstructing the crime."

"I should call it reconstructing the punishment," said Mrs. Thackenbury; "and, anyhow, I don't see how you could introduce a system of primitive schoolboy vengeance into civilised adult life. We haven't outgrown our passions, but we are supposed to have learned how to keep them within strictly decorous limits."

"Of course the thing would have to be done furtively and politely," said Clovis; "the charm of it would be that it would never be perfunctory like the other thing. Now, for instance, you say to yourself: 'I must show the Webleys some attention at Christmas, they were kind to dear Bertie at Bournemouth,' and you send them a calendar, and daily for six days after Christmas the male Webley asks the female Webley if she has remembered to thank you for the calendar you sent them. Well, transplant that idea to the other and more human side of your nature, and say to yourself: 'Next Thursday is Nemesis Day; what on earth can I do to those odious people next door who made such an absurd fuss when Ping Yang bit their youngest child?' Then you'd get up awfully early on the allotted day and climb over into their garden and dig for truffles on their tennis court with a good gardening fork, choosing, of course, that part of the court that was screened from observation by the laurel bushes. You wouldn't find any truffles but you would find a great peace, such as no amount of present-giving could ever bestow."

"I shouldn't," said Mrs. Thackenbury, though her air of protest sounded a bit forced; "I should feel rather a worm for doing such a thing."

"You exaggerate the power of upheaval which a worm would be able to bring into play in the limited time available," said Clovis; "if you put in a strenuous ten minutes with a really useful fork, the result ought to suggest the operations of an unusually masterful mole or a badger in a hurry."

"They might guess I had done it," said Mrs. Thackenbury.

"Of course they would," said Clovis; "that would be half the satisfaction of the thing, just as you like people at Christmas to know what presents or cards you've sent them. The thing would be much easier to manage, of course, when you were on outwardly friendly terms with the object of your dislike. That greedy little Agnes Blaik, for instance, who thinks of nothing but her food, it would be quite simple to ask her to a picnic in some wild woodland spot and lose her just before lunch was served; when you found her again every morsel of food could have been eaten up."

"It would require no ordinary human strategy to lose Agnes Blaik when luncheon was imminent: in fact, I don't believe it could be done."

"Then have all the other guests, people whom you dislike, and lose the luncheon. It could have been sent by accident in the wrong direction."

"It would be a ghastly picnic," said Mrs. Thackenbury.

"For them, but not for you," said Clovis; "you would have had an early and comforting lunch before you started, and you could improve the occasion by mentioning in detail the items of the missing banquet – the lobster Newburg and the egg mayonnaise, and the curry that was to have been heated in a chafing-dish. Agnes Blaik would be delirious long before you got to the list of wines, and in the long interval of waiting, before they had quite abandoned hope of the lunch turning up, you could induce them to play silly games, such as that idiotic one of 'the Lord Mayor's dinner-party,' in which every one has to choose the name of a dish and do something futile when it is called out. In this case they would probably burst into tears when their dish is mentioned. It would be a heavenly picnic."

Mrs. Thackenbury was silent for a moment; she was probably making a mental list of the people she would like to invite to the Duke Humphrey picnic. Presently she asked: "And that odious young man, Waldo Plubley, who is always coddling himself – have you thought of anything that one could do to him?" Evidently she was beginning to see the possibilities of Nemesis Day.

"If there was anything like a general observance of the festival," said Clovis, "Waldo would be in such demand that you would have to bespeak him weeks beforehand, and even then, if there were an east wind blowing or a cloud or two in the sky he might be too careful of his precious self to come out. It would be rather jolly if you could lure him into a hammock in the orchard, just near the spot where there is a wasps' nest every summer. A comfortable hammock on a warm afternoon would appeal to his indolent tastes, and then, when he was getting drowsy, a lighted fusee thrown into the nest would bring the wasps out in an indignant mass, and they would soon find a 'home away from home' on Waldo's fat body. It takes some doing to get out of a hammock in a hurry."

"They might sting him to death," protested Mrs. Thackenbury.

"Waldo is one of those people who would be enormously improved by death," said Clovis; "but if you didn't want to go as far as that, you could have some wet straw ready to hand, and set it alight under the hammock at the same time that the fusee was thrown into the nest; the smoke would keep all but the most militant of the wasps just outside the stinging line, and as long as Waldo remained within its protection he would escape serious damage, and could be eventually restored to his mother, kippered all over and swollen in places, but still perfectly recognisable."

"His mother would be my enemy for life," said Mrs. Thackenbury.

"That would be one greeting less to exchange at Christmas," said Clovis

35. The Dreamer

It was the season of sales. The august establishment of Walpurgis and Nettlepink had lowered its prices for an entire week as a concession to trade observances, much as an Archduchess might protestingly contract an attack of influenza for the unsatisfactory reason that influenza was locally prevalent. Adela Chemping, who considered herself in some measure superior to the allurements of an ordinary bargain sale, made a point of attending the reduction week at Walpurgis and Nettlepink's.

"I'm not a bargain hunter," she said, "but I like to go where bargains are."

Which showed that beneath her surface strength of character there flowed a gracious undercurrent of human weakness.

With a view to providing herself with a male escort Mrs. Chemping had invited her youngest nephew to accompany her on the first day of the shopping expedition, throwing in the additional allurement of a cinematograph theatre and the prospect of light refreshment. As Cyprian was not yet eighteen she hoped he might not have reached that stage in masculine development when parcel-carrying is looked on as a thing abhorrent.

"Meet me just outside the floral department," she wrote to him, "and don't be a moment later than eleven."

Cyprian was a boy who carried with him through early life the wondering look of a dreamer, the eyes of one who sees things that are not visible to ordinary mortals, and invests the commonplace things of this world with qualities unsuspected by plainer folk – the eyes of a poet or a house agent. He was quietly dressed – that sartorial quietude which frequently accompanies early adolescence, and is usually attributed by novel-writers to the influence of a widowed mother. His hair was brushed back in a smoothness as of ribbon seaweed and seamed with a narrow furrow that scarcely aimed at being a parting. His aunt particularly noted this item of his toilet when they met at the appointed rendezvous, because he was standing waiting for her bare-headed.

"Where is your hat?" she asked.

"I didn't bring one with me," he replied.

Adela Chemping was slightly scandalised.

"You are not going to be what they call a Nut, are you?" she inquired with some anxiety, partly with the idea that a Nut would be an extravagance which her sister's small household would scarcely be justified in incurring, partly, perhaps, with the instinctive apprehension that a Nut, even in its embryo stage, would refuse to carry parcels.

Cyprian looked at her with his wondering, dreamy eyes.

"I didn't bring a hat," he said, "because it is such a nuisance when one is shopping; I mean it is so awkward if one meets anyone one knows and has to take one's hat off when one's hands are full of parcels. If one hasn't got a hat on one can't take it off."

Mrs. Chemping sighed with great relief; her worst fear had been laid at rest.

"It is more orthodox to wear a hat," she observed, and then turned her attention briskly to the business in hand.

"We will go first to the table-linen counter," she said, leading the way in that direction; "I should like to look at some napkins."

The wondering look deepened in Cyprian's eyes as he followed his aunt; he belonged to a generation that is supposed to be over-fond of the role of mere spectator, but looking at napkins that one did not mean to buy was a pleasure beyond his comprehension. Mrs. Chemping held one or two napkins up to the light and stared fixedly at them, as though she half expected to find some revolutionary cypher written on them in scarcely visible ink; then she suddenly broke away in the direction of the glassware department.

"Millicent asked me to get her a couple of decanters if there were any going really cheap," she explained on the way, "and I really do want a salad bowl. I can come back to the napkins later on."

She handled and scrutinised a large number of decanters and a long series of salad bowls, and finally bought seven chrysanthemum vases.

"No one uses that kind of vase nowadays," she informed Cyprian, "but they will do for presents next Christmas."

Two sunshades that were marked down to a price that Mrs. Chemping considered absurdly cheap were added to her purchases.

"One of them will do for Ruth Colson; she is going out to the Malay States, and a sunshade will always be useful there. And I must get her some thin writing paper. It takes up no room in one's baggage."

Mrs. Chemping bought stacks of writing paper; it was so cheap, and it went so flat in a trunk or portmanteau. She also bought a few envelopes – envelopes somehow seemed rather an extravagance compared with notepaper.

"Do you think Ruth will like blue or grey paper?" she asked Cyprian.

"Grey," said Cyprian, who had never met the lady in question.

"Have you any mauve notepaper of this quality?" Adela asked the assistant.

"We haven't any mauve," said the assistant, "but we've two shades of green and a darker shade of grey."

Mrs. Chemping inspected the greens and the darker grey, and chose the blue.

"Now we can have some lunch," she said.

Cyprian behaved in an exemplary fashion in the refreshment department, and cheerfully accepted a fish cake and a mince pie and a small cup of coffee as adequate restoratives after two hours of concentrated shopping. He was adamant, however, in resisting his aunt's suggestion that a hat should be bought for him at the counter where men's headwear was being disposed of at temptingly reduced prices.

"I've got as many hats as I want at home," he said, "and besides, it rumples one's hair so, trying them on."

Perhaps he was going to develop into a Nut after all. It was a disquieting symptom that he left all the parcels in charge of the cloak-room attendant.

"We shall be getting more parcels presently," he said, "so we need not collect these till we have finished our shopping."

His aunt was doubtfully appeased; some of the pleasure and excitement of a shopping expedition seemed to evaporate when one was deprived of immediate personal contact with one's purchases.

"I'm going to look at those napkins again," she said, as they descended the stairs to the ground floor. "You need not come," she added, as the dreaming look in the boy's eyes changed for a moment into one of mute protest, "you can meet me afterwards in the cutlery department; I've just remembered that I haven't a corkscrew in the house that can be depended on."

Cyprian was not to be found in the cutlery department when his aunt in due course arrived there, but in the crush and bustle of anxious shoppers and busy attendants it was an easy matter to miss anyone. It was in the leather goods department some quarter of an hour later that Adela Chemping caught sight of her nephew, separated from her by a rampart of suitcases and portmanteaux and hemmed in by the jostling crush of human beings that now invaded every corner of the great shopping emporium. She was just in time to witness a pardonable but rather embarrassing mistake on the part of a lady who had wriggled her way with unstayable determination towards the bareheaded Cyprian, and was now breathlessly demanding the sale price of a handbag which had taken her fancy.

"There now," exclaimed Adela to herself, "she takes him for one of the shop assistants because he hasn't got a hat on. I wonder it hasn't happened before."

Perhaps it had. Cyprian, at any rate, seemed neither startled nor embarrassed by the error into which the good lady had fallen. Examining the ticket on the bag, he announced in a clear, dispassionate voice:

"Black seal, thirty-four shillings, marked down to twenty-eight. As a matter of fact, we are clearing them out at a special reduction price of twenty-six shillings. They are going off rather fast."

"I'll take it," said the lady, eagerly digging some coins out of her purse.

"Will you take it as it is?" asked Cyprian; "it will be a matter of a few minutes to get it wrapped up, there is such a crush."

"Never mind, I'll take it as it is," said the purchaser, clutching her treasure and counting the money into Cyprian's palm.

Several kind strangers helped Adela into the open air.

"It's the crush and the heat," said one sympathiser to another; "it's enough to turn anyone giddy."

When she next came across Cyprian he was standing in the crowd that pushed and jostled around the counters of the book department. The dream look was deeper than ever in his eyes. He had just sold two books of devotion to an elderly Canon.

36. A Defensive Diamond

Treddleford sat in an easeful arm-chair in front of a slumberous fire, with a volume of verse in his hand and the comfortable consciousness that outside the club windows the rain was dripping and pattering with persistent purpose. A chill, wet October afternoon was merging into a bleak, wet October evening, and the club smoking-room seemed warmer and cosier by contrast. It was an afternoon on which to be wafted away from one's climatic surroundings, and "The Golden journey to Samarkand" promised to bear Treddleford well and bravely into other lands and under other skies. He had already migrated from London the rain-swept to Bagdad the Beautiful, and stood by the Sun Gate "in the olden time" when an icy breath of imminent annoyance seemed to creep between the book and himself. Amblecope, the man with the restless, prominent eyes and the mouth ready mobilised for conversational openings, had planted himself in a neighbouring arm-chair. For a twelvemonth and some odd weeks Treddleford had skilfully avoided making the acquaintance of his voluble fellow-clubman; he had marvellously escaped from the infliction of his relentless record of tedious personal achievements, or alleged achievements, on golf links, turf, and gaming table, by flood and field and covert-side. Now his season of immunity was coming to an end. There was no escape; in another moment he would be numbered among those who knew Amblecope to speak to – or rather, to suffer being spoken to.

The intruder was armed with a copy of *Country Life*, not for purposes of reading, but as an aid to conversational ice-breaking.

"Rather a good portrait of Throstlewing," he remarked explosively, turning his large challenging eyes on Treddleford; "somehow it reminds me very much of Yellowstep, who was supposed to be such a good thing for the Grand Prix in 1903. Curious race that was; I suppose I've seen every race for the Grand Prix for the last –"

"Be kind enough never to mention the Grand Prix in my hearing," said Treddleford desperately; "it awakens acutely distressing memories. I can't explain why without going into a long and complicated story."

"Oh, certainly, certainly," said Amblecope hastily; long and complicated stories that were not told by himself were abominable in his eyes. He turned the pages of Country Life and became spuriously interested in the picture of a Mongolian pheasant.

"Not a bad representation of the Mongolian variety," he exclaimed, holding it up for his neighbour's inspection. "They do very well in some covers. Take some stopping too, once they're fairly on the wing. I suppose the biggest bag I ever made in two successive days –"

"My aunt, who owns the greater part of Lincolnshire," broke in Treddleford, with dramatic abruptness, "possesses perhaps the most remarkable record in the way of a pheasant bag that has ever been achieved. She is seventy-five and can't hit a thing, but she always goes out with the guns. When I say she can't hit a thing, I don't mean to say that she doesn't occasionally endanger the lives of her fellow-guns, because that wouldn't be true. In fact, the chief Government Whip won't allow Ministerial M.P.'s to go out with her; 'We don't want to incur by-elections needlessly,' he quite reasonably observed. Well, the other day she winged a pheasant, and brought it to earth with a feather or two knocked out of it; it was a runner, and my aunt saw herself in danger of being done out of about the only bird she'd hit during the present reign. Of course she wasn't going to stand that; she followed it through bracken and brushwood, and when it took to the open country and started across a ploughed field she jumped on to the shooting pony and went after it. The chase was a long one, and when my aunt at last ran the bird to a standstill she was nearer home than she was to the shooting party; she had left that some five miles behind her."

"Rather a long run for a wounded pheasant," snapped Amblecope.

"The story rests on my aunt's authority," said Treddleford coldly, "and she is local vice-president of the Young Women's Christian Association. She trotted three miles or so to her home, and it was not till the middle of the afternoon that it was discovered that the lunch for the entire shooting party was in a pannier attached to the pony's saddle. Anyway, she got her bird."

"Some birds, of course, take a lot of killing," said Amblecope; "so do some fish. I remember once I was fishing in the Exe, lovely trout stream, lots of fish, though they don't run to any great size –"

"One of them did," announced Treddleford, with emphasis. "My uncle, the Bishop of Southmolton, came across a giant trout in a pool just off the main stream of the Exe near Ugworthy; he tried it with every kind of fly and worm every day for three weeks without an atom of success, and then Fate intervened on his behalf. There was a low stone bridge just over this pool, and on the last day of his fishing holiday a motor van ran violently into the parapet and turned completely over; no one was hurt, but part of the parapet was knocked away, and the entire load that the van was carrying was pitched over and fell a little way into the pool. In a couple of minutes the giant trout was flapping and twisting on bare mud at the bottom of a waterless pool, and my uncle was able to walk down to him and fold him to his breast. The van-load consisted of blotting-paper, and every drop of water in that pool had been sucked up into the mass of spilt cargo."

There was silence for nearly half a minute in the smoking-room, and Treddleford began to let his mind steal back towards the golden road that led to Samarkand. Amblecope, however, rallied, and remarked in a rather tired and dispirited voice:

"Talking of motor accidents, the narrowest squeak I ever had was the other day, motoring with old Tommy Yarby in North Wales. Awfully good sort, old Yarby, thorough good sportsman, and the best –"

"It was in North Wales," said Treddleford, "that my sister met with her sensational carriage accident last year. She was on her way to a garden-party at Lady Nineveh's, about the only garden-party that ever comes to pass in those parts in the course of the year, and therefore a thing that she would have been very sorry to miss. She was driving a young horse that she'd only bought a week or two previously, warranted to be perfectly steady with motor traffic, bicycles, and other common objects of the roadside. The animal lived up to its reputation, and passed the most explosive of motorbikes with an indifference that almost amounted to apathy. However, I suppose we all draw the line somewhere, and this particular cob drew it at travelling wild beast shows. Of course my sister didn't know that, but she knew it very distinctly when she turned a sharp corner and found herself in a mixed company of camels, piebald horses, and canary-coloured vans. The dogcart was overturned in a ditch and kicked to splinters, and the cob went home across country. Neither my sister nor the groom was hurt, but the problem of how to get to the Nineveh garden-party, some three miles distant, seemed rather difficult to solve; once there, of course, my sister would easily find some one to drive her home. 'I suppose you wouldn't care for the loan of a couple of my camels?' the showman suggested, in humorous sympathy. 'I would,' said my sister, who had ridden camel-back in Egypt, and she overruled the objections of the groom, who hadn't. She picked out two of the most presentable-looking of the beasts and had them dusted and made as tidy as was possible at short notice, and set out for the Nineveh mansion. You may imagine the sensation that her small but imposing caravan created when she arrived at the hall door. The entire garden-party flocked up to gape. My sister was rather glad to slip down from her camel, and the groom was thankful to scramble down from his. Then young Billy Doulton, of the Dragoon Guards, who has been a lot at Aden and thinks he knows camel-language backwards, thought he would show off by making the beasts kneel down in orthodox fashion. Unfortunately camel words-of-command are not the same all the world over; these were magnificent Turkestan camels, accustomed to stride up the stony terraces of mountain passes, and when Doulton shouted at them they went side by side up the front steps, into the entrance hall, and up the grand staircase. The German governess met them just at the turn of the corridor. The Ninevehs nursed her with devoted attention for weeks, and when I last heard from them she was well enough to go about her duties again, but the doctor says she will always suffer from Hagenbeck heart."

Amblecope got up from his chair and moved to another part of the room. Treddleford reopened his book and betook himself once more across

The dragon-green, the luminous, the dark, the serpent-haunted sea.

For a blessed half-hour he disported himself in imagination by the "gay Aleppo-Gate," and listened to the bird-voiced singing-man. Then the world of to-day called him back; a page summoned him to speak with a friend on the telephone.

As Treddleford was about to pass out of the room he encountered Amblecope, also passing out, on his way to the billiard-room, where, perchance, some luckless wight might be secured and held fast to listen to the number of his attendances at the Grand Prix, with subsequent remarks on Newmarket and the Cambridgeshire. Amblecope made as if to pass out first, but a new-born pride was surging in Treddleford's breast and he waved him back.

"I believe I take precedence," he said coldly; "you are merely the club Bore; I am the club Liar."

37. The Lumber Room

The children were to be driven, as a special treat, to the sands at Jagborough. Nicholas was not to be of the party; he was in disgrace. Only that morning he had refused to eat his wholesome bread-and-milk on the seemingly frivolous ground that there was a frog in it. Older and wiser and better people had told him that there could not possibly be a frog in his bread-and-milk and that he was not to talk nonsense; he continued, nevertheless, to talk what seemed the veriest nonsense, and described with much detail the colouration and markings of the alleged frog. The dramatic part of the incident was that there really was a frog in Nicholas' basin of bread-and-milk; he had put it there himself, so he felt entitled to know something about it. The sin of taking a frog from the garden and putting it into a bowl of wholesome bread-and-milk was enlarged on at great length, but the fact that stood out clearest in the whole affair, as it presented itself to the mind of Nicholas, was that the older, wiser, and better people had been proved to be profoundly in error in matters about which they had expressed the utmost assurance.

"You said there couldn't possibly be a frog in my bread-and-milk; there *was* a frog in my bread-and-milk," he repeated, with the insistence of a skilled tactician who does not intend to shift from favourable ground.

So his boy-cousin and girl-cousin and his quite uninteresting younger brother were to be taken to Jagborough sands that afternoon and he was to stay at home. His cousins' aunt, who insisted, by an unwarranted stretch of imagination, in styling herself his aunt also, had hastily invented the Jagborough expedition in order to impress on Nicholas the delights that he had justly forfeited by his disgraceful conduct at the breakfast-table. It was her habit, whenever one of the children fell from grace, to improvise something of a festival nature from which the offender would be rigorously debarred; if all the children sinned collectively they were suddenly informed of a circus in a neighbouring town, a circus of unrivalled merit and uncounted elephants, to which, but for their depravity, they would have been taken that very day.

A few decent tears were looked for on the part of Nicholas when the moment for the departure of the expedition arrived. As a matter of fact, however, all the crying was done by his girl-cousin, who scraped her knee rather painfully against the step of the carriage as she was scrambling in.

"How she did howl," said Nicholas cheerfully, as the party drove off without any of the elation of high spirits that should have characterised it.

"She'll soon get over that," said the *soi-disant* aunt; "it will be a glorious afternoon for racing about over those beautiful sands. How they will enjoy themselves!"

"Bobby won't enjoy himself much, and he won't race much either," said Nicholas with a grim chuckle; his boots are hurting him. They're too tight."

"Why didn't he tell me they were hurting?" asked the aunt with some asperity.

"He told you twice, but you weren't listening. You often don't listen when we tell you important things."

"You are not to go into the gooseberry garden," said the aunt, changing the subject.

"Why not?" demanded Nicholas.

"Because you are in disgrace," said the aunt loftily.

Nicholas did not admit the flawlessness of the reasoning; he felt perfectly capable of being in disgrace and in a gooseberry garden at the same moment. His face took on an expression of considerable obstinacy. It was clear to his aunt that he was determined to get into the gooseberry garden, "only," as she remarked to herself, "because I have told him he is not to."

Now the gooseberry garden had two doors by which it might be entered, and once a small person like Nicholas could slip in there he could effectually disappear from view amid the masking growth of artichokes, raspberry canes, and fruit bushes. The aunt had many other things to do that afternoon, but she spent an hour or two in trivial gardening operations among flower beds and shrubberies, whence she could keep a watchful eye on the two doors that led to the forbidden paradise. She was a woman of few ideas, with immense powers of concentration.

Nicholas made one or two sorties into the front garden, wriggling his way with obvious stealth of purpose towards one or other of the doors, but never able for a moment to evade the aunt's watchful eye. As a matter of fact, he had no intention of trying to get into the gooseberry garden, but it was extremely convenient for him that his aunt should believe that he had; it was a belief that would keep her on self-imposed sentry-duty for the greater part of the afternoon. Having thoroughly confirmed and fortified her suspicions Nicholas slipped back into the house and rapidly put into execution a plan of action that had long germinated in his brain. By standing on a chair in the library one could reach a shelf on which reposed a fat, important-looking key. The key was as important as it looked; it was the instrument which kept the mysteries of the lumber-room secure from unauthorised intrusion, which opened a way only for aunts and such-like privileged persons. Nicholas had not had much experience of the art of fitting keys into keyholes and turning locks, but for some days past he had practised with the key of the schoolroom door; he did not believe in trusting too much to luck and accident. The key turned stiffly in the lock, but it turned. The door opened, and Nicholas was in an unknown land, compared with which the gooseberry garden was a stale delight, a mere material pleasure.

Often and often Nicholas had pictured to himself what the lumber-room might be like, that region that was so carefully sealed from youthful eyes and concerning which no questions were ever answered. It came up to his expectations. In the first place it was large and dimly lit, one high window opening on to the forbidden garden being its only source of illumination. In the second place it was a storehouse of unimagined treasures. The aunt-by-assertion was one of those people who think that things spoil by use and consign them to dust and damp by way of preserving them. Such parts of the house as Nicholas knew best were rather bare and cheerless, but here there were wonderful things for the eye to feast on. First and foremost there was a piece of framed tapestry that was evidently meant to be a fire-screen. To Nicholas it was a living, breathing story; he sat down on a roll of Indian hangings, glowing in wonderful colours beneath a layer of dust, and took in all the details of the tapestry picture. A man, dressed in the hunting costume of some remote period, had just transfixed a stag with an arrow; it could not have been a difficult shot because the stag was only one or two paces away from him; in the thickly-growing vegetation that the picture suggested it would not have been difficult to creep up to a feeding stag, and the two spotted dogs that were springing forward to join in the chase had evidently been trained to keep to heel till the arrow was discharged. That part of the picture was simple, if interesting, but did the huntsman see, what Nicholas saw, that four galloping wolves were coming in his direction through the wood? There might be more than four of them hidden behind the trees, and in any case would the man and his dogs be able to cope with the four wolves if they made an attack? The man had only two arrows left in his quiver, and he might miss with one or both of them; all one knew about his skill in shooting was that he could hit a large stag at a ridiculously short range. Nicholas sat for many golden minutes revolving the possibilities of the scene; he was inclined to think that there were more than four wolves and that the man and his dogs were in a tight corner.

But there were other objects of delight and interest claiming his instant attention: there were quaint twisted candlesticks in the shape of snakes, and a teapot fashioned like a china duck, out of whose open beak the tea was supposed to come. How dull and shapeless the nursery teapot seemed in comparison!

And there was a carved sandal-wood box packed tight with aromatic cotton wool, and between the layers of cotton wool were little brass figures, hump-necked bulls, and peacocks and goblins, delightful to see and to handle. Less promising in appearance was a large square book with plain black covers; Nicholas peeped into it, and, behold, it was full of coloured pictures of birds. And such birds! In the garden, and in the lanes when he went for a walk, Nicholas came across a few birds, of which the largest were an occasional magpie or wood-pigeon; here were herons and bustards, kites, toucans, tiger-bitterns, brush turkeys, ibises, golden pheasants, a whole portrait gallery of undreamed-of creatures. And as he was admiring the colouring of the mandarin duck and assigning a life-history to it, the voice of his aunt in shrill vociferation of his name came from the gooseberry garden without. She had grown suspicious at his long disappearance, and had leapt to the conclusion that he had climbed over the wall behind the sheltering screen of the lilac bushes; she was now engaged in energetic and rather hopeless search for him among the artichokes and raspberry canes.

"Nicholas, Nicholas!" she screamed, "you are to come out of this at once. It's no use trying to hide there; I can see you all the time."

It was probably the first time for twenty years that anyone had smiled in that lumber-room.

Presently the angry repetitions of Nicholas' name gave way to a shriek, and a cry for somebody to come quickly. Nicholas shut the book, restored it carefully to its place in a corner, and shook some dust from a neighbouring pile of newspapers over it. Then he crept from the room, locked the door, and replaced the key exactly where he had found it. His aunt was still calling his name when he sauntered into the front garden.

"Who's calling?" he asked.

"Me," came the answer from the other side of the wall; "didn't you hear me? I've been looking for you in the gooseberry garden, and I've slipped into the rainwater tank. Luckily there's no water in it, but the sides are slippery and I can't get out. Fetch the little ladder from under the cherry tree –"

"I was told I wasn't to go into the gooseberry garden," said Nicholas promptly.

"I told you not to, and now I tell you that you may," came the voice from the rain-water tank, rather impatiently.

"Your voice doesn't sound like aunt's," objected Nicholas; "you may be the Evil One tempting me to be disobedient. Aunt often tells me that the Evil One tempts me and that I always yield. This time I'm not going to yield."

"Don't talk nonsense," said the prisoner in the tank; "go and fetch the ladder."

"Will there be strawberry jam for tea?" asked Nicholas innocently.

"Certainly there will be," said the aunt, privately resolving that Nicholas should have none of it.

"Now I know that you are the Evil One and not aunt," shouted Nicholas gleefully; "when we asked aunt for strawberry jam yesterday she said there wasn't any. I know there are four jars of it in the store cupboard, because I looked, and of course you know it's there, but she doesn't, because she said there wasn't any. Oh, Devil, you *have* sold yourself!"

There was an unusual sense of luxury in being able to talk to an aunt as though one was talking to the Evil One, but Nicholas knew, with childish discernment, that such luxuries were not to be over-indulged in. He walked noisily away, and it was a kitchen maid, in search of parsley, who eventually rescued the aunt from the rainwater tank.

Tea that evening was partaken of in a fearsome silence. The tide had been at its highest when the children had arrived at Jagborough Cove, so there had been no sands to play on – a circumstance that the aunt had overlooked in the haste of organising her punitive expedition. The tightness of Bobby's boots had had disastrous effect on his temper the whole of the afternoon, and altogether the children could not have been said to have enjoyed themselves. The aunt maintained the frozen muteness of one who has suffered undignified and unmerited detention in a rain-water tank for thirty-five minutes. As for Nicholas, he, too, was silent, in the absorption of one who has much to think about; it was just possible, he considered, that the huntsman would escape with his hounds while the wolves feasted on the stricken stag.

38. Louise

"The tea will be quite cold, you'd better ring for some more," said the Dowager Lady Beanford.

Susan Lady Beanford was a vigorous old woman who had coquetted with imaginary ill-health for the greater part of a lifetime; Clovis Sangrail irreverently declared that she had caught a chill at the Coronation of Queen Victoria and had never let it go again. Her sister, Jane Thropplestance, who was some years her junior, was chiefly remarkable for being the most absent-minded woman in Middlesex.

"I've really been unusually clever this afternoon," she remarked gaily, as she rang for the tea. "I've called on all the people I meant to call on; and I've done all the shopping that I set out to do. I even remembered to try and match that silk for you at Harrod's, but I'd forgotten to bring the pattern with me, so it was no use. I really think that was the only important thing I forgot during the whole afternoon. Quite wonderful for me, isn't it?"

"What have you done with Louise?" asked her sister. "Didn't you take her out with you? You said you were going to."

"Good gracious," exclaimed Jane, "what have I done with Louise? I must have left her somewhere."

"But where?"

"That's just it. Where have I left her? I can't remember if the Carrywoods were at home or if I just left cards. If there were at home I may have left Louise there to play bridge. I'll go and telephone to Lord Carrywood and find out."

"Is that you, Lord Carrywood?" she queried over the telephone; "it's me, Jane Thropplestance. I want to know, have you seen Louise?"

"'Louise,'" came the answer, "it's been my fate to see it three times. At first, I must admit, I wasn't impressed by it, but the music grows on one after a bit. Still, I don't think I want to see it again just at present. Were you going to offer me a seat in your box?"

"Not the opera 'Louise' – my niece, Louise Thropplestance. I thought I might have left her at your house."

"You left cards on us this afternoon, I understand, but I don't think you left a niece. The footman would have been sure to have mentioned it if you had. Is it going to be a fashion to leave nieces on people as well as cards? I hope not; some of these houses in Berkeley-square have practically no accommodation for that sort of thing."

"She's not at the Carrywoods'," announced Jane, returning to her tea; "now I come to think of it, perhaps I left her at the silk counter at Selfridge's. I may have told her to wait there a moment while I went to look at the silks in a better light, and I may easily have forgotten about her when I found I hadn't your pattern with me. In that case she's still sitting there. She wouldn't move unless she was told to; Louise has no initiative."

"You said you tried to match the silk at Harrod's," interjected the dowager.

"Did I? Perhaps it was Harrod's. I really don't remember. It was one of those places where every one is so kind and sympathetic and devoted that one almost hates to take even a reel of cotton away from such pleasant surroundings."

"I think you might have taken Louise away. I don't like the idea of her being there among a lot of strangers. Supposing some unprincipled person was to get into conversation with her."

"Impossible. Louise has no conversation. I've never discovered a single topic on which she'd anything to say beyond 'Do you think so? I dare say you're right.' I really thought her reticence about the fall of the Ribot Ministry was ridiculous, considering how much her dear mother used to visit Paris. This bread and butter is cut far too thin; it crumbles away long before you can get it to your mouth. One feels so absurd, snapping at one's food in mid-air, like a trout leaping at mayfly."

"I am rather surprised," said the dowager, "that you can sit there making a hearty tea when you've just lost a favourite niece."

"You talk as if I'd lost her in a churchyard sense, instead of having temporarily mislaid her. I'm sure to remember presently where I left her."

"You didn't visit any place of devotion, did you? If you've left her mooning about Westminster Abbey or St. Peter's, Eaton Square, without being able to give any satisfactory reason why she's there, she'll be seized under the Cat and Mouse Act and sent to Reginald McKenna."

"That would be extremely awkward," said Jane, meeting an irresolute piece of bread and butter halfway; "we hardly know the McKennas, and it would be very tiresome having to telephone to some unsympathetic private secretary, describing Louise to him and asking to have her sent back in time for dinner. Fortunately, I didn't go to any place of devotion, though I did get mixed up with a Salvation Army procession. It was quite interesting to be at close quarters with them, they're so absolutely different to what they used to be when I first remember them in the 'eighties. They used to go about then unkempt and dishevelled, in a sort of smiling rage with the world, and now they're spruce and jaunty and flamboyantly decorative, like a geranium bed with religious convictions. Laura Kettleway was going on about them in the lift of the Dover Street Tube the other day, saying what a lot of good work they did, and what a loss it would have been if they'd never existed. 'If they had never existed,' I said, 'Granville Barker would have been certain to have invented something that looked exactly like them.' If you say things like that, quite loud, in a Tube lift, they always sound like epigrams."

"I think you ought to do something about Louise," said the dowager.

"I'm trying to think whether she was with me when I called on Ada Spelvexit. I rather enjoyed myself there. Ada was trying, as usual, to ram that odious Koriatoffski woman down my throat, knowing perfectly well that I detest her, and in an unguarded moment she said: 'She's leaving her present house and going to

Lower Seymour Street.' 'I dare say she will, if she stays there long enough,' I said. Ada didn't see it for about three minutes, and then she was positively uncivil. No, I am certain I didn't leave Louise there."

"If you could manage to remember where you DID leave her, it would be more to the point than these negative assurances," said Lady Beanford; "so far, all we know is that she is not at the Carrywoods', or Ada Spelvexit's, or Westminster Abbey."

"That narrows the search down a bit," said Jane hopefully; "I rather fancy she must have been with me when I went to Mornay's. I know I went to Mornay's, because I remember meeting that delightful Malcolm What's-his-name there – you know whom I mean. That's the great advantage of people having unusual first names, you needn't try and remember what their other name is. Of course I know one or two other Malcolms, but none that could possibly be described as delightful. He gave me two tickets for the Happy Sunday Evenings in Sloane Square. I've probably left them at Mornay's, but still it was awfully kind of him to give them to me."

"Do you think you left Louise there?"

"I might telephone and ask. Oh, Robert, before you clear the tea things away I wish you'd ring up Mornay's, in Regent Street, and ask if I left two theatre tickets and one niece in their shop this afternoon."

"A niece, ma'am?" asked the footman.

"Yes, Miss Louise didn't come home with me, and I'm not sure where I left her."

"Miss Louise has been upstairs all the afternoon, ma'am, reading to the second kitchen-maid, who has the neuralgia. I took up tea to Miss Louise at a quarter to five o'clock, ma'am."

"Of course, how silly of me. I remember now, I asked her to read the Faerie Queene to poor Emma, to try to send her to sleep. I always get some one to read the Faerie Queene to me when I have neuralgia, and it usually sends me to sleep. Louise doesn't seem to have been successful, but one can't say she hasn't tried. I expect after the first hour or so the kitchenmaid would rather have been left alone with her neuralgia, but of course Louise wouldn't leave off till some one told her to. Anyhow, you can ring up Mornay's, Robert, and ask whether I left two theatre tickets there. Except for your silk, Susan, those seem to be the only things I've forgotten this afternoon. Quite wonderful for me."

39. The Phantom Luncheon

"The Smithly-Dubbs are in Town," said Sir James. "I wish you would show them some attention. Ask them to lunch with you at the Ritz or somewhere."

"From the little I've seen of the Smithly-Dubbs I don't thing I want to cultivate their acquaintance," said Lady Drakmanton.

"They always work for us at election times," said her husband; "I don't suppose they influence very many votes, but they have an uncle who is on one of my ward committees, and another uncle speaks sometimes at some of our less important meetings. Those sort of people expect some return in the shape of hospitality."

"Expect it!" exclaimed Lady Drakmanton; "the Misses Smithly-Dubb do more than that; they almost demand it. They belong to my club, and hang about the lobby just about lunch-time, all three of them, with their tongues hanging out of their mouths and the six-course look in their eyes. If I were to breathe the word 'lunch' they would hustle me into a taxi and scream 'Ritz' or 'Dieudonne's' to the driver before I knew what was happening."

"All the same, I think you ought to ask them to a meal of some sort," persisted Sir James.

"I consider that showing hospitality to the Smithly-Dubbs is carrying Free Food principles to a regrettable extreme," said Lady Drakmanton; "I've entertained the Joneses and the Browns and the Snapheimers and the Lubrikoffs, and heaps of others whose names I forget, but I don't see why I should inflict the society of the Misses Smithly-Dubb on myself for a solid hour. Imagine it, sixty minutes, more or less, of unrelenting gobble and gabble. Why can't *you* take them on, Milly?" she asked, turning hopefully to her sister.

"I don't know them," said Milly hastily.

"All the better; you can pass yourself off as me. People say that we are so alike that they can hardly tell us apart, and I've only spoken to these tiresome young women about twice in my life, at committee-rooms, and bowed to them in the club. Any of the club page-boys will point them out to you; they're always to be found lolling about the hall just before lunch-time."

"My dear Betty, don't be absurd," protested Milly; "I've got some people lunching with me at the Carlton to-morrow, and I'm leaving Town the day afterwards."

"What time is your lunch to-morrow?" asked Lady Drakmanton reflectively.

"Two o'clock," said Milly.

"Good," said her sister; "the Smithly-Dubbs shall lunch with me to-morrow. It shall be rather an amusing lunch-party. At least, I shall be amused."

The last two remarks she made to herself. Other people did not always appreciate her ideas of humour. Sir James never did.

The next day Lady Drakmanton made some marked variations in her usual toilet effects. She dressed her hair in an unaccustomed manner, and put on a hat that added to the transformation of her appearance. When she had made one or two minor alterations she was sufficiently unlike her usual smart self to produce some hesitation in the greeting which the Misses Smithly-Dubb bestowed on her in the club-lobby. She responded, however, with a readiness which set their doubts at rest.

"What is the Carlton like for lunching in?" she asked breezily.

The restaurant received an enthusiastic recommendation from the three sisters.

"Let's go and lunch there, shall we?" she suggested, and in a few minutes' time the Smithly-Dubb mind was contemplating at close quarters a happy vista of baked meats and approved vintage.

"Are you going to start with caviare? I am," confided Lady Drakmanton, and the Smithly-Dubbs started with caviare. The subsequent dishes were chosen in the same ambitious spirit, and by the time they had arrived at the wild duck course it was beginning to be a rather expensive lunch.

The conversation hardly kept pace with the brilliancy of the menu. Repeated references on the part of the guests to the local political conditions and prospects in Sir James's constituency were met with vague "ahs" and "indeeds" from Lady Drakmanton, who might have been expected to be specially interested.

"I think when the Insurance Act is a little better understood it will lose some of its present unpopularity," hazarded Cecilia Smithly-Dubb.

"Will it? I dare say. I'm afraid politics don't interest me very much," said Lady Drakmanton.

The three Miss Smithly-Dubbs put down their cups of Turkish coffee and stared. Then they broke into protesting giggles.

"Of course, you're joking," they said.

"Not me," was the disconcerting answer; "I can't make head or tail of these bothering old politics. Never could, and never want to. I've quite enough to do to manage my own affairs, and that's a fact."

"But," exclaimed Amanda Smithly-Dubb, with a squeal of bewilderment breaking into her voice, "I was told you spoke so informingly about the Insurance Act at one of our social evenings."

It was Lady Drakmanton who stared now. "Do you know," she said, with a scared look around her, "rather a dreadful thing is happening. I'm suffering from a complete loss of memory. I can't even think who I am. I remember meeting you somewhere, and I remember you asking me to come and lunch with you here, and that I accepted your kind invitation. Beyond that my mind is a positive blank."

The scared look was transferred with intensified poignancy to the faces of her companions.

"*You* asked *us* to lunch," they exclaimed hurriedly. That seemed a more immediately important point to clear up than the question of identity.

"Oh, no," said the vanishing hostess, "*That* I do remember about. You insisted on my coming here because the feeding was so good, and I must say it comes up to all you said about it. A very nice lunch it's been. What I'm worrying about is who on earth am I? I haven't the faintest notion?"

"You are Lady Drakmanton," exclaimed the three sisters in chorus.

"Now, don't make fun of me," she replied, crossly, "I happen to know her quite well by sight, and she isn't a bit like me. And it's an odd thing you should have mentioned her, for it so happens she's just come into the room. That lady in black, with the yellow plume in her hat, there over by the door."

The Smithly-Dubbs looked in the indicated direction, and the uneasiness in their eyes deepened into horror. In outward appearance the lady who had just entered the room certainly came rather nearer to their recollection of their Member's wife than the individual who was sitting at table with them.

"Who ARE you, then, if that is Lady Drakmanton?" they asked in panic-stricken bewilderment.

"That is just what I don't know," was the answer; "and you don't seem to know much better than I do."

"You came up to us in the club –"

"In what club?"

"The New Didactic, in Calais Street."

"The New Didactic!" exclaimed Lady Drakmanton with an air of returning illumination; "thank you so much. Of course, I remember now who I am. I'm Ellen Niggle, of the Ladies' Brasspolishing Guild. The Club employs me to come now and then and see to the polishing of the brass fittings. That's how I came to know Lady Drakmanton by sight; she's very often in the Club. And you are the ladies who so kindly asked me out to lunch. Funny how it should all have slipped my memory, all of a sudden. The unaccustomed good food and wine must have been too much for me; for the moment I really couldn't call to mind who I was. Good gracious," she broke off suddenly, "it's ten past two; I should be at a polishing job in Whitehall. I must scuttle off like a giddy rabbit. Thanking you ever so."

She left the room with a scuttle sufficiently suggestive of the animal she had mentioned, but the giddiness was all on the side of her involuntary hostesses. The restaurant seemed to be spinning round them; and the bill when it appeared did nothing to restore their composure. They were as nearly in tears as it is permissible to be during the luncheon hour in a really good restaurant. Financially speaking, they were well able to afford the luxury of an elaborate lunch, but their ideas on the subject of entertaining differed very sharply, according to the circumstances of whether they were dispensing or receiving hospitality. To have fed themselves liberally at their own expense was, perhaps, an extravagance to be deplored, but, at any rate, they had had something for their money; to have drawn an unknown and socially unremunerative Ellen Niggle into the net of their hospitality was a catastrophe that they could not contemplate with any degree of calmness.

The Smithly-Dubbs never quite recovered from their unnerving experience. They have given up politics and taken to doing good.

40. The Interlopers

In a forest of mixed growth somewhere on the eastern spurs of the Karpathians, a man stood one winter night watching and listening, as though he waited for some beast of the woods to come within the range of his vision, and, later, of his rifle. But the game for whose presence he kept so keen an outlook was none that figured in the sportsman's calendar as lawful and proper for the chase; Ulrich von Gradwitz patrolled the dark forest in quest of a human enemy.

The forest lands of Gradwitz were of wide extent and well stocked with game; the narrow strip of precipitous woodland that lay on its outskirt was not remarkable for the game it harboured or the shooting it afforded, but it was the most jealously guarded of all its owner's territorial possessions. A famous law suit, in the days of his grandfather, had wrested it from the illegal possession of a neighbouring family of petty landowners; the dispossessed party had never acquiesced in the judgment of the Courts, and a long series of poaching affrays and similar scandals had embittered the relationships between the families for three generations. The neighbour feud had grown into a personal one since Ulrich had come to be head of his family; if there was a man in the world whom he detested and wished ill to it was Georg Znaeym, the inheritor of the quarrel and the tireless game-snatcher and raider of the disputed border-forest. The feud might, perhaps, have died down or been compromised if the personal ill-will of the two men had not stood in the way; as boys they had thirsted for one another's blood, as men each prayed that misfortune might fall on the other, and this wind-scourged winter night Ulrich had banded together his foresters to watch the dark forest, not in quest of four-footed quarry, but to keep a look-out for the prowling thieves whom he suspected of being afoot from across the land boundary. The roebuck, which usually kept in the sheltered hollows during a storm-wind, were running like driven things to-night, and there was movement and unrest among the creatures that were wont to sleep through the dark hours. Assuredly there was a disturbing element in the forest, and Ulrich could guess the quarter from whence it came.

He strayed away by himself from the watchers whom he had placed in ambush on the crest of the hill, and wandered far down the steep slopes amid the wild tangle of undergrowth, peering through the tree trunks and listening through the whistling and skirling of the wind and the restless beating of the branches for sight and sound of the marauders. If only on this wild night, in this dark, lone spot, he might come across Georg Znaeym, man to man, with none to witness – that was the wish that was uppermost in his thoughts. And as he stepped round the trunk of a huge beech he came face to face with the man he sought.

The two enemies stood glaring at one another for a long silent moment. Each had a rifle in his hand, each had hate in his heart and murder uppermost in his mind. The chance had come to give full play to the passions of a lifetime. But a man who has been brought up under the code of a restraining civilisation cannot easily nerve himself to shoot down his neighbour in cold blood and without word spoken, except for an offence against his hearth and honour. And before the moment of hesitation had given way to action a deed of Nature's own violence overwhelmed them both. A fierce shriek of the storm had been answered by a splitting crash over their heads, and ere they could leap aside a mass of falling beech tree had thundered down on them. Ulrich von Gradwitz found himself stretched on the ground, one arm numb beneath him and the other held almost as helplessly in a tight tangle of forked branches, while both legs were pinned beneath the fallen mass. His heavy shooting-boots had saved his feet from being crushed to pieces, but if his fractures were not as serious as they might have been, at least it was evident that he could not move from his present position till some one came to release him. The descending twig had slashed the skin of his face, and he had to wink away some drops of blood from his eyelashes before he could take in a general view of the disaster. At his side, so near that under ordinary circumstances he could almost have touched him, lay Georg Znaeym, alive and struggling, but obviously as helplessly pinioned down as himself. All round them lay a thick-strewn wreckage of splintered branches and broken twigs.

Relief at being alive and exasperation at his captive plight brought a strange medley of pious thank-offerings and sharp curses to Ulrich's lips. Georg, who was early blinded with the blood which trickled across his eyes, stopped his struggling for a moment to listen, and then gave a short, snarling laugh.

"So you're not killed, as you ought to be, but you're caught, anyway," he cried; "caught fast. Ho, what a jest, Ulrich von Gradwitz snared in his stolen forest. There's real justice for you!"

And he laughed again, mockingly and savagely.

"I'm caught in my own forest-land," retorted Ulrich. "When my men come to release us you will wish, perhaps, that you were in a better plight than caught poaching on a neighbour's land, shame on you."

Georg was silent for a moment; then he answered quietly:

"Are you sure that your men will find much to release? I have men, too, in the forest to-night, close behind me, and *they* will be here first and do the releasing. When they drag me out from under these damned branches it won't need much clumsiness on their part to roll this mass of trunk right over on the top of you. Your men will find you dead under a fallen beech tree. For form's sake I shall send my condolences to your family."

"It is a useful hint," said Ulrich fiercely. "My men had orders to follow in ten minutes time, seven of which must have gone by already, and when they get me out – I will remember the hint. Only as you will have met your death poaching on my lands I don't think I can decently send any message of condolence to your family."

"Good," snarled Georg, "good. We fight this quarrel out to the death, you and I and our foresters, with no cursed interlopers to come between us. Death and damnation to you, Ulrich von Gradwitz."

"The same to you, Georg Znaeym, forest-thief, game-snatcher."

Both men spoke with the bitterness of possible defeat before them, for each knew that it might be long before his men would seek him out or find him; it was a bare matter of chance which party would arrive first on the scene.

Both had now given up the useless struggle to free themselves from the mass of wood that held them down; Ulrich limited his endeavours to an effort to bring his one partially free arm near enough to his outer coat-pocket to draw out his wine-flask. Even when he had accomplished that operation it was long before he could manage the unscrewing of the stopper or get any of the liquid down his throat. But what a Heaven-sent draught it seemed! It was an open winter, and little snow had fallen as yet, hence the captives suffered less from the cold than might have been the case at that season of the year; nevertheless, the wine was warming and reviving to the wounded man, and he looked across with something like a throb of pity to where his enemy lay, just keeping the groans of pain and weariness from crossing his lips.

"Could you reach this flask if I threw it over to you?" asked Ulrich suddenly; "there is good wine in it, and one may as well be as comfortable as one can. Let us drink, even if to-night one of us dies."

"No, I can scarcely see anything; there is so much blood caked round my eyes," said Georg, "and in any case I don't drink wine with an enemy."

Ulrich was silent for a few minutes, and lay listening to the weary screeching of the wind. An idea was slowly forming and growing in his brain, an idea that gained strength every time that he looked across at the man who was fighting so grimly against pain and exhaustion. In the pain and languor that Ulrich himself was feeling the old fierce hatred seemed to be dying down.

"Neighbour," he said presently, "do as you please if your men come first. It was a fair compact. But as for me, I've changed my mind. If my men are the first to come you shall be the first to be helped, as though you were my guest. We have quarrelled like devils all our lives over this stupid strip of forest, where the trees can't even stand upright in a breath of wind. Lying here to-night thinking I've come to think we've been rather fools; there are better things in life than getting the better of a boundary dispute. Neighbour, if you will help me to bury the old quarrel I – I will ask you to be my friend."

Georg Znaeym was silent for so long that Ulrich thought, perhaps, he had fainted with the pain of his injuries. Then he spoke slowly and in jerks.

"How the whole region would stare and gabble if we rode into the market-square together. No one living can remember seeing a Znaeym and a von Gradwitz talking to one another in friendship. And what peace there would be among the forester folk if we ended our feud to-night. And if we choose to make peace among our people there is none other to interfere, no interlopers from outside... You would come and keep the Sylvester night beneath my roof, and I would come and feast on some high day at your castle... I would never fire a shot on your land, save when you invited me as a guest; and you should come and shoot with me down in the marshes where the wildfowl are. In all the countryside there are none that could hinder if we willed to make peace. I never thought to have wanted to do other than hate you all my life, but I think I have changed my mind about things too, this last half-hour. And you offered me your wineflask... Ulrich von Gradwitz, I will be your friend."

For a space both men were silent, turning over in their minds the wonderful changes that this dramatic reconciliation would bring about. In the cold, gloomy forest, with the wind tearing in fitful gusts through the naked branches and whistling round the tree trunks, they lay and waited for the help that would now bring release and succour to both parties. And each prayed a private prayer that his men might be the first to arrive, so that he might be the first to show honourable attention to the enemy that had become a friend.

Presently, as the wind dropped for a moment, Ulrich broke silence.

"Let's shout for help," he said; he said; "in this lull our voices may carry a little way."

"They won't carry far through the trees and undergrowth," said Georg, "but we can try. Together, then."

The two raised their voices in a prolonged hunting call.

"Together again," said Ulrich a few minutes later, after listening in vain for an answering halloo.

"I heard nothing but the pestilential wind," said Georg hoarsely.

There was silence again for some minutes, and then Ulrich gave a joyful cry.

"I can see figures coming through the wood. They are following in the way I came down the hillside."

Both men raised their voices in as loud a shout as they could muster.

"They hear us! They've stopped. Now they see us. They're running down the hill towards us," cried Ulrich.

"How many of them are there?" asked Georg.

"I can't see distinctly," said Ulrich; "nine or ten,"

"Then they are yours," said Georg; "I had only seven out with me."

"They are making all the speed they can, brave lads," said Ulrich gladly.

"Are they your men?" asked Georg. "Are they your men?" he repeated impatiently as Ulrich did not answer.

"No," said Ulrich with a laugh, the idiotic chattering laugh of a man unstrung with hideous fear.

"Who are they?" asked Georg quickly, straining his eyes to see what the other would gladly not have seen.

"Wolves."

41. The Threat

Sir Lulworth Quayne sat in the lounge of his favourite restaurant, the Gallus Bankiva, discussing the weaknesses of the world with his nephew, who had lately returned from a much-enlivened exile in the wilds of Mexico. It was that blessed season of the year when the asparagus and the plover's egg are abroad in the land, and the oyster has not yet withdrawn into it's summer entrenchments, and Sir Lulworth and his nephew were in that enlightened after-dinner mood when politics are seen in their right perspective, even the politics of Mexico.

"Most of the revolutions that take place in this country nowadays," said Sir Lulworth, "are the product of moments of legislative panic. Take, for instance, one of the most dramatic reforms that has been carried through Parliament in the lifetime of this generation. It happened shortly after the coal strike, of unblessed memory. To you, who have been plunged up to the neck in events of a more tangled and tumbled description, the things I am going to tell you of may seem of secondary interest, but after all we had to live in the midst of them."

Sir Lulworth interrupted himself for a moment to say a few kind words to the liqueur brandy he had just tasted, and them resumed his narrative.

"Whether one sympathises with the agitation for female suffrage or not one has to admit that its promoters showed tireless energy and considerable enterprise in devising and putting into action new methods for accomplishing their ends. As a rule they were a nuisance and a weariness to the flesh, but there were times when they verged on the picturesque. There was the famous occasion when they enlivened and diversified the customary pageantry of the Royal progress to open Parliament by letting loose thousands of parrots, which had been carefully trained to scream 'Votes for women,' and which circled round his Majesty's coach in a clamorous cloud of green, and grey and scarlet. It was really rather a striking episode from the spectacular point of view; unfortunately, however, for its devisers, the secret of their intentions had not been well kept, and their opponents let loose at the same moment a rival swarm of parrots, which screeched 'I *don't* think' and other hostile cries, thereby robbing the demonstration of the unanimity which alone could have made it politically impressive. In the process of recapture the birds learned a quantity of additional language which unfitted them for further service in the Suffragette cause; some of the green ones were secured by ardent Home Rule propagandists and trained to disturb the serenity of Orange meetings by pessimistic reflections on Sir Edward Carson's destination in the life to come. In fact, the bird in politics is a factor that seems to have come to stay; quite recently, at a political gathering held in a dimly-lighted place of worship, the congregation gave a respectful hearing for nearly ten minutes to a jackdaw from Wapping, under the impression that they were listening to the Chancellor of the Exchequer, who was late in arriving."

"But the Suffragettes," interrupted the nephew; "what did they do next?"

"After the bird fiasco," said Sir Lulworth, "the militant section made a demonstration of a more aggressive nature; they assembled in force on the opening day of the Royal Academy Exhibition and destroyed some three or four hundred of the pictures. This proved an even worse failure than the parrot business; every one agreed that there was always far too many pictures in the Academy Exhibition, and the drastic weeding out of a few hundred canvases was regarded as a positive improvement. Moreover, from the artists' point of view it was realised that the outrage constituted a sort of compensation for those whose works were persistently 'skied', since out of sight meant also out of reach. Altogether it was one of the most successful and popular exhibitions that the Academy had held for many years. Then the fair agitators fell back on some of their earlier methods; they wrote sweetly argumentative plays to prove that they ought to have the vote, they smashed windows to show that they must have the vote, and they kicked Cabinet Ministers to demonstrate that they'd better have the vote, and still the coldly reasoned or unreasoned reply was that they'd better not. Their plight might have been summed up in a perversion of Gilbert's lines –

"Twenty voteless millions we,
Voteless all against our will,
Twenty years hence we shall be
Twenty voteless millions still."

And of course the great idea for their master-stroke of strategy came from a masculine source. Lena Dubarri, who was the captain-general of their thinking department, met Waldo Orpington in the Mall one afternoon, just at a time when the fortunes of the Cause were at their lowest ebb. Waldo Orpington is a frivolous little fool who chirrups at drawing-room concerts and can recognise bits from different composers without referring to the programme, but all the same he occasionally has ideas. He didn't care a twopenny fiddlestring about the Cause, but he rather enjoyed the idea of having his finger in the political pie. Also it is possible, though I should think highly improbable, that he admired Lena Dubarri. Anyhow, when Lena gave a rather gloomy account of the existing state of things in the Suffragette World, Waldo was not merely sympathetic but ready with a practical suggestion. Turning his gaze westward along the Mall, towards the setting sun and Buckingham Palace, he was silent for a moment, and then said significantly, 'You have expended your energies and enterprise on labours of destruction; why has it never occurred to you to attempt something far more terrific?'

'What do you mean?' she asked him eagerly.

'Create.'

'Do you mean create disturbances? We've been doing nothing else for months,' she said.

"Waldo shook his head, and continued to look westward along the Mall. He's rather good at acting in an amateur sort of fashion. Lena followed his gaze, and then turned to him with a puzzled look of inquiry.

'Exactly,' said Waldo, in answer to her look.

'But – how can we create?' she asked; 'it's been done already.'

'Do it *again*,' said Waldo, 'and again and again –'

Before he could finish the sentence she had kissed him. She declared afterwards that he was the first man she had ever kissed, and he declared that she was the first woman who had ever kissed him in the Mall, so they both secured a record of a kind.

Within the next day or two a new departure was noticeable in Suffragette tactics. They gave up worrying Ministers and Parliament and took to worrying their own sympathisers and supporters – for funds. The ballot-box was temporarily forgotten in the cult of the collecting-box. The daughters of the horseleech were not more persistent in their demands, the financiers of the tottering ancient regime were not more desperate in their expedients for raising money than the Suffragist workers of all sections at this juncture, and in one way and another, by fair means and normal, they really got together a very useful sum. What they were going to do with it no one seemed to know, not even those who were most active in collecting work. The secret on this occasion had been well kept. Certain transactions that leaked out from time to time only added to the mystery of the situation.

'Don't you long to know what we are going to do with our treasure hoard?' Lena asked the Prime Minister one day when she happened to sit next to him at a whist drive at the Chinese Embassy.

'I was hoping you were going to try a little personal bribery,' he responded banteringly, but some genuine anxiety and curiosity lay behind the lightness of his chaff; 'of course I know,' he added, 'that you have been buying up building sites in commanding situations in and around the Metropolis. Two or three, I'm told, are on the road to Brighton, and another near Ascot. You don't mean to fortify them, do you?'

'Something more insidious than that,' she said; 'you could prevent us from building forts; you can't prevent us from erecting an exact replica of the Victoria Memorial on each of those sites. They're all private property, with no building restrictions attached.'

'Which memorial?' he asked; 'not the one in front of Buckingham Palace? Surely not that one?'

'That one,' she said.

'My dear lady,' he cried, 'you can't be serious. It is a beautiful and imposing work of art – at any rate one is getting accustomed to it, and even if one doesn't happen to admire it one can always look in another direction. But imagine what life would be like if one saw that erection confronting one wherever one went. Imagine the effect on people with tired, harassed nerves who saw it three times on the way to Brighton and three times on the way back. Imagine seeing it dominate the landscape at Ascot, and trying to keep your eye off it on the Sandwich golf links. What have your countrymen done to deserve such a thing?'

'They have refused us the vote,' said Lena bitterly.

'The Prime Minister always declared himself an opponent of anything savouring of panic legislation, but he brought a Bill into Parliament forthwith and successfully appealed to both Houses to pass it through all its stages within the week. And that is how we got one of the most glorious measures of the century.'

'A measure conferring the vote on women?' asked the nephew.

'Oh dear, no. An Act which made it a penal offence to erect commemorative statuary anywhere within three miles of a public highway.'

42. The Hedgehog

A "Mixed Double" of young people were contesting a game of lawn tennis at the Rectory garden party; for the past five-and-twenty years at least mixed doubles of young people had done exactly the same thing on exactly the same spot at about the same time of year. The young people changed and made way for others in the course of time, but very little else seemed to alter. The present players were sufficiently conscious of the social nature of the occasion to be concerned about their clothes and appearance, and sufficiently sport-loving to be keen on the game. Both their efforts and their appearance came under the fourfold scrutiny of a quartet of ladies sitting as official spectators on a bench immediately commanding the court. It was one of the accepted conditions of the Rectory garden party that four ladies, who usually knew very little about tennis and a great deal about the players, should sit at that particular spot and watch the game. It had also come to be almost a tradition that two ladies should be amiable, and that the other two should be Mrs. Dole and Mrs. Hatch-Mallard.

"What a singularly unbecoming way Eva Jonelet has taken to doing her hair in," said Mrs. Hatch-Mallard; "it's ugly hair at the best of times, but she needn't make it look ridiculous as well. Someone ought to tell her."

Eva Jonelet's hair might have escaped Mrs. Hatch-Mallard's condemnation if she could have forgotten the more glaring fact that Eva was Mrs. Dole's favourite niece. It would, perhaps, have been a more comfortable arrangement if Mrs. Hatch-Mallard and Mrs. Dole could have been asked to the Rectory on separate occasions, but there was only one garden party in the course of the year, and neither lady could have been omitted from the list of invitations without hopelessly wrecking the social peace of the parish.

"How pretty the yew trees look at this time of year," interposed a lady with a soft, silvery voice that suggested a chinchilla muff painted by Whistler.

"What do you mean by this time of year?" demanded Mrs. Hatch-Mallard. "Yew trees look beautiful at all times of the year. That is their great charm."

"Yew trees never look anything but hideous under any circumstances or at any time of year," said Mrs. Dole, with the slow, emphatic relish of one who contradicts for the pleasure of the thing. "They are only fit for graveyards and cemeteries."

Mrs. Hatch-Mallard gave a sardonic snort, which, being translated, meant that there were some people who were better fitted for cemeteries than for garden parties.

"What is the score, please?" asked the lady with the chinchilla voice.

The desired information was given her by a young gentleman in spotless white flannels, whose general toilet effect suggested solicitude rather than anxiety.

"What an odious young cub Bertie Dykson has become!" pronounced Mrs. Dole, remembering suddenly that Bertie was a favourite with Mrs. Hatch-Mallard. "The young men of to-day are not what they used to be twenty years ago."

"Of course not," said Mrs. Hatch-Mallard; "twenty years ago Bertie Dykson was just two years old, and you must expect some difference in appearance and manner and conversation between those two periods."

"Do you know," said Mrs. Dole, confidentially, "I shouldn't be surprised if that was intended to be clever."

"Have you any one interesting coming to stay with you, Mrs. Norbury?" asked the chinchilla voice, hastily; "you generally have a house party at this time of year."

"I've got a most interesting woman coming," said Mrs. Norbury, who had been mutely struggling for some chance to turn the conversation into a safe channel; "an old acquaintance of mine, Ada Bleek –"

"What an ugly name," said Mrs. Hatch-Mallard.

"She's descended from the de la Bliques, an old Huguenot family of Touraine, you know."

"There weren't any Huguenots in Touraine," said Mrs. Hatch-Mallard, who thought she might safely dispute any fact that was three hundred years old.

"Well, anyhow, she's coming to stay with me," continued Mrs. Norbury, bringing her story quickly down to the present day, "she arrives this evening, and she's highly clairvoyante, a seventh daughter of a seventh daughter, you now, and all that sort of thing."

"How very interesting," said the chinchilla voice; "Exwood is just the right place for her to come to, isn't it? There are supposed to be several ghosts there."

"That is why she was so anxious to come," said Mrs. Norbury; "she put off another engagement in order to accept my invitation. She's had visions and dreams, and all those sort of things, that have come true in a most marvellous manner, but she's never actually seen a ghost, and she's longing to have that experience. She belongs to that Research Society, you know."

"I expect she'll see the unhappy Lady Cullumpton, the most famous of all the Exwood ghosts," said Mrs. Dole; "my ancestor, you know, Sir Gervase Cullumpton, murdered his young bride in a fit of jealousy while they were on a visit to Exwood. He strangled her in the stables with a stirrup leather, just after they had come in from riding, and she is seen sometimes at dusk going about the lawns and the stable yard, in a long green habit, moaning and trying to get the thong from round her throat. I shall be most interested to hear if your friend sees –"

"I don't know why she should be expected to see a trashy, traditional apparition like the so-called Cullumpton ghost, that is only vouched for by housemaids and tipsy stable-boys, when my uncle, who was the owner of Exwood, committed suicide there under the most tragical circumstances, and most certainly haunts the place."

"Mrs. Hatch-Mallard has evidently never read Popple's County History," said Mrs. Dole icily, "or she would know that the Cullumpton ghost has a wealth of evidence behind it –"

"Oh, Popple!" exclaimed Mrs. Hatch-Mallard scornfully; "any rubbishy old story is good enough for him. Popple, indeed! Now my uncle's ghost was seen by a Rural Dean, who was also a Justice of the Peace. I should think that would be good enough testimony for any one. Mrs. Norbury, I shall take it as a deliberate personal affront if your clairvoyante friend sees any other ghost except that of my uncle."

"I daresay she won't see anything at all; she never has yet, you know," said Mrs. Norbury hopefully.

"It was a most unfortunate topic for me to have broached," she lamented afterwards to the owner of the chinchilla voice; "Exwood belongs to Mrs. Hatch-Mallard, and we've only got it on a short lease. A nephew of hers has been wanting to live there for some time, and if we offend her in any way she'll refuse to renew the lease. I sometimes think these garden-parties are a mistake."

The Norburys played bridge for the next three nights till nearly one o'clock; they did not care for the game, but it reduced the time at their guest's disposal for undesirable ghostly visitations.

"Miss Bleek is not likely to be in a frame of mind to see ghosts," said Hugo Norbury, "if she goes to bed with her brain awhirl with royal spades and no trumps and grand slams."

"I've talked to her for hours about Mrs. Hatch-Mallard's uncle," said his wife, "and pointed out the exact spot where he killed himself, and invented all sorts of impressive details, and I've found an old portrait of Lord John Russell and put it in her room, and told her that it's supposed to be a picture of the uncle in middle age. If Ada does see a ghost at all it certainly ought to be old Hatch-Mallard's. At any rate, we've done our best."

The precautions were in vain. On the third morning of her stay Ada Bleek came down late to breakfast, her eyes looking very tired, but ablaze with excitement, her hair done anyhow, and a large brown volume hugged under her arm.

"At last I've seen something supernatural!" she exclaimed, and gave Mrs. Norbury a fervent kiss, as though in gratitude for the opportunity afforded her.

"A ghost!" cried Mrs. Norbury, "not really!"

"Really and unmistakably!"

"Was it an oldish man in the dress of about fifty years ago?" asked Mrs. Norbury hopefully.

"Nothing of the sort," said Ada; "it was a white hedgehog."

"A white hedgehog!" exclaimed both the Norburys, in tones of disconcerted astonishment.

"A huge white hedgehog with baleful yellow eyes," said Ada; "I was lying half asleep in bed when suddenly I felt a sensation as of something sinister and unaccountable passing through the room. I sat up and looked round, and there, under the window, I saw an evil, creeping thing, a sort of monstrous hedgehog, of a dirty white colour, with black, loathsome claws that clicked and scraped along the floor, and narrow, yellow eyes of indescribable evil. It slithered along for a yard or two, always looking at me with its cruel, hideous eyes, then, when it reached the second window, which was open it clambered up the sill and vanished. I got up at once and went to the window; there wasn't a sign of it anywhere. Of course, I knew it must be something from another world, but it was not till I turned up Popple's chapter on local traditions that I realised what I had seen."

She turned eagerly to the large brown volume and read: "'Nicholas Herison, an old miser, was hung at Batchford in 1763 for the murder of a farm lad who had accidentally discovered his secret hoard. His ghost is supposed to traverse the countryside, appearing sometimes as a white owl, sometimes as a huge white hedgehog.'"

"I expect you read the Popple story overnight, and that made you *think* you saw a hedgehog when you were only half awake," said Mrs. Norbury, hazarding a conjecture that probably came very near the truth.

Ada scouted the possibility of such a solution of her apparition.

"This must be hushed up," said Mrs. Norbury quickly; "the servants –"

"Hushed up!" exclaimed Ada, indignantly; "I'm writing a long report on it for the Research Society."

It was then that Hugo Norbury, who is not naturally a man of brilliant resource, had one of the really useful inspirations of his life.

"It was very wicked of us, Miss Bleek," he said, "but it would be a shame to let it go further. That white hedgehog is an old joke of ours; stuffed albino hedgehog, you know, that my father brought home from Jamaica, where they grow to enormous size. We hide it in the room with a string on it, run one end of the string through the window; then we pull if from below and it comes scraping along the floor, just as you've described, and finally jerks out of the window. Taken in heaps of people; they all read up Popple and think it's old Harry Nicholson's ghost; we always stop them from writing to the papers about it, though. That would be carrying matters too far."

Mrs. Hatch-Mallard renewed the lease in due course, but Ada Bleek has never renewed her friendship.

43. The Bull

Tom Yorkfield had always regarded his half-brother, Laurence, with a lazy instinct of dislike, toned down, as years went on, to a tolerant feeling of indifference. There was nothing very tangible to dislike him for; he was just a blood-relation, with whom Tom had no single taste or interest in common, and with whom, at the same time, he had had no occasion for quarrel. Laurence had left the farm early in life, and had lived for a few years on a small sum of money left him by his mother; he had taken up painting as a profession, and was reported to be doing fairly well at it, well enough, at any rate, to keep body and soul together. He specialised in painting animals, and he was successful in finding a certain number of people to buy his pictures. Tom felt a comforting sense of assured superiority in contrasting his position with that of his half-brother; Laurence was an artist-chap, just that and nothing more, though you might make it sound more important by calling an animal painter; Tom was a farmer, not in a very big way, it was true, but the Helsery farm had been in the family for some generations, and it had a good reputation for the stock raised on it. Tom had done his best, with the little capital at his command, to maintain and improve the standard of his small herd of cattle, and in Clover Fairy he had bred a bull which was something rather better than any that his immediate neighbours could show. It would not have made a sensation in the judging-ring at an important cattle show, but it was as vigorous, shapely, and healthy a young animal as any small practical farmer could wish to possess. At the King's Head on market days Clover Fairy was very highly spoken of, and

Yorkfield used to declare that he would not part with him for a hundred pounds; a hundred pounds is a lot of money in the small farming line, and probably anything over eighty would have tempted him.

It was with some especial pleasure that Tom took advantage of one of Laurence's rare visits to the farm to lead him down to the enclosure where Clover Fairy kept solitary state – the grass widower of a grazing harem. Tom felt some of his old dislike for his half-brother reviving; the artist was becoming more languid in his manner, more unsuitably turned-out in attire, and he seemed inclined to impart a slightly patronising tone to his conversation. He took no heed of a flourishing potato crop, but waxed enthusiastic over a clump of yellow-flowering weed that stood in a corner by a gateway, which was rather galling to the owner of a really very well weeded farm; again, when he might have been duly complimentary about a group of fat, black-faced lambs, that simply cried aloud for admiration, he became eloquent over the foliage tints of an oak copse on the hill opposite. But now he was being taken to inspect the crowning pride and glory of Helsery; however grudging he might be in his praises, however backward and niggardly with his congratulations, he would have to see and acknowledge the many excellences of that redoubtable animal. Some weeks ago, while on a business journey to Taunton, Tom had been invited by his half-brother to visit a studio in that town, where Laurence was exhibiting one of his pictures, a large canvas representing a bull standing knee-deep in some marshy ground; it had been good of its kind, no doubt, and Laurence had seemed inordinately pleased with it; "the best thing I've done yet," he had said over and over again, and Tom had generously agreed that it was fairly life-like. Now, the man of pigments was going to be shown a real picture, a living model of strength and comeliness, a thing to feast the eyes on, a picture that exhibited new pose and action with every shifting minute, instead of standing glued into one unvarying attitude between the four walls of a frame. Tom unfastened a stout wooden door and led the way into a straw-bedded yard.

"Is he quiet?" asked the artist, as a young bull with a curly red coat came inquiringly towards them.

"He's playful at times," said Tom, leaving his half-brother to wonder whether the bull's ideas of play were of the catch-as-catch-can order. Laurence made one or two perfunctory comments on the animal's appearance and asked a question or so as to his age and such-like details; then he coolly turned the talk into another channel.

"Do you remember the picture I showed you at Taunton?" he asked.

"Yes," grunted Tom; "a white-faced bull standing in some slush. Don't admire those Herefords much myself; bulky-looking brutes, don't seem to have much life in them. Daresay they're easier to paint that way; now, this young beggar is on the move all the time, aren't you, Fairy?"

"I've sold that picture," said Laurence, with considerable complacency in his voice.

"Have you?" said Tom; "glad to hear it, I'm sure. Hope you're pleased with what you've got for it."

"I got three hundred pounds for it," said Laurence.

Tom turned towards him with a slowly rising flush of anger in his face. Three hundred pounds! Under the most favourable market conditions that he could imagine his prized Clover Fairy would hardly fetch a hundred, yet here was a piece of varnished canvas, painted by his half-brother, selling for three times that sum. It was a cruel insult that went home with all the more force because it emphasised the triumph of the patronising, self-satisfied Laurence. The young farmer had meant to put his relative just a little out of conceit with himself by displaying the jewel of his possessions, and now the tables were turned, and his valued beast was made to look cheap and insignificant beside the price paid for a mere picture. It was so monstrously unjust; the painting would never be anything more than a dexterous piece of counterfeit life, while Clover Fairy was the real thing, a monarch in his little world, a personality in the countryside. After he was dead, even, he would still be something of a personality; his descendants would graze in those valley meadows and hillside pastures, they would fill stall and byre and milking-shed, their good red coats would speckle the landscape and crowd the market-place; men would note a promising heifer or a well-proportioned steer, and say: "Ah, that one comes of good old Clover Fairy's stock." All that time the picture would be hanging, lifeless and unchanging, beneath its dust and varnish, a chattel that ceased to mean anything if you chose to turn it with its back to the wall. These thoughts chased themselves angrily through Tom Yorkfield's mind, but he could not put them into words. When he gave tongue to his feelings he put matters bluntly and harshly.

"Some soft-witted fools may like to throw away three hundred pounds on a bit of paintwork; can't say as I envy them their taste. I'd rather have the real thing than a picture of it."

He nodded towards the young bull, that was alternately staring at them with nose held high and lowering its horns with a half-playful, half-impatient shake of the head.

Laurence laughed a laugh of irritating, indulgent amusement.

"I don't think the purchaser of my bit of paintwork, as you call it, need worry about having thrown his money away. As I get to be better known and recognised my pictures will go up in value. That particular one will probably fetch four hundred in a sale-room five or six years hence; pictures aren't a bad investment if you know enough to pick out the work of the right men. Now you can't say your precious bull is going to get more valuable the longer you keep him; he'll have his little day, and then, if you go on keeping him, he'll come down at last to a few shillings' worth of hoofs and hide, just at a time, perhaps, when my bull is being bought for a big sum for some important picture gallery."

It was too much. The united force of truth and slander and insult put over heavy a strain on Tom Yorkfield's powers of restraint. In his right hand he held a useful oak cudgel, with his left he made a grab at the loose collar of Laurence's canary-coloured silk shirt. Laurence was not a fighting man; the fear of physical violence threw him off his balance as completely as overmastering indignation had thrown Tom off his, and thus it came to pass that Clover Fairy was regaled with the unprecedented sight of a human being scudding and squawking across the enclosure, like the hen that would persist in trying to establish a nesting-place in the manger. In another crowded happy moment the bull was trying to jerk Laurence over his left shoulder, to prod him in the ribs while still in the air, and to kneel on him when he reached the ground. It was only the vigorous intervention of Tom that induced him to relinquish the last item of his programme.

Tom devotedly and ungrudgingly nursed his half-brother to a complete recovery from his injuries, which consisted of nothing more serious than a dislocated shoulder, a broken rib or two, and a little nervous prostration. After all, there was no further occasion for rancour in the young farmer's mind; Laurence's bull might sell for three hundred, or for six hundred, and be admired by thousands in some big picture gallery, but it would never toss a man over one shoulder and catch him a jab in the ribs before he had fallen on the other side. That was Clover Fairy's noteworthy achievement, which could never be taken away from him.

Laurence continues to be popular as an animal artist, but his subjects are always kittens or fawns or lambkins – never bulls.

44. Shock Tactics

On a late spring afternoon Ella McCarthy sat on a green-painted chair in Kensington Gardens, staring listlessly at an uninteresting stretch of park landscape, that blossomed suddenly into tropical radiance as an expected figure appeared in the middle distance.

"Hullo, Bertie!" she exclaimed sedately, when the figure arrived at the painted chair that was the nearest neighbour to her own, and dropped into it eagerly, yet with a certain due regard for the set of its trousers; "hasn't it been a perfect spring afternoon?"

The statement was a distinct untruth as far as Ella's own feelings were concerned; until the arrival of Bertie the afternoon had been anything but perfect.

Bertie made a suitable reply, in which a questioning note seemed to hover.

"Thank you ever so much for those lovely handkerchiefs," said Ella, answering the unspoken question; "they were just what I've been wanting. There's only one thing spoilt my pleasure in your gift," she added, with a pout.

"What was that?" asked Bertie anxiously, fearful that perhaps he had chosen a size of handkerchief that was not within the correct feminine limit.

"I should have liked to have written and thanked you for them as soon as I got them," said Ella, and Bertie's sky clouded at once.

"You know what mother is," he protested; "she opens all my letters, and if she found I'd been giving presents to any one there'd have been something to talk about for the next fortnight."

"Surely, at the age of twenty –" began Ella.

"I'm not twenty till September," interrupted Bertie.

"At the age of nineteen years and eight months," persisted Ella, "you might be allowed to keep your correspondence private to yourself."

"I ought to be, but things aren't always what they ought to be. Mother opens every letter that comes into the house, whoever it's for. My sisters and I have made rows about it time and again, but she goes on doing it."

"I'd find some way to stop her if I were in your place," said Ella valiantly, and Bertie felt that the glamour of his anxiously deliberated present had faded away in the disagreeable restriction that hedged round its acknowledgment.

"Is anything the matter?" asked Bertie's friend Clovis when they met that evening at the swimming-bath.

"Why do you ask?" said Bertie.

"When you wear a look of tragic gloom in a swimming-bath," said Clovis, "it's especially noticeable from the fact that you're wearing very little else. Didn't she like the handkerchiefs?"

Bertie explained the situation.

"It is rather galling, you know," he added, "when a girl has a lot of things she wants to write to you and can't send a letter except by some roundabout, underhand way."

"One never realises one's blessings while one enjoys them," said Clovis; "now I have to spend a considerable amount of ingenuity inventing excuses for not having written to people."

"It's not a joking matter," said Bertie resentfully: "you wouldn't find it funny if your mother opened all your letters."

"The funny thing to me is that you should let her do it."

"I can't stop it. I've argued about it –"

"You haven't used the right kind of argument, I expect. Now, if every time one of your letters was opened you lay on your back on the dining-table during dinner and had a fit, or roused the entire family in the middle of the night to hear you recite one of Blake's 'Poems of Innocence,' you would get a far more respectful hearing for future protests. People yield more consideration to a mutilated mealtime or a broken night's rest, than ever they would to a broken heart."

"Oh, dry up," said Bertie crossly, inconsistently splashing Clovis from head to foot as he plunged into the water.

It was a day or two after the conversation in the swimming-bath that a letter addressed to Bertie Heasant slid into the letter-box at his home, and thence into the hands of his mother. Mrs. Heasant was one of those empty-minded individuals to whom other people's affairs are perpetually interesting. The more private they are intended to be the more acute is the interest they arouse. She would have opened this particular letter in any case; the fact that it was marked "private," and diffused a delicate but penetrating aroma merely caused her to open it with headlong haste rather than matter-of-course deliberation. The harvest of sensation that rewarded her was beyond all expectations.

"Bertie, carissimo," it began, "I wonder if you will have the nerve to do it: it will take some nerve, too. Don't forget the jewels. They are a detail, but details interest me.

"Yours as ever, Clotilde."

"Your mother must not know of my existence. If questioned swear you never heard of me."

For years Mrs. Heasant had searched Bertie's correspondence diligently for traces of possible dissipation or youthful entanglements, and at last the suspicions that had stimulated her inquisitorial zeal were justified by this one splendid haul. That any one wearing the exotic name "Clotilde" should write to Bertie under the incriminating announcement "as ever" was sufficiently electrifying, without the astounding allusion to the jewels. Mrs. Heasant could recall novels and dramas wherein jewels played an exciting and commanding role, and here, under her own roof, before her very eyes as it were, her own son was carrying on an intrigue in which jewels were merely an interesting detail. Bertie was not due home for another hour, but his sisters were available for the immediate unburdening of a scandal-laden mind.

"Bertie is in the toils of an adventuress," she screamed; "her name is Clotilde," she added, as if she thought they had better know the worst at once. There are occasions when more harm than good is done by shielding young girls from a knowledge of the more deplorable realities of life.

By the time Bertie arrived his mother had discussed every possible and improbable conjecture as to his guilty secret; the girls limited themselves to the opinion that their brother had been weak rather than wicked.

"Who is Clotilde?" was the question that confronted Bertie almost before he had got into the hall. His denial of any knowledge of such a person was met with an outburst of bitter laughter.

"How well you have learned your lesson!" exclaimed Mrs. Heasant. But satire gave way to furious indignation when she realised that Bertie did not intend to throw any further light on her discovery.

"You shan't have any dinner till you've confessed everything," she stormed.

Bertie's reply took the form of hastily collecting material for an impromptu banquet from the larder and locking himself into his bedroom. His mother made frequent visits to the locked door and shouted a succession of interrogations with the persistence of one who thinks that if you ask a question often enough an answer will eventually result. Bertie did nothing to encourage the supposition. An hour had passed in fruitless one-sided palaver when another letter addressed to Bertie and marked "private" made its appearance in the letter-box. Mrs. Heasant pounced on it with the enthusiasm of a cat that has missed its mouse and to whom a second has been unexpectedly vouchsafed. If she hoped for further disclosures assuredly she was not disappointed.

"So you have really done it!" the letter abruptly commenced; "Poor Dagmar. Now she is done for I almost pity her. You did it very well, you wicked boy, the servants all think it was suicide, and there will be no fuss. Better not touch the jewels till after the inquest.

"Clotilde."

Anything that Mrs. Heasant had previously done in the way of outcry was easily surpassed as she raced upstairs and beat frantically at her son's door.

"Miserable boy, what have you done to Dagmar?"

"It's Dagmar now, is it?" he snapped; "it will be Geraldine next."

"That it should come to this, after all my efforts to keep you at home of an evening," sobbed Mrs. Heasant; "it's no use you trying to hide things from me; Clotilde's letter betrays everything."

"Does it betray who she is?" asked Bertie; "I've heard so much about her, I should like to know something about her home-life. Seriously, if you go on like this I shall fetch a doctor; I've often enough been preached at about nothing, but I've never had an imaginary harem dragged into the discussion."

"Are these letters imaginary?" screamed Mrs. Heasant; "what about the jewels, and Dagmar, and the theory of suicide?"

No solution of these problems was forthcoming through the bedroom door, but the last post of the evening produced another letter for Bertie, and its contents brought Mrs. Heasant that enlightenment which had already dawned on her son.

"Dear Bertie," it ran; "I hope I haven't distracted your brain with the spoof letters I've been sending in the name of a fictitious Clotilde. You told me the other day that the servants, or somebody at your home, tampered with your letters, so I thought I would give any one that opened them something exciting to read. The shock might do them good.

"Yours, Clovis Sangrail."

Mrs. Heasant knew Clovis slightly, and was rather afraid of him. It was not difficult to read between the lines of his successful hoax. In a chastened mood she rapped once more at Bertie's door.

"A letter from Mr. Sangrail. It's all been a stupid hoax. He wrote those other letters. Why, where are you going?"

Bertie had opened the door; he had on his hat and overcoat.

"I'm going for a doctor to come and see if anything's the matter with you. Of course it was all a hoax, but no person in his right mind could have believed all that rubbish about murder and suicide and jewels. You've been making enough noise to bring the house down for the last hour or two."

"But what was I to think of those letters?" whimpered Mrs. Heasant.

"I should have known what to think of them," said Bertie; "if you choose to excite yourself over other people's correspondence it's your own fault. Anyhow, I'm going for a doctor."

It was Bertie's great opportunity, and he knew it. His mother was conscious of the fact that she would look rather ridiculous if the story got about. She was willing to pay hush-money.

"I'll never open your letters again," she promised. And Clovis has no more devoted slave than Bertie Heasant.

45. The Seven Cream Jugs

"I suppose we shall never see Wilfred Pigeoncote here now that he has become heir to the baronetcy and to a lot of money," observed Mrs. Peter Pigeoncote regretfully to her husband.

"Well, we can hardly expect to," he replied, "seeing that we always choked him off from coming to see us when he was a prospective nobody. I don't think I've set eyes on him since he was a boy of twelve."

"There was a reason for not wanting to encourage his acquaintanceship," said Mrs. Peter. "With that notorious failing of his he was not the sort of person one wanted in one's house."

"Well, the failing still exists, doesn't it?" said her husband; "or do you suppose a reform of character is entailed along with the estate?"

"Oh, of course, there is still that drawback," admitted the wife, "but one would like to make the acquaintance of the future head of the family, if only out of mere curiosity. Besides, cynicism apart, his being rich will make a difference in the way people will look at his failing. When a man is absolutely wealthy, not merely well-to-do, all suspicion of sordid motive naturally disappears; the thing becomes merely a tiresome malady."

Wilfrid Pigeoncote had suddenly become heir to his uncle, Sir Wilfrid Pigeoncote, on the death of his cousin, Major Wilfrid Pigeoncote, who had succumbed to the after-effects of a polo accident. (A Wilfrid Pigeoncote had covered himself with honours in the course of Marlborough's campaigns, and the name Wilfrid had been a baptismal weakness in the family ever since.) The new heir to the family dignity and estates was a young man of about five-and-twenty, who was known more by reputation than by person to a wide circle of cousins and kinsfolk. And the reputation was an unpleasant one. The numerous other Wilfrids in the family were distinguished one from another chiefly by the names of their residences or professions, as Wilfrid of Hubbledown, and young Wilfrid the Gunner, but this particular scion was known by the ignominious and expressive label of Wilfrid the Snatcher. From his late schooldays onward he had been possessed by an acute and obstinate form of kleptomania; he had the acquisitive instinct of the collector without any of the collector's discrimination. Anything that was smaller and more portable than a sideboard, and above the value of ninepence, had an irresistible attraction for him, provided that it fulfilled the necessary condition of belonging to someone else. On the rare occasions when he was included in a country-house party, it was usual and almost necessary for his host, or some member of the family, to make a friendly inquisition through his baggage on the eve of his departure, to see if he had packed up "by mistake" anyone else's property. The search usually produced a large and varied yield.

"This is funny," said Peter Pigeoncote to his wife, some half-hour after their conversation; "here's a telegram from Wilfrid, saying he's passing through here in his motor, and would like to stop and pay us his respects. Can stay for the night if it doesn't inconvenience us. Signed 'Wilfrid Pigeoncote.' Must be the Snatcher; none of the others have a motor. I suppose he's bringing us a present for the silver wedding."

"Good gracious!" said Mrs. Peter, as a thought struck her; "this is rather an awkward time to have a person with his failing in the house. All those silver presents set out in the drawing-room, and others coming by every post; I hardly know what we've got and what are still to come. We can't lock them all up; he's sure to want to see them."

"We must keep a sharp look-out, that's all," said Peter reassuringly.

"But these practised kleptomaniacs are so clever," said his wife, apprehensively, "and it will be so awkward if he suspects that we are watching him."

Awkwardness was indeed the prevailing note that evening when the passing traveller was being entertained. The talk flitted nervously and hurriedly from one impersonal topic to another. The guest had none of the furtive, half-apologetic air that his cousins had rather expected to find; he was polite, well-assured, and, perhaps, just a little inclined to "put on side". His hosts, on the other hand, wore an uneasy manner that might have been the hallmark of conscious depravity. In the drawing-room, after dinner, their nervousness and awkwardness increased.

"Oh, we haven't shown you the silver-wedding presents," said Mrs. Peter, suddenly, as though struck by a brilliant idea for entertaining the guest; "here they all are. Such nice, useful gifts. A few duplicates, of course."

"Seven cream jugs," put in Peter.

"Yes, isn't it annoying," went on Mrs. Peter; "seven of them. We feel that we must live on cream for the rest of our lives. Of course, some of them can be changed."

Wilfrid occupied himself chiefly with such of the gifts as were of antique interest, carrying one or two of them over to the lamp to examine their marks. The anxiety of his hosts at these moments resembled the solicitude of a cat whose newly born kittens are being handed round for inspection.

"Let me see; did you give me back the mustard-pot? This is its place here," piped Mrs. Peter.

"Sorry. I put it down by the claret-jug," said Wilfrid, busy with another object.

"Oh, just let me have the sugar-sifter again," asked Mrs. Peter, dogged determination showing through her nervousness; "I must label it who it comes from before I forget."

Vigilance was not completely crowned with a sense of victory. After they had said "Good-night" to their visitor, Mrs. Peter expressed her conviction that he had taken something.

"I fancy, by his manner, that there was something up," corroborated her husband; "do you miss anything?"

Mrs. Peters hastily counted the array of gifts.

"I can only make it thirty-four, and I think it should be thirty-five," she announced; "I can't remember if thirty-five includes the Archdeacon's cruet-stand that hasn't arrived yet."

"How on earth are we to know?" said Peter. "The mean pig hasn't brought us a present, and I'm hanged if he shall carry one off."

"Tomorrow, when's he having his bath," said Mrs. Peter excitedly, "he's sure to leave his keys somewhere, and we can go through his portmanteau. It's the only thing to do."

On the morrow an alert watch was kept by the conspirators behind half-closed doors, and when Wilfrid, clad in a gorgeous bath-robe, had made his way to the bath-room, there was a swift and furtive rush by two excited individuals towards the principal guest-chamber. Mrs. Peter kept guard outside, while her husband first made a hurried and successful search for the keys, and then plunged at the portmanteau with the air of a disagreeably conscientious Customs official. The quest was a brief one; a silver cream jug lay embedded in the folds of some zephyr shirts.

"The cunning brute," said Mrs. Peters; "he took a cream jug because there were so many; he thought one wouldn't be missed. Quick, fly down with it and put it back among the others."

Wilfrid was late in coming down to breakfast, and his manner showed plainly that something was amiss.

"It's an unpleasant thing to have to say," he blurted out presently, "but I'm afraid you must have a thief among your servants. Something's been taken out of my portmanteau. It was a little present from my mother and myself for your silver wedding. I should have given it to you last night after dinner, only it happened to be a cream jug, and you seemed annoyed at having so many duplicates, so I felt rather awkward about giving you another. I thought I'd get it changed for something else, and now it's gone."

"Did you say it was from your *mother* and yourself?" asked Mr. and Mrs. Peter almost in unison. The Snatcher had been an orphan these many years.

"Yes, my mother's at Cairo just now, and she wrote to me at Dresden to try and get you something quaint and pretty in the old silver line, and I pitched on this cream jug."

Both the Pigeoncotes had turned deadly pale. The mention of Dresden had thrown a sudden light on the situation. It was Wilfrid the Attache, a very superior young man, who rarely came within their social horizon, whom they had been entertaining unawares in the supposed character of Wilfrid the Snatcher. Lady Ernestine Pigeoncote, his mother, moved in circles which were entirely beyond their compass or ambitions, and the son would probably one day be an Ambassador. And they had rifled and despoiled his portmanteau! Husband and wife looked blankly and desperately at one another. It was Mrs. Peter who arrived first at an inspiration.

"How dreadful to think there are thieves in the house! We keep the drawing-room locked up at night, of course, but anything might be carried off while we are at breakfast."

She rose and went out hurriedly, as though to assure herself that the drawing-room was not being stripped of its silverware, and returned a moment later, bearing a cream jug in her hands.

"There are eight cream jugs now, instead of seven," she cried; "this one wasn't there before. What a curious trick of memory, Mr. Wilfrid! You must have slipped downstairs with it last night and put it there before we locked up, and forgotten all about having done it in the morning."

"One's mind often plays one little tricks like that," said Mr. Peter, with desperate heartiness. "Only the other day I went into the town to pay a bill, and went in again next day, having clean forgotten that I'd –"

"It is certainly the jug I bought for you," said Wilfrid, looking closely at it; "it was in my portmanteau when I got my bath-robe out this morning, before going to my bath, and it was not there when I unlocked the portmanteau on my return. Some one had taken it while I was away from the room."

The Pigeoncotes had turned paler than ever. Mrs. Peter had a final inspiration.

"Get me my smelling-salts, dear," she said to her husband; "I think they're in the dressing-room."

Peter dashed out of the room with glad relief; he had lived so long during the last few minutes that a golden wedding seemed within measurable distance.

Mrs. Peter turned to her guest with confidential coyness.

"A diplomat like you will know how to treat this as if it hadn't happened. Peter's little weakness; it runs in the family."

"Good Lord! Do you mean to say he's a kleptomaniac, like Cousin Snatcher?"

"Oh, not exactly," said Mrs. Peter, anxious to whitewash her husband a little greyer than she was painting him. "He would never touch anything he found lying about, but he can't resist making a raid on things that are locked up. The doctors have a special name for it. He must have pounced on your portmanteau the moment you went to your bath, and taken the first thing he came across. Of course, he had no motive for taking a cream jug; we've already got seven, as you know – not, of course, that we don't value the kind of gift you and your mother – hush here's Peter coming."

Mrs. Peter broke off in some confusion, and tripped out to meet her husband in the hall.

"It's all right," she whispered to him; "I've explained everything. Don't say anything more about it."

"Brave little woman," said Peter, with a gasp of relief; "I could never have done it."

~

Diplomatic reticence does not necessarily extend to family affairs. Peter Pigeoncote was never able to understand why Mrs.

Consuelo van Bullyon, who stayed with them in the spring, always carried two very obvious jewel-cases with her to the bathroom, explaining them to any one she chanced to meet in the corridor as her manicure and face-massage set.

46. The Sheep

The enemy had declared "no trumps." Rupert played out his ace and king of clubs and cleared the adversary of that suit; then the Sheep, whom the Fates had inflicted on him for a partner, took the third round with the queen of clubs, and, having no other club to lead back, opened another suit. The enemy won the remainder of the tricks – and the rubber.

"I had four more clubs to play; we only wanted the odd trick to win the rubber," said Rupert.

"But I hadn't another club to lead you," exclaimed the Sheep, with his ready, defensive smile.

"It didn't occur to you to throw your queen away on my king and leave me with the command of the suit," said Rupert, with polite bitterness.

"I suppose I ought to have – I wasn't certain what to do. I'm awfully sorry," said the Sheep.

Being awfully and uselessly sorry formed a large part of his occupation in life. If a similar situation had arisen in a subsequent hand he would have blundered just as certainly, and he would have been just as irritatingly apologetic.

Rupert stared gloomily across at him as he sat smiling and fumbling with his cards. Many men who have good brains for business do not possess the rudiments of a card-brain, and Rupert would not have judged and condemned his prospective brother-in-law on the evidence of his bridge play alone. The tragic part of it was that he smiled and fumbled through life just as fatuously and apologetically as he did at the card-table. And behind the defensive smile and the well-worn expressions of regret there shone a scarcely believable but quite obvious self-satisfaction. Every sheep of the pasture probably imagines that in an emergency it could become terrible as an army with banners – one has only to watch how they stamp their feet and stiffen their necks when a minor object of suspicion comes into view and behaves meekly. And probably the majority of human sheep see themselves in imagination taking great parts in the world's more impressive dramas, forming swift, unerring decisions in moments of crisis, cowing mutinies, allaying panics, brave, strong, simple, but, in spite of their natural modesty, always slightly spectacular.

"Why in the name of all that is unnecessary and perverse should Kathleen choose this man for her future husband?" was the question that Rupert asked himself ruefully. There was young Malcolm Athling, as nice-looking, decent, level-headed a fellow as any one could wish to meet, obviously her very devoted admirer, and yet she must throw herself away on this pale-eyed, weak-mouthed embodiment of self-approving ineptitude. If it had been merely Kathleen's own affair Rupert would have shrugged his shoulders and philosophically hoped that she might make the best of an undeniably bad bargain. But Rupert had no heir; his own boy lay underground somewhere on the Indian frontier, in goodly company. And the property would pass in due curse to Kathleen and Kathleen's husband. The Sheep would live there in the beloved old home, rearing up other little Sheep, fatuous and rabbit-faced and self-satisfied like himself, to dwell in the land and possess it. It was not a soothing prospect.

Towards dusk on the afternoon following the bridge experience Rupert and the Sheep made their way homeward after a day's mixed shooting. The Sheep's cartridge bag was nearly empty, but his game bag showed no signs of over-crowding. The birds he had shot at had seemed for the most part as impervious to death or damage as the hero of a melodrama. And for each failure to drop his bird he had some explanation or apology ready on his lips. Now he was striding along in front of his host, chattering happily over his shoulder, but obviously on the look-out for some belated rabbit or wood-pigeon that might haply be secured as an eleventh-hour addition to his bag. As they passed the edge of a small copse a large bird rose from the ground and flew slowly towards the trees, offering an easy shot to the oncoming sportsmen. The Sheep banged forth with both barrels, and gave an exultant cry.

"Horray! I've shot a thundering big hawk!"

"To be exact, you've shot a honey-buzzard. That is the hen bird of one of the few pairs of honey-buzzards breeding in the United Kingdom. We've kept them under the strictest preservation for the last four years; every game-keeper and village gun loafer for twenty miles round has been warned and bribed and threatened to respect their sanctity, and egg-snatching agents have been carefully guarded against during the breeding season. Hundreds of lovers of rare birds have delighted in seeing their snap-shotted portraits in Country Life, and now you've reduced the hen bird to a lump of broken feathers."

Rupert spoke quietly and evenly, but for a moment or two a gleam of positive hatred shone in his eyes.

"I say, I'm so sorry," said the Sheep, with his apologetic smile. "Of course I remember hearing about the buzzards, but somehow I didn't connect this bird with them. And it was such an east shot –"

"Yes," said Rupert; "that was the trouble."

Kathleen found him in the gun-room smoothing out the feathers of the dead bird. She had already been told of the catastrophe.

"What a horrid misfortune," she said sympathetically.

"It was my dear Robbie who first discovered them, the last time he was home on leave. Don't you remember how excited he was about them? Let's go and have some tea."

Both bridge and shooting were given a rest for the next two or three weeks. Death, who enters into no compacts with party whips, had forced a Parliamentary vacancy on the neighbourhood at the least convenient season, and the local partisans on either side found themselves immersed in the discomforts of a mid-winter election. Rupert took his politics seriously and keenly. He belonged to that type of strangely but rather happily constituted individuals which these islands seem to produce in a fair plenty; men and women who for no personal profit or gain go forth from their comfortable firesides or club card-rooms to hunt to and fro in the mud and rain and wind for the capture or tracking of a stray vote here and there on their party's behalf – not because they think they ought to, but because they want to. And his energies were welcome enough on this occasion, for the seat was a closely disputed possession, and its loss or retention would count for much in the present position of the Parliamentary game. With Kathleen to help him, he had worked his corner of the constituency with tireless, well-directed zeal, taking his share of the dull routine work as well as of the livelier episodes. The talking part of the campaign wound up on the eve of the poll with a meeting in a centre where more undecided votes were supposed to be concentrated than anywhere else in the division. A good final meeting here would mean everything. And the speakers, local and imported, left nothing undone to improve the occasion. Rupert was down for the unimportant task of moving the complimentary vote to the chairman which should close the proceedings.

"I'm so hoarse," he protested, when the moment arrived; "I don't believe I can make my voice heard beyond the platform."

"Let me do it," said the Sheep; "I'm rather good at that sort of thing."

The chairman was popular with all parties, and the Sheep's opening words of complimentary recognition received a round of applause. The orator smiled expansively on his listeners and seized the opportunity to add a few words of political wisdom on his own account. People looked at the clock or began to grope for umbrellas and discarded neckwraps. Then, in the midst of a string of meaningless platitudes, the Sheep delivered himself of one of those blundering remarks which travel from one end of a constituency to the other in half an hour, and are seized on by the other side as being more potent on their behalf than a ton of election literature. There was a general shuffling and muttering across the length and breadth of the hall, and a few hisses made themselves heard. The Sheep tried to whittle down his remark, and the chairman unhesitatingly threw him over in his speech of thanks, but the damage was done.

"I'm afraid I lost touch with the audience rather over that remark," said the Sheep afterwards, with his apologetic smile abnormally developed.

"You lost us the election," said the chairman, and he proved a true prophet.

A month or so of winter sport seemed a desirable pick-me-up after the strenuous work and crowning discomfiture of the election. Rupert and Kathleen hied them away to a small Alpine resort that was just coming into prominence, and thither the Sheep followed them in due course, in his role of husband-elect. The wedding had been fixed for the end of March.

It was a winter of early and unseasonable thaws, and the far end of the local lake, at a spot where swift currents flowed into it, was decorated with notices, written in three languages, warning skaters not to venture over certain unsafe patches. The folly of approaching too near these danger spots seemed to have a natural fascination for the Sheep.

"I don't see what possible danger there can be," he protested, with his inevitable smile, when Rupert beckoned him away from the proscribed area; "the milk that I put out on my window-sill last night was frozen an inch deep."

"It hadn't got a strong current flowing through it," said Rupert; "in any case, there is not much sense in hovering round a doubtful piece of ice when there are acres of good ice to skate over. The secretary of the ice-committee has warned you once already."

A few minutes later Rupert heard a loud squeal of fear, and saw a dark spot blotting the smoothness of the lake's frozen surface. The Sheep was struggling helplessly in an ice-hole of his own making. Rupert gave one loud curse, and then dashed full tilt for the shore; outside a low stable building on the lake's edge he remembered having seen a ladder. If he could slide it across the ice-hole before the Sheep went under the rescue would be comparatively simple work. Other skaters were dashing up from a distance, and, with the ladder's help, they could get him out of his death-trap without having to trust themselves on the margin of rotten ice. Rupert sprang on to the surface of lumpy, frozen snow, and staggered to where the ladder lay. He had already lifted it when the rattle of a chain and a furious outburst of growls burst on his hearing, and he was dashed to the ground by a mass of white and tawny fur. A sturdy young yard-dog, frantic with the pleasure of performing his first piece of actice guardian service, was ramping and snarling over him, rendering the task of regaining his feet or securing the ladder a matter of considerable difficulty. When he had at last succeeded in both efforts he was just by a hair's-breadth too late to be of any use. The Sheep had definitely disappeared under the ice-rift.

Kathleen Athling and her husband stay the greater part of the year with Rupert, and a small Robbie stands in some danger of being idolised by a devoted uncle. But for twelve months of the year Rupert's most inseparable and valued companion is a sturdy tawny and white yard-dog

47. Hyacinth

"The new fashion of introducing the candidate's children into an election contest is a pretty one," said Mrs. Panstreppon; "it takes away something from the acerbity of party warfare, and it makes an interesting experience for children to look back on in after years. Still, if you will listen to my advice, Matilda, you will not take Hyacinth with you down to Luffbridge on election day."

"Not take Hyacinth!" exclaimed his mother; "but why not? Jutterly is bringing his three children, and they are going to drive a pair of Nubian donkeys about the town, to emphasise the fact that their father has been appointed Colonial Secretary. We are making the demand for a strong Navy a special feature in our campaign, and it will be particularly appropriate to have Hyacinth dressed in his sailor suit. He'll look heavenly."

"The question is, not how he'll look, but how he'll behave. He's a delightful child, of course, but there is a strain of unbridled pugnacity in him that breaks out at times in a really alarming fashion. You may have forgotten the affair of the little Gaffin children; I haven't."

"I was in India at the time, and I've only a vague recollection of what happened; he was very naughty, I know."

"He was in his goat-carriage, and met the Gaffins in their perambulator, and he drove the goat full tilt at them and sent the perambulator spinning. Little Jacky Gaffin was pinned down under the wreckage, and while the nurse had her hands full with the goat Hyacinth was laying into Jacky's legs with his belt like a small fury."

"I'm not defending him," said Matilda, "but they must have done something to annoy him."

"Nothing intentionally, but some one had unfortunately told him that they were half French – their mother was a Duboc, you know – and he had been having a history lesson that morning, and had just heard of the final loss of Calais by the English, and was furious about it. He said he'd teach the little toads to go snatching towns from us, but we didn't know at the time that he was referring to the Gaffins. I told him afterwards that all bad feeling between the two nations had died out long ago, and that anyhow the Gaffins were only half French, and he said that it was only the French half of Jacky that he had been hitting; the rest had been buried under the perambulator. If the loss of Calais unloosed such fury in him, I tremble to think what the possible loss of the election might entail."

"All that happened when he was eight; he's older now and knows better."

"Children with Hyacinth's temperament don't know better as they grow older; they merely know more."

"Nonsense. He will enjoy the fun of the election, and in any case he'll be tired out by the time the poll is declared, and the new sailor suit that I've had made for him is just in the right shade of blue for our election colours, and it will exactly match the blue of his eyes. He will be a perfectly charming note of colour."

"There is such a thing as letting one's aesthetic sense override one's moral sense," said Mrs. Panstreppon. "I believe you would have condoned the South Sea Bubble and the persecution of the Albigenses if they had been carried out in effective colour schemes. However, if anything unfortunate should happen down at Luffbridge, don't say it wasn't foreseen by one member of the family."

The election was keenly but decorously contested. The newly-appointed Colonial Secretary was personally popular, while the Government to which he adhered was distinctly unpopular, and there was some expectancy that the majority of four hundred, obtained at the last election, would be altogether wiped out. Both sides were hopeful, but neither could feel confident. The children were a great success; the little Jutterlys drove their chubby donkeys solemnly up and down the main streets, displaying posters which advocated the claims of their father on the broad general grounds that he was their father, while as for Hyacinth, his conduct might have served as a model for any seraph-child that had strayed unwittingly on to the scene of an electoral contest. Of his own accord, and under the delighted eyes of half a dozen camera operators, he had gone up to the Jutterly children and presented them with a packet of butterscotch; "we needn't be enemies because we're wearing the opposite colours," he said with engaging friendliness, and the occupants of the donkey-cart accepted his offering with polite solemnity. The grown-up members of both political camps were delighted at the incident – with the exception of Mrs. Panstreppon, who shuddered.

"Never was Clytemnestra's kiss sweeter than on the night she slew me," she quoted, but made the quotation to herself.

The last hour of the poll was a period of unremitting labour for both parties; it was generally estimated that not more than a dozen votes separated the candidates, and every effort was made to bring up obstinately wavering electors. It was with a feeling of relaxation and relief that every one heard the clocks strike the hour for the close of the poll. Exclamations broke out from the tired workers, and corks flew out from bottles.

"Well, if we haven't won; we've done our level best." "It has been a clean straight fight, with no rancour." "The children were quite a charming feature, weren't they?"

The children? It suddenly occurred to everybody that they had seen nothing of the children for the last hour. What had become of the three little Jutterlys and their donkey-cart, and, for the matter of that, what had become of Hyacinth. Hurried, anxious embassies went backwards and forwards between the respective party headquarters and the various committee-rooms, but there was blank ignorance everywhere as to the whereabouts of the children. Every one had been too busy in the closing moments of the poll to bestow a thought on them. Then there came a telephone call at the Unionist Women's Committee-rooms, and the voice of Hyacinth was heard demanding when the poll would be declared.

"Where are you, and where are the Jutterly children?" asked his mother.

"I've just finished having high-tea at a pastry-cook's," came the answer, "and they let me telephone. I've had a poached egg and a sausage roll and four meringues."

"You'll be ill. Are the little Jutterlys with you?"

"Rather not. They're in a pigstye."

"A pigstye? Why? What pigstye?"

"Near the Crawleigh Road. I met them driving about a back road, and told them they were to have tea with me, and put their donkeys in a yard that I knew of. Then I took them to see an old sow that had got ten little pigs. I got the sow into the outer stye by giving her bits of bread, while the Jutterlys went in to look at the litter, then I bolted the door and left them there."

"You wicked boy, do you mean to say you've left those poor children there alone in the pigstye?"

"They're not alone, they've got ten little pigs in with them; they're jolly well crowded. They were pretty mad at being shut in, but not half as mad as the old sow is at being shut out from her young ones. If she gets in while they're there she'll bite them into mincemeat. I can get them out by letting a short ladder down through the top window, and that's what I'm going to do *if we win*. If their blighted father gets in, I'm just going to open the door for the sow, and let her do what she dashed well likes to them. That's why I want to know when the poll will be declared."

Here the narrator rang off. A wild stampede and a frantic sending-off of messengers took place at the other end of the telephone. Nearly all the workers on either side had disappeared to their various club-rooms and public-house bars to await the declaration of the poll, but enough local information could be secured to determine the scene of Hyacinth's exploit. Mr. John Ball had a stable yard down near the Crawleigh Road, up a short lane, and his sow was known to have a litter of ten young ones. Thither went in headlong haste both the candidates, Hyacinth's mother, his aunt (Mrs. Panstreppon), and two or three hurriedly-summoned friends. The two Nubian donkeys, contentedly munching at bundles of hay, met their gaze as they entered the yard. The hoarse savage grunting of an enraged animal and the shriller note of thirteen young voices, three of them human, guided them to the stye, in the outer yard of which a huge Yorkshire sow kept up a ceaseless raging patrol before a closed door. Reclining on the broad ledge of an open window, from which point of vantage he could reach down and shoot the bolt of the door, was Hyacinth, his blue sailor-suit somewhat the worse of wear, and his angel smile exchanged for a look of demoniacal determination.

"If any of you come a step nearer," he shouted, "the sow will be inside in half a jiffy."

A storm of threatening, arguing, entreating expostulation broke from the baffled rescue party, but it made no more impression on Hyacinth than the squealing tempest that raged within the stye.

"If Jutterly heads the poll I'm going to let the sow in. I'll teach the blighters to win elections from us."

"He means it," said Mrs. Panstreppon; "I feared the worst when I saw that butterscotch incident."

"It's all right, my little man," said Jutterly, with the duplicity to which even a Colonial Secretary can sometimes stoop, "your father has been elected by a large majority."

"Liar!" retorted Hyacinth, with the directness of speech that is not merely excusable, but almost obligatory, in the political profession; "the votes aren't counted yet. You won't gammon me as to the result, either. A boy that I've palled with is going to fire a gun when the poll is declared; two shots if we've won, one shot if we haven't."

The situation began to look critical. "Drug the sow," whispered Hyacinth's father.

Some one went off in the motor to the nearest chemist's shop and returned presently with two large pieces of bread, liberally dosed with narcotic. The bread was thrown deftly and unostentatiously into the stye, but Hyacinth saw through the manoeuvre. He set up a piercing imitation of a small pit in Purgatory, and the infuriated mother ramped round and round the stye; the pieces of bread were trampled into slush.

At any moment now the poll might be declared. Jutterly flew back to the Town Hall, where the votes were being counted. His agent met him with a smile of hope.

"You're eleven ahead at present, and only about eighty more to be counted; you're just going to squeak through."

"I mustn't squeak through," exclaimed Jutterly, hoarsely. "You must object to every doubtful vote on our side that can possibly be disallowed. I must *not* have the majority."

Then was seen the unprecedented sight of a party agent challenging the votes on his own side with a captiousness that his opponents would have hesitated to display. One or two votes that would have certainly passed muster under ordinary circumstances were disallowed, but even so Jutterly was six ahead with only thirty more to be counted.

To the watchers by the stye the moments seemed intolerable. As a last resort some one had been sent for a gun with which to shoot the sow, though Hyacinth would probably draw the bolt the moment such a weapon was brought into the yard. Nearly all the men were away from their homes, however, on election night, and the messenger had evidently gone far afield in his search. It must be a matter of minutes now to the declaration of the poll.

A sudden roar of shouting and cheering was heard from the direction of the Town Hall. Hyacinth's father clutched a pitchfork and prepared to dash into the stye in the forlorn hope of being in time.

A shot rang out in the evening air. Hyacinth stooped down from his perch and put his finger on the bolt. The sow pressed furiously against the door.

"Bang," came another shot.

Hyacinth wriggled back, and sent a short ladder down through the window of the inner stye.

"Now you can come up, you unclean little blighters," he sang out; "my daddy's got in, not yours. Hurry up, I can't keep the sow waiting much longer. And don't you jolly well come butting into any election again where I'm on the job."

In the reaction that set in after the deliverance furious recrimination were indulged in by the lately opposed candidates, their women folk, agents, and party helpers. A recount was demanded, but failed to establish the fact that the Colonial Secretary had obtained a majority. Altogether the election left a legacy of soreness behind it, apart from any that was experienced by Hyacinth in person.

"It is the last time I shall let him go to an election," exclaimed his mother.

"There I think you are going to extremes," said Mrs. Panstreppon; "if there should be a general election in Mexico I think you might safely let him go there, but I doubt whether our English politics are suited to the rough and tumble of an angel-child."

48. The Image Of The Lost Soul

There were a number of carved stone figures placed at intervals along the parapets of the old Cathedral; some of them represented angels, others kings and bishops, and nearly all were in attitudes of pious exaltation and composure. But one figure, low down on the cold north side of the building, had neither crown, mitre, not nimbus, and its face was hard and bitter and downcast; it must be a demon, declared the fat blue pigeons that roosted and sunned themselves all day on the ledges of the parapet; but the old belfry jackdaw, who was an authority on ecclesiastical architecture, said it was a lost soul. And there the matter rested.

One autumn day there fluttered on to the Cathedral roof a slender, sweet-voiced bird that had wandered away from the bare fields and thinning hedgerows in search of a winter roosting-place. It tried to rest its tired feet under the shade of a great angel-wing or to nestle in the sculptured folds of a kingly robe, but the fat pigeons hustled it away from wherever it settled, and the noisy sparrow-folk drove it off the ledges. No respectable bird sang with so much feeling, they cheeped one to another, and the wanderer had to move on.

Only the effigy of the Lost Soul offered a place of refuge. The pigeons did not consider it safe to perch on a projection that leaned so much out of the perpendicular, and was, besides, too much in the shadow. The figure did not cross its hands in the pious attitude of the other graven dignitaries, but its arms were folded as in defiance and their angle made a snug resting-place for the little bird. Every evening it crept trustfully into its corner against the stone breast of the image, and the darkling eyes seemed to keep watch over its slumbers. The lonely bird grew to love its lonely protector, and during the day it would sit from time to time on some rainshoot or other abutment and trill forth its sweetest music in grateful thanks for its nightly shelter. And, it may have been the work of wind and weather, or some other influence, but the wild drawn face seemed gradually to lose some of its hardness and unhappiness. Every day, through the long monotonous hours, the song of his little guest would come up in snatches to the lonely watcher, and at evening, when the vesper-bell was ringing and the great grey bats slid out of their hiding-places in the belfry roof, the bright-eyed bird would return, twitter a few sleepy notes, and nestle into the arms that were waiting for him. Those were happy days for the Dark Image. Only the great bell of the Cathedral rang out daily its mocking message, "After joy...sorrow."

The folk in the verger's lodge noticed a little brown bird flitting about the Cathedral precincts, and admired its beautiful singing. "But it is a pity," said they, "that all that warbling should be lost and wasted far out of hearing up on the parapet." They were poor, but they understood the principles of political economy. So they caught the bird and put it in a little wicker cage outside the lodge door.

That night the little songster was missing from its accustomed haunt, and the Dark Image knew more than ever the bitterness of loneliness. Perhaps his little friend had been killed by a prowling cat or hurt by a stone. Perhaps...perhaps he had flown elsewhere. But when morning came there floated up to him, through the noise and bustle of the Cathedral world, a faint heart-aching message from the prisoner in the wicker cage far below. And every day, at high noon, when the fat pigeons were stupefied into silence after their midday meal and the sparrows were washing themselves in the street-puddles, the song of the little bird came up to the parapets – a song of hunger and longing and hopelessness, a cry that could never be answered. The pigeons remarked, between mealtimes, that the figure leaned forward more than ever out of the perpendicular.

One day no song came up from the little wicker cage. It was the coldest day of the winter, and the pigeons and sparrows on the Cathedral roof looked anxiously on all sides for the scraps of food which they were dependent on in hard weather.

"Have the lodge-folk thrown out anything on to the dust-heap?" inquired one pigeon of another which was peering over the edge of the north parapet.

"Only a little dead bird," was the answer.

There was a crackling sound in the night on the Cathedral roof and a noise as of falling masonry. The belfry jackdaw said the frost was affecting the fabric, and as he had experienced many frosts it must have been so. In the morning it was seen that the Figure of the Lost Soul had toppled from its cornice and lay now in a broken mass on the dust-heap outside the verger's lodge.

"It is just as well," cooed the fat pigeons, after they had peered at the matter for some minutes; "now we shall have a nice angel put up there. Certainly they will put an angel there."

"After joy…sorrow," rang out the great bell.

49. The Purple Of The Balkan Kings

Luitpold Wolkenstein, financier and diplomat on a small, obtrusive, self-important scale, sat in his favoured cafe in the world-wise Habsburg capital, confronted with the Neue Freie Presse and the cup of cream-topped coffee and attendant glass of water that a sleek-headed piccolo had just brought him. For years longer than a dog's lifetime sleek-headed piccolos had placed the Neue Freie Presse and a cup of cream-topped coffee on his table; for years he had sat at the same spot, under the dust-coated, stuffed eagle, that had once been a living, soaring bird on the Styrian mountains, and was now made monstrous and symbolical with a second head grafted on to its neck and a gilt crown planted on either dusty skull. To-day Luitpold Wolkenstein read no more than the first article in his paper, but read it again and again.

"The Turkish fortress of Kirk Kilisseh has fallen... The Serbs, it is officially announced, have taken Kumanovo... The fortress of Kirk Kilisseh lost, Kumanovo taken by the Serbs, these are tiding for Constantinople resembling something out of Shakspeare's tragedies of the kings... The neighbourhood of Adrianople and the Eastern region, where the great battle is now in progress, will not reveal merely the future of Turkey, but also what position and what influence the Balkan States are to have in the world."

For years longer than a dog's lifetime Luitpold Wolkenstein had disposed of the pretensions and strivings of the Balkan States over the cup of cream-topped coffee that sleek-headed piccolos had brought him. Never travelling further eastward than the horse-fair at Temesvar, never inviting personal risk in an encounter with anything more potentially desperate than a hare or partridge, he had constituted himself the critical appraiser and arbiter of the military and national prowess of the small countries that fringed the Dual Monarchy on its Danube border. And his judgment had been one of unsparing contempt for small-scale efforts, of unquestioning respect for the big battalions and full purses. Over the whole scene of the Balkan territories and their troubled histories had loomed the commanding magic of the words "the Great Powers" – even more imposing in their Teutonic rendering, *"Die Grossmächte."*

Worshipping power and force and money-mastery as an elderly nerve-ridden woman might worship youthful physical energy, the comfortable, plump-bodied café-oracle had jested and gibed at the ambitions of the Balkan kinglets and their peoples, had unloosed against them that battery of strange lip-sounds that a Viennese employs almost as an auxiliary language to express the thoughts when his thoughts are not complimentary. British travellers had visited the Balkan lands and reported high things of the Bulgarians and their future, Russian officers had taken peeps at their army and confessed "this is a thing to be reckoned with, and it is not we who have created it, they have done it by themselves." But over his cups of coffee and his hour-long games of dominoes the oracle had laughed and wagged his head and distilled the worldly wisdom of his castle. The Grossmachte had not succeeded in stifling the roll of the war-drum, that was true; the big battalions of the Ottoman Empire would have to do some talking, and then the big purses and big threatenings of the Powers would speak and the last word would be with them. In imagination Luitpold heard the onward tramp of the red-fezzed bayonet bearers echoing through the Balkan passes, saw the little sheepskin-clad mannikins driven back to their villages, saw the augustly chiding spokesman of the Powers dictating, adjusting, restoring, settling things once again in their allotted places, sweeping up the dust of conflict, and now his ears had to listen to the war-drum rolling in quite another direction, had to listen to the tramp of battalions that were bigger and bolder and better skilled in war-craft than he had deemed possible in that quarter;

his eyes had to read in the columns of his accustomed newspaper a warning to the Grossmachte that they had something new to learn, something new to reckon with, much that was time-honoured to relinquish. "The Great Powers will have not little difficulty in persuading the Balkan States of the inviolability of the principle that Europe cannot permit any fresh partition of territory in the East without her approval. Even now, while the campaign is still undecided, there are rumours of a project of fiscal unity, extending over the entire Balkan lands, and further of a constitutional union in imitation of the German Empire. That is perhaps only a political straw blown by the storm, but it is not possible to dismiss the reflection that the Balkan States leagued together command a military strength with which the Great Powers will have to reckon... The people who have poured out their blood on the battlefields and sacrificed the available armed men of an entire generation in order to encompass a union with their kinsfolk will not remain any longer in an attitude of dependence on the Great Powers or on Russia, but will go their own ways ... The blood that has been poured forth to-day gives for the first time a genuine tone to the purple of the Balkan Kings. The Great Powers cannot overlook the fact that a people that has tasted victory will not let itself be driven back again within its former limits. Turkey has lost to-day not only Kirk Kilisseh and Kumanovo, but Macedonia also."

Luitpold Wolkenstein drank his coffee, but the flavour had somehow gone out of it. His world, his pompous, imposing, dictating world, had suddenly rolled up into narrower dimensions. The big purses and the big threats had been pushed unceremoniously on one side; a force that he could not fathom, could not comprehend, had made itself rudely felt. The august Caesars of Mammon and armament had looked down frowningly on the combat, and those about to die had not saluted, had no intention of saluting. A lesson was being imposed on unwilling learners, a lesson of respect for certain fundamental principles, and it was not the small struggling States who were being taught the lesson.

Luitpold Wolkenstein did not wait for the quorum of domino players to arrive. They would all have read the article in the Freie Presse. And there are moments when an oracle finds its greatest salvation in withdrawing itself from the area of human questioning.

50. The Cupboard Of The Yesterdays

"War is a cruelly destructive thing," said the Wanderer, dropping his newspaper to the floor and staring reflectively into space.

"Ah, yes, indeed," said the Merchant, responding readily to what seemed like a safe platitude; "when one thinks of the loss of life and limb, the desolated homesteads, the ruined –"

"I wasn't thinking of anything of the sort," said the Wanderer; "I was thinking of the tendency that modern war has to destroy and banish the very elements of picturesqueness and excitement that are its chief excuse and charm. It is like a fire that flares up brilliantly for a while and then leaves everything blacker and bleaker than before. After every important war in South-East Europe in recent times there has been a shrinking of the area of chronically disturbed territory, a stiffening of the area of chronically disturbed territory, a stiffening of frontier lines, an intrusion of civilised monotony. And imagine what may happen at the conclusion of this war if the Turk should really be driven out of Europe."

"Well, it would be a gain to the cause of good government, I suppose," said the Merchant.

"But have you counted the loss?" said the other. "The Balkans have long been the last surviving shred of happy hunting-ground for the adventurous, a playground for passions that are fast becoming atrophied for want of exercise. In old bygone days we had the wars in the Low Countries always at our doors, as it were; there was no need to go far afield into malaria-stricken wilds if one wanted a life of boot and saddle and licence to kill and be killed. Those who wished to see life had a decent opportunity for seeing death at the same time."

"It is scarcely right to talk of killing and bloodshed in that way," said the Merchant reprovingly; "one must remember that all men are brothers."

"One must also remember that a large percentage of them are younger brothers; instead of going into bankruptcy, which is the usual tendency of the younger brother nowadays, they gave their families a fair chance of going into mourning. Every bullet finds a billet, according to a rather optimistic proverb, and you must admit that nowadays it is becoming increasingly difficult to find billets for a lot of young gentlemen who would have adorned, and probably thoroughly enjoyed, one of the old-time happy-go-lucky wars. But that is not exactly the burden of my complaint. The Balkan lands are especially interesting to us in these rapidly-moving days because they afford us the last remaining glimpse of a vanishing period of European history. When I was a child one of the earliest events of the outside world that forced itself coherently under my notice was a war in the Balkans; I remember a sunburnt, soldierly man putting little pin-flags in a war-map, red flags for the Turkish forces and yellow flags for the Russians. It seemed a magical region, with its mountain passes and frozen rivers and grim battlefields, its drifting snows, and prowling wolves; there was a great stretch of water that bore the sinister but engaging name of the Black Sea – nothing that I ever learned before or after in a geography lesson made the same impression on me as that strange-named inland sea, and I don't think its magic has ever faded out of my imagination. And there was a battle called Plevna that went on and on with varying fortunes for what seemed like a great part of a lifetime; I remember the day of wrath and mourning when the little red flag had to be taken away from Plevna-like other maturer judges, I was backing the wrong horse, at any rate the losing horse. And now today we are putting little pin-flags again into maps of the Balkan region, and the passions are being turned loose once more in their playground."

"The war will be localised," said the Merchant vaguely; "at least every one hopes so."

"It couldn't wish for a better locality," said the Wanderer; "there is a charm about those countries that you find nowhere else in Europe, the charm of uncertainty and landslide, and the little dramatic happenings that make all the difference between the ordinary and the desirable."

"Life is held very cheap in those parts," said the Merchant.

"To a certain extent, yes," said the Wanderer. "I remember a man at Sofia who used to teach me Bulgarian in a rather inefficient manner, interspersed with a lot of quite wearisome gossip. I never knew what his personal history was, but that was only because I didn't listen; he told it to me many times. After I left Bulgaria he used to send me Sofia newspapers from time to time. I felt that he would be rather tiresome if I ever went there again. And then I heard afterwards that some men came in one day from Heaven knows where, just as things do happen in the Balkans, and murdered him in the open street, and went away as quietly as they had come. You will not understand it, but to me there was something rather piquant in the idea of such a thing happening to such a man; after his dullness and his long-winded small-talk it seemed a sort of brilliant *esprit d'escalier* on his part to meet with an end of such ruthlessly planned and executed violence."

The Merchant shook his head; the piquancy of the incident was not within striking distance of his comprehension.

"I should have been shocked at hearing such a thing about any one I had known," he said.

"The present war," continued his companion, without stopping to discuss two hopelessly divergent points of view, "may be the beginning of the end of much that has hitherto survived the resistless creeping-in of civilisation. If the Balkan lands are to be finally parcelled out between the competing Christian Kingdoms and the haphazard rule of the Turk banished to beyond the Sea of Marmora, the old order, or disorder if you like, will have received its death-blow. Something of its spirit will linger perhaps for a while in the old charmed regions where it bore sway; the Greek villagers will doubtless be restless and turbulent and unhappy where the Bulgars rule, and the Bulgars will certainly be restless and turbulent and unhappy under Greek administration, and the rival flocks of the Exarchate and Patriarchate will make themselves intensely disagreeable to one another wherever the opportunity offers; the habits of a lifetime, of several lifetimes, are not laid aside all at once. And the Albanians, of course, we shall have with us still, a troubled Moslem pool left by the receding wave of Islam in Europe. But the old atmosphere will have changed, the glamour will have gone; the dust of formality and bureaucratic neatness will slowly settle down over the time-honoured landmarks; the Sanjak of Novi Bazar, the Muersteg Agreement, the Komitadje bands, the Vilayet of Adrianople, all those familiar outlandish names and things and places, that we have known so long as part and parcel of the Balkan Question, will have passed away into the cupboard of yesterdays, as completely as the Hansa League and the wars of the Guises.

"They were the heritage that history handed down to us, spoiled and diminished no doubt, in comparison with yet earlier days that we never knew, but still something to thrill and enliven one little corner of our Continent, something to help us to conjure up in our imagination the days when the Turk was thundering at the gates of Vienna. And what shall we have to hand down to our children? Think of what their news from the Balkans will be in the course of another ten or fifteen years. Socialist Congress at Uskub, election riot at Monastir, great dock strike at Salonika, visit of the Y.M.C.A. to Varna. Varna – on the coast of that enchanted sea! They will drive out to some suburb to tea, and write home about it as the Bexhill of the East.

"War is a wickedly destructive thing."

"Still, you must admit –" began the Merchant. But the Wanderer was not in the mood to admit anything. He rose impatiently and walked to where the tape-machine was busy with the news from Adrianople.

Other Titles In This Series

9 789352 762767

9 789352 762910

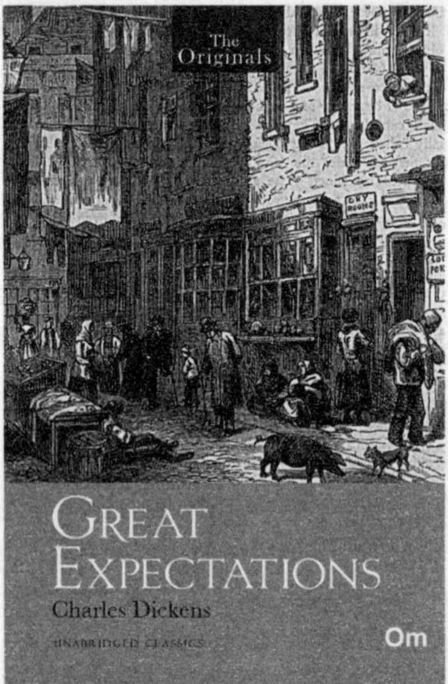

9 789352 763153

Other Titles In This Series

9 789352 763375

9 789352 763382

9 789352 763399

Other Titles In This Series

9 789352 763337

9 789352 762897

9 789352 762774

9 789352 762934

9 789352 762880

9 789352 762897

9 789352 760015